PLEASURE BOUND

Books by Anne Rainey

Pleasure Bound

So Sensitive

Body Rush

"Cherry on Top" in *Some Like It Rough*

PLEASURE BOUND

ANNE RAINEY

APHRODISIA

KENSINGTON PUBLISHING CORP.

www.kensingtonbooks.com

APHRODISIA BOOKS are published by

Kensington Publishing Corp.
119 West 40th Street
New York, NY 10018

All Kensington titles, imprints, and distributed lines are available at special quantity discounts for bulk purchases for sales promotion, premiums, fund-raising, and educational or institutional use.

Special book excerpts or customized printings can also be created to fit specific needs. For details, write or phone the office of the Kensington Special Sales Manager: Kensington Publishing Corp., 119 West 40th Street, New York, NY 10018. Attn. Special Sales Department. Phone: 1-800-221-2647.

Aphrodisia and the A logo Reg. U.S. Pat. & TM Off.

ISBN-13: 978-0-7582-6902-7
ISBN-10: 0-7582-6902-1

First Kensington Trade Paperback Printing: November 2011

10 9 8 7 6 5 4 3 2 1

Printed in the United States of America

Prologue

Five years earlier . . .

Jonas got out of Wade's truck and stared at the white ranch-style house. It was big, but not ostentatious. Wade's family home, Jonas reminded himself. He clenched and unclenched his fists, wishing for the hundredth time that he'd kept his big mouth shut when Wade had asked if he'd had plans for the day.

It was Saturday, and the only thing on his agenda had been getting in a good, hard workout at the gym. He was man enough to admit that the uncomfortable feeling skating down his spine now was fear. Pure, unadulterated fear. Jonas was damn tempted to get back in the truck and get the hell out of Dodge.

Wade and his big idea to introduce him to his family. Christ. Although, he couldn't blame his buddy entirely. Curiosity had gotten the better of Jonas and he'd caved. Wade always went on and on about his fabulous family. The brother with the new construction company, the little sister who'd just graduated from nursing school. Hell, even Wade's parents intrigued Jonas. They were wildly in love even after thirty years of marriage. In

Jonas's family, a loving marriage was an oddity, considering his own parents barely tolerated each other.

Now, as he stared at the house, his palms started to sweat. Shit. Why had he decided to torture himself? He could be at home, drinking a beer and watching a game. Any game.

As Jonas stepped onto the porch, he turned and stared at Wade. He'd become like a brother to him. They'd met a few years before in the army, during basic training. For some reason that Jonas couldn't recall now, he'd called Wade a pussy. Of course, Wade had responded with an uppercut to Jonas's jaw. They'd been buddies ever since.

"Are you sure about this, Wade? I mean, I don't want to crash your family get-together."

"Don't be such a pain in the ass," Wade said as he slapped Jonas on the back and tried to push him through the front door. "You've been trying to get out of this the entire way over here. Jesus, you're getting on my last nerve!"

Jonas still didn't budge. "Why'd I let you talk me into this? It's a family picnic, Wade. I'm not family. I don't know a damn thing about families, much less family picnics."

"Blah, blah," Wade said as he rolled his eyes.

Several voices filtered through the screen door. "Who's in there anyway?"

"My parents, my brother and sister, some cousins. Uncles and aunts. You know, family."

Yep, Jonas definitely wanted to make a break for it.

Wade sighed. "Trust me. Everyone will be glad to finally meet you."

Jonas quirked a brow. "Finally?"

"I've talked about you in my letters," Wade admitted. "Mostly about what a dumbass you are. So, naturally they're curious."

Jonas chuckled. "You wrote about me? How romantic."

"Quit stalling," Wade growled.

"Fine, but I'm not staying long."

"Yeah, yeah, families give you hives. I get it. Now go."

Jonas grunted and stepped over the threshold. The house was bursting with activity. A petite woman with shoulder-length, dark brown hair sprinkled with gray looked toward them and grinned. "It's about time you showed up."

Wade closed the distance and enveloped her in a big bear hug. Jonas took a step back, all but ready to dart through the door as he watched the warm display. Wade's mother? As Jonas pondered the identity of the woman, several others surrounded the pair. Jonas felt a pang of envy toward his friend. Hugs and kisses? Yeah, right. Jonas's parents didn't operate that way. The day Jonas had left for the army, his dad had awkwardly patted him on the shoulder and his mother had simply stood by, impatiently waiting and checking her watch. She'd been more concerned about being late for a business meeting than seeing her only child off to the military.

"Hey, Jonas," Wade shouted. "Come over here and meet my mom."

As Jonas shoved the shitty memory to the background, he realized everyone in the room was staring at him. He grimaced. It was going to be a long day.

"You look like you're having a root canal."

The warm, bedroom voice tore Jonas's attention away from the bottle cap he'd been mindlessly spinning on the picnic table. The first thing to catch his gaze was the hourglass figure encased in a black one-piece swimsuit. Damn, talk about built! Jonas let himself enjoy the slow route to the woman's perfect oval-shaped face. Long, wind-tossed, dark brown hair, ruby-red lips, and sexy brown eyes gave Jonas some seriously dirty thoughts.

"Things are definitely looking up." He dropped the cap and stood. "Jonas Phoenix and you are . . . ?"

"Deanna—and I'm late."

Jonas froze when he heard the name. "Deanna? As in, Wade's little sister?"

"Not so little, but yeah. You're the friend from the army, right?"

He'd heard about Deanna quite often. Wade had talked about his sister, who'd recently graduated from nursing school. The pride and love his friend felt for Deanna had come through loud and clear. Jonas had never once imagined Deanna looking anything like the hot, curvy woman in front of him now. "Uh, the army, yeah."

She nodded and pushed a heavy section of hair behind her shoulder. "He's talked about you."

"All good stuff, I hope."

She winked and Jonas wondered if maybe he was drooling. "Mostly good. He told us you're a whiz on the computer. I confess, I expected you to look a bit more . . . geeky."

"Let me guess, you figured I'd be wearing a tie, a pocket protector, and maybe a pair of thick glasses?"

She laughed and Jonas couldn't help grinning. Christ, even her laughter went straight to his groin. "That's pretty close, but you actually look more like the guy in that movie I saw recently."

Jonas cocked his head to the side. "Is that good or bad?"

"Good. The actor played a sniper out for revenge on the gang who'd killed his wife."

He stepped closer, his voice lowering to a more intimate level as he said, "You don't look a thing like I imagined either, Deanna."

She quirked a brow at him. "Oh?"

"Actually, you—" A hand slapped Jonas on the back, and he wanted to curse the interruption.

Just barely tamping down the urge to search out a more private spot to continue their conversation, Jonas turned to find

Wade and his brother Dean. Jonas immediately put some space between himself and Deanna. Christ, had he really just been flirting with Wade's baby sister? What the hell had he been thinking?

"Don't you own a cover-up, Dee?" Dean asked, frowning at his sister.

Deanna gave herself a once-over before looking back at Dean, color staining her cheeks. "Uh, yeah, but I didn't really think I needed it." Her gaze shot to his as she said, "It was nice meeting you, Jonas."

"You too." Jonas wanted to punch Dean for making Deanna feel so self-conscious in the swimsuit. Then again, Dean could say whatever the hell he wanted to the woman, considering they were related. *You're the outsider here*, Jonas reminded himself.

Offering Deanna a smile, Jonas said, "Maybe we can finish our conversation later."

She smiled, but it didn't quite meet her eyes this time. "Yeah, maybe."

Jonas didn't take his gaze off Deanna as she walked across the deck. When she disappeared inside the house, Dean muttered, "She forgets sometimes."

Curious, Jonas asked, "Forgets what?"

"That she's not a little girl any longer."

No, Deanna definitely wasn't a little girl, Jonas thought, as her image popped back into his head. She was all woman, and he had the crazy urge to possess her.

"Cut her some slack, Dean," Wade said. "You're too protective of her."

"And you aren't?" Dean asked as he turned to face Wade.

Jonas stayed silent as he listened to the two brothers argue. He couldn't believe Dean and Deanna were actually twins. While they did share many of the same features—same dark hair and eyes, even the same height—Dean had a big, muscular build. Deanna was all soft hills and valleys and sweet, feminine curves. And damn if he didn't wish like hell she wasn't his best friend's little sister.

Sometimes life just sucked.

Deanna watched Jonas from the safety of the kitchen window. "Holy smokes, he's hot," she mumbled to herself.

From his shaggy, dark hair right on down to his lean, powerful frame. Everything about him appealed to her. She'd never experienced such a strong reaction to a man. It frightened her a little. There was just something in the way he'd looked at her. As if he'd wanted to devour her. Inch by inch. And Deanna knew deep down that she would've let him.

Then her brothers had come along and ruined the moment. Score another one for the Harrison men. Geez, what else was new? And her twin was the worst. Dean seemed to have a sixth sense where she was concerned. A guy couldn't look at her twice without Dean sticking his big, crooked nose into the mix. When would he realize she wasn't a little kid any longer?

Deanna moved away from the window—away from the appealing sight of Jonas Phoenix—and went to the fridge. Grabbing a bottle of water, she glanced down at her swimsuit and cursed under her breath. She didn't see anything wrong with wearing a one-piece. It's not as if she were parading around in a bikini, for crying out loud. And it was a family picnic!

"Brothers are annoying," she muttered.

"You're glaring."

The deep baritone so close to her ear made Deanna jump. Her water bottle sloshed around, and a little of it spilled onto her mother's tile floor. "Dang it," she grumbled.

"It was my fault."

The sexy voice had her looking to her right. Jonas stood there, staring at her, his lips tilted sideways. "Oh, no," she rushed to say. "I get lost in thought sometimes, that's all." So lost in her own angry musings that she hadn't even heard the back door open and close.

He leaned around her and grabbed a couple of napkins sitting in a holder on the counter. Then he bent to clean up the mess. When he looked at her from his kneeling position, Deanna's heart beat faster. He licked his lips. Deanna froze in place as his gaze roamed over her body. "I see you didn't put on a cover-up," he stated in a low voice.

"N-no. My brother can stuff it."

His sinful smile turned her legs to rubber. "I'm glad. You shouldn't let him tell you what to do."

"It's okay. I'll get him back later. I'm thinking the water hose."

He stood and went to the trash to toss out the wet napkins. Deanna couldn't help but stare at his butt. It was a really great butt.

When he came back over to her, he said, "Well, I'm sorry I startled you." He paired the apology with a delicious grin.

As he shoved his big hands into the front pockets of his jeans, Deanna felt goose bumps popping up all over her skin. Oh, yes, definitely yummy.

"Like I said, it's not your fault," she replied, hoping to sound unaffected by the six-foot-plus hottie. "We'll blame Dean for this one."

"I thought I heard you curse." He frowned. "Is there something wrong?"

"Nothing a good beating can't fix," she grumbled, still perturbed at her siblings. "My twin can be annoying sometimes."

He chuckled as he pulled a set of keys out of his front pocket. "Remind me never to piss you off."

Deanna pointed to them. "You're leaving already?" Her stomach sank at the thought, and she didn't understand why. She'd only just met the guy.

"Yeah. I need to be at the other end of town for a meeting."

He looked at his watch. "I'm already running behind, I'm afraid."

She wondered if the meeting was with a woman but quickly banished the thought. *It's none of my concern.* "Will I see you again?"

Jonas stepped forward and cupped her chin in his palm. The bold move surprised her into remaining still, curious what he'd do next. "I hope so, Deanna," he murmured.

"I hope so too," she answered, feeling a little overheated all of a sudden. Would he kiss her? She really wanted him to kiss her.

He rubbed his thumb over her bottom lip and groaned. "Meeting you has easily been the highlight of my summer," he whispered. Then, as if for her ears alone, Jonas leaned close to her ear and added, "I have a feeling I'm not going to forget you anytime soon either."

Before she could reply, Jonas dropped his hand and left the kitchen. Her heart thundered in her chest as she pondered his hushed words. Something about the way he'd spoken made Deanna feel rejected—even though she hadn't actually done any asking. Not a pleasant thought.

Right about then, Dean came in the back door. "I thought you were going to put on a cover-up."

Deanna cursed and went outside in search of the hose.

1
_____

Present day . . .

She had sweet, gentle curves that the tight black skirt and light pink tank top couldn't even begin to hide. Short blond hair framed a cute oval-shaped face. Pretty. Flirty too. Her smiles should've been pulling him across the room. *Do it, dumbass. Walk over to her, whisper some lame shit in her ear, and get laid.* Great fucking advice. So, why wasn't he listening to it? Easy. His dick wanted only one woman—and she was nowhere in sight.

Jonas slammed back the last of his light beer and stepped away from the bar. The neon lights, crowded room, and booming bass should've been exactly what he needed to get his mind off one Deanna Harrison. He had a feeling an earthquake couldn't even manage to accomplish that goal.

After giving the little blonde a parting grin, Jonas headed out of the bar into the cold winter night. As he slid behind the wheel of his new black Dodge Charger, he felt marginally better, but not enough. Not nearly enough. He sighed and stared out at the darkness. Friday night and more than enough honeys to fill his bed for a week, and where was he? Alone. Again. "Christ, I'm an idiot."

Shoving the key into the ignition, Jonas started the car. Listening to the hum of the engine as the beautiful machine came to life sent a shot of pride through him. He loved his car, but as he drove out of the parking lot and headed toward the highway, Jonas's mind turned toward another beauty, Deanna. The way her eyes lit with mischief whenever she saw him. Only Deanna could make a smart-ass comment sound sexy. What would it take to slip past that exterior? To reach the passionate woman beneath? And she would be passionate; Jonas felt it in his gut. A woman like Deanna would burn him alive in bed. If he could ever get her to stop rejecting him.

Without thinking, Jonas automatically took the on ramp, which brought him in the direction of Deanna's house. "Ah, hell. Clearly my dick is now in complete control." The part of his brain that controlled rational thought seemed to switch off the minute the woman's image slipped through the cracks.

As he approached her house, Jonas stiffened. There weren't any lights on, which meant she was out. "It's Friday night—of course she's out." With a guy? "Now that's a hell of an ugly thought."

Jonas drove up the street a little ways, then parked along the curb. No reason why he couldn't wait for her to return home. He needed to be sure she was safe, didn't he? Jonas got out of the car and locked it. Jogging the short distance to her front porch gave him a chance to think about his actions. Deanna was a grown woman. She had every right to date whomever she chose. To come home late. Hell, stay out all night. None of his business, of course. The logical discussion didn't stop him from selecting the chair situated in the shadows of her porch. Dropping into it, Jonas pulled his leather coat around him tighter and relaxed, waited. His head started swirling with images of Deanna and some faceless stranger. Kissing. Touching. Another man's hands stroking her alabaster skin. Another man's tongue teasing her plump lips. His temper flared.

Please, for both their sakes, let her be out with friends.

When a car pulled into her drive, Jonas stiffened. Definitely not Deanna's red coupe. The big, silver Lexus looked expensive, fancy. Is that the type Deanna went for? The clean-shaven, suit-wearing type? Jonas rubbed his jaw, then cursed when he felt the rough stubble there. Watching from the shadows, he saw Deanna lean toward the driver. He couldn't make out any more than their shapes. Was she kissing him? Was the asshole staying the night?

Not damn likely.

When she opened the passenger door and stepped out, Jonas breathed a sigh of relief. She waved and the car started a slow glide back out of the driveway. Jonas waited. When she stepped onto the porch, he got a better look at her. She wore a pair of red heels and a matching slip dress with a little black shawl wrap. The dress hit above the knee. Classy, but sexy—and too freaking revealing for his peace of mind.

"Even though it's winter and that dress is clearly not designed to keep a body warm, you sure are heating me up pretty damn fast."

At his words, Deanna jumped and screamed. Jonas shot out of the chair and grabbed her by the shoulders in time to keep her from tumbling off the porch. "What the hell, Jonas? You scared the crap out of me!"

Feeling like an idiot, he mumbled, "Sorry. I didn't mean to startle you."

She shoved out of his arms and slapped his chest. "Why are you lurking in the dark? Are you spying on me?"

Her eyes flashed fire and ice at the same time. How did she do that? It captivated the hell out of him. "Who's spying? I just came for a friendly visit."

"You know very well you're spying." She bit the words out between clenched teeth.

He leaned close, inhaling her floral scent. Lilacs. She always smelled like lilacs. Delicate and gentle. Two things Jonas didn't know shit about. If he had any decency at all, he'd leave.

"A visit, Deanna." He stepped back and let her pass. "I'm not allowed to visit?"

She pulled open the screen door and shoved her key into the dead bolt. "No, you aren't. Now go away. I'm tired."

Her voice had lowered to a quiet, husky tone. It snaked up Jonas's chest like a caress. It pissed him off that she could get to him so easily. "Is that why you sent your date home? Because you're tired?"

She pushed her door open, then turned to him. "That's none of your business." She crossed her arms over her chest. "Go home, Jonas."

Jonas closed the distance separating them. "Let me come inside, Deanna. We need to talk."

"No, we don't," she gritted out, her voice not quite as steady as before. "You need to go home and I need to sleep."

His temper flared. "Why won't you give me the time of day?"

Deanna shook her head and looked away.

Jonas cupped her cheek and forced her back around. He wouldn't let her hide from him. Not ever. "This isn't all one-sided," he whispered. "This desire, you feel it too. I know you do."

On a sigh, Deanna closed her eyes tight. "Just because there's an itch doesn't mean we should scratch it."

Damn, her skin was as soft as flower petals. He stroked his thumb over her lower lip and found it plump, inviting. His dick hardened beneath his jeans as he imagined those full pink lips wrapped snug around his cock.

"An itch, huh?" he growled. "Is that the way you see it?"

She opened her eyes and stared up at him. The angry glare she shot him wasn't at all what he expected. "You had your chance once. You blew it."

Genuinely confused, Jonas dropped his hand. "Chance? You've shot me down at every turn, Deanna."

She squinted and pointed her finger at his chest. "You took my brother's side."

He shoved a hand through his hair and prayed for patience. "Wade?"

"Yes. At Gracie's apartment. When we were there helping clean up the mess that freak left behind. You sided with Wade. Some stupid nonsense about the sister code. Remember?"

Ah, it was all coming together finally. Gracie had been a client of his and Wade's investigation business, but she'd quickly become the love of Wade's life. Unfortunately, she'd been having trouble with a deranged stalker. When the creep had broken into Gracie's apartment and torn it all to hell, they'd all rallied together to help Gracie put things back in order. Once again, Jonas had seen a chance to ask Deanna out, but she'd shot him down. Then Dean and Wade, her two over-protective brothers, had gotten involved. Jonas and Wade were not only business partners but also friends—an annoying little fact that forced Jonas to back off in his pursuit.

"Wade is like a brother to me," he explained, "and he re-minded me of that. It's not cool to chase after your friend's baby sister, Deanna."

She quirked a brow at him. "And yet here you are."

"Yes, smart-ass, here I am," he said softly. "I talked to Wade. He's still not crazy about the fact that I'm hot for you, but he's not going to stand in my way either."

If anything, her frown turned darker. "You asked for his blessing?"

"Uh, something like that, yeah."

"He's not my father, Jonas. I'm a grown woman. Wade has no right to interfere in my personal life."

"Right or wrong, Deanna, Wade will always look out for you. Dean, too, for that matter."

She sighed. "And let me guess, Wade threatened to castrate you if you hurt me. Is that it?"

Jonas propped a fist against the doorjamb, then wrapped his other hand around her waist to keep her from bolting through the open door. "The last thing I want is to hurt you, Deanna."

Deanna's slender fingers gripped onto his forearm. "No," she whispered, "you just want to get me into bed."

He let his hand move lower, until he was mere inches from the sweet curve of her ass. "I want you like hell. Just looking at you makes my dick hard. But there's more than that between us."

She shook her head, maybe a little too vehemently, Jonas thought. "No, there isn't."

"There could be," he murmured as he dipped his head and brushed her lips with his. "If you'd stop playing so hard to get."

The hand she had on his forearm tightened, but she wasn't pushing him away. "I don't want to be another in a long line of conquests, Jonas. This isn't a game for me."

"If all I wanted was a few hours between the sheets with a warm, willing woman, I would've taken that cute little blonde up on her offer at the bar I went to tonight."

Her nails dug into his skin. "Cute little blonde?"

He nodded, enjoying the note of jealousy in her voice. It served her right, considering how jealous he'd been when he'd seen her in that Lexus. "She sent me all the right signals too. But the only woman I want isn't in some bar."

"She's not?"

"Uh-uh. She's standing right in front of me." He looked

down her body, his gaze snagging on the fullness of her breasts pressing so enticingly against the thin material of the dress. "And she's so pretty too."

Deanna dropped her hands and sighed. "I can't do this, Jonas. Please."

"Why? It's just a date. We can go real slow, I swear."

The satin skin over her cheekbones, the same skin he wanted to press his lips against, tautened. Jonas ached to take the starch right out of her. He wanted to watch her go all soft and rosy for him.

"It's not going to work," she said. "I've known guys like you. You're an oversexed playboy. You aren't the serious type, Jonas. You like to play, and I'm not willing to be your plaything."

He snorted at her description. "Plaything?"

Deanna stiffened and dropped her hands from his arms. Jonas instantly missed the warm touch. "Do you deny you're a player?"

Damn, she was serious. "That's what you think of me? That I'm a player?"

She pointed a finger at his chest. "I've watched you with women. None of them are ever around for long either."

Jonas felt his own anger rise. Only Deanna could get to him so quickly and with so little effort. "You think you have me all figured out, but you don't."

Her lips twitched. "Oh, really?"

Jonas scowled. "Really."

She crossed her arms over her chest, and Jonas's gaze shot to the plump swells. She might well be trying to hide them from his view, but Jonas could've told her not to waste her time. The woman put new meaning to the word *stacked*. A man would have to be blind not to notice Deanna's voluptuous curves. Jonas groaned. So fucking close, and yet he may as well be miles away.

"How long was your last relationship?"

Her question jarred Jonas back to the conversation. He had to think back quite a few months before he could answer. "Her name was Marissa, and it lasted two months."

She quirked a brow at him in that regal, slightly bitchy way she had. His dick, which always hardened the instant she came within view, perked right up. "Gee, a whole two months, huh?"

Jonas reached out and tweaked her nose. "Yeah, smart-ass, two months. Sweet lady, but not the one for me." He chose to leave off the part about not having had a serious relationship ever since the day he'd met one hardheaded, dark-haired vixen, who just happened to be his best friend's baby sister. "Now you," he murmured. "How long was your last relationship, Deanna?"

To his surprise, she looked away. As if uncomfortable with the conversation all of a sudden. "I've been busy with work lately. Dating has been the last thing on my mind."

"That doesn't answer my question. I was honest, sweetheart. Don't you think you owe me the same courtesy?"

"Fine. I haven't had a serious relationship since Roger and I broke up."

Jonas remembered Roger. Deanna had dated him for six months. It'd been six months of pure hell for Jonas as he imagined Roger touching Deanna. Touching, tasting, and loving. Jonas had gotten drunk more than once during those six months. Christ, just the thought sent Jonas's temperature into the red zone. "That was a year ago."

She rolled her eyes. "I'm well aware of that, but thanks for the reminder."

Jonas propped his hand against the doorjamb. "Did you love him?"

"I thought so at the time."

"Are you pining away for him, Deanna?"

She laughed. *"Pining?"*

At the sound of her quiet laughter, a dam inside Jonas burst and warmth flooded his system. "You're beautiful when you do that," he whispered as he lifted his hand and cupped her cheek in his palm.

"What?"

"Laugh. I love to hear you laugh."

"Jonas, don't." She shook her head and covered his hand with her own, but she didn't remove it. To his way of thinking, it was another step in the right direction.

Jonas dipped his head, slowly, afraid if he moved too fast she'd bolt through the open door. "Are you sure, Deanna?"

Her soft lips parted and Jonas swept in.

2

The instant their lips touched, Deanna's heart did a little cart-wheel. Geez, *good-looking* only scratched the surface with Jonas. She could also add *talented* to the list. There was a rather lethal sort of appeal to Jonas that she had the hardest time ig-noring. Danger oozed from his every pore. He seemed more animal than man. The image of a leopard sprang to Deanna's mind. The skillful, quiet way he moved reminded her of a great jungle cat stalking its prey.

Deanna was a breath away from pushing him back when she felt his arms come around her middle, pulling her closer. Too close. His hard body pressed against hers. God, that felt good. Deanna surrendered. Just this once she wanted to taste him. Feel him. To see if he would be as good in real life as in her fan-tasies. She'd had a lot of them. Putting everything she had into the kiss, Deanna touched the seam of his mouth with her tongue, prodding him to open and let her play. Jonas groaned and tightened his hold. She nipped his lower lip with her teeth, eager for more. He angled his head and dipped his tongue be-tween her lips. Finally, she got her first real taste of the man.

She detected a hint of alcohol, but most of all she simply savored Jonas. Hot and masculine. He was like Swiss chocolate, tempting and sweet; Deanna wanted to gorge herself on him.

Jonas rotated his hips, and Deanna felt the hard length of his cock against her stomach. Her pussy throbbed and dampened. She wanted to feel him, deep and hot, filling her. When his hands skimmed over the swell of her bottom, Deanna knew she had to put a stop to things before it was too late. Heck, much more and she'd be too far gone. She'd be begging him to take her.

Pulling back, but still close enough to feel his heavy breathing against her kiss-swollen lips, Deanna whispered, "Enough, Jonas."

"You want me, and we both know I'm desperate for you," he growled. "Why stop now? Just when things were getting interesting too."

Deanna had no answers for him. Her head felt too fuzzy to try to speak with any degree of intelligence. Instead, she attempted to step through the doorway, into her house, where she would be safe from big, hard men bent on turning her into a begging wanton. She needed distance between them. She needed to gain control over her raging hormones.

Jonas's fingers tugged at the length of her hair. "Uh-uh. You don't get off that easily, Deanna. We started something here tonight, you and I. The least you can do is give me a reason for leaving me standing here like some schmuck."

His low voice heated the blood in her veins. He was annoyed with her, and it should've cooled her down. The deep rumble so close to her ear only served to make her body burn hotter. Crap, even angry he exuded sex appeal. As if she needed him to wield more power over her!

Deanna turned slowly on her heel, all too aware of the hold he had on her hair. "Yes, we started something, but it was a mistake and I'm rectifying it."

He loosened his fist a fraction, and his mouth crooked up at the corners. "A damn delicious mistake in my opinion." He paused before adding, "You shouldn't tease a man like that, kitten."

Kitten? She reached a hand up and gently moved his hand out of her hair. "I didn't initiate the kiss—you did. And I'm not your kitten."

He chuckled. "You haven't kissed a lot of men, have you?"

His quiet, tender voice wrapped her in a layer of warmth, but the question slapped at her pride all the same. "Good night, Jonas. Find another corner to hang out on. Give this one a rest." She quickly turned, afraid she'd lose her nerve, and darted through the door. Unfortunately for Deanna's dignity, her foot caught on the entry rug and she stumbled. Yelping, she pitched forward. Before she landed on her face, Jonas caught her in his strong arms.

He swept her off her feet and took her into the house, then kicked the door closed behind him. As he stared down at her, his eyes full of mischief, he murmured, "That's twice you nearly fell. Next time maybe you should wear lower heels."

Deanna exhaled as embarrassment swamped her. Her face flamed red-hot, and she buried her nose into his black T-shirt. His masculine scent filled her nostrils, which made everything worse. Crap.

"Deanna?"

She squirmed in an attempt to get him to put her down, but he was too determined. His arms were steel bands around her. She lifted her head. Refusing to look at him, she said, "Jonas, please put me down. I feel enough like an idiot as it is."

He narrowed his eyes. "Did you twist your ankle? Does it hurt?"

"No. Please, I'm fine."

He kept his hold on her and took her into the living room. After placing her on the couch, Jonas knelt in front of her and cupped her cheek, forcing her to look at him. His hard jaw set in a rigid line, all but daring her to protest. "I can see you're in pain. Don't lie to me. Never lie to me, Deanna."

She slumped against the cushions. "The only thing in pain is my self-respect."

He cursed as he took hold of her foot and inspected it. "This is my fault," he growled. "If I'd let you go, you wouldn't have nearly twisted your ankle trying to run from me."

"I'm clumsy. Always have been. And I was not running."

"More lies." He tsked. "Stay put while I get some ice."

"I can ice my own ankle. I'm a nurse, remember?" Well, at least she'd been a nurse until recently.

He stood and stared down at her. "Where's your kitchen?"

Must he be so impossibly persistent? "Straight to the back. There's an ice pack in the freezer door."

He winked. "Be back in a jiffy."

Strangulation suddenly started to sound like a great way to commit murder. She could suffocate the man and be done with it. She'd probably get off on an insanity defense.

True to his word, Jonas strode back in, then folded his huge frame into the chair opposite her. He patted his thigh and said, "Give me your foot."

Her foot on his thigh? And why did that turn her on? "No."

He cursed under his breath. "I really wish you'd stop saying that word." He patted his thigh again. "I'm not leaving until this ice pack has been on your ankle at least fifteen minutes."

Deanna couldn't have him in her home. Much too private and he was simply too overwhelming. Besides, she would never be able to keep him at arm's length if she kept thinking about her bed. Her close, comfortable bed, plenty big enough for two. One flight of stairs and, boom, she'd be that much closer to satisfaction. Self-preservation caused her to cave and lift her leg. His large hand wrapped around her calf, and the heat of his palm went straight to her core. Jonas stared at her with such intensity, his eyes unblinking. She couldn't discern his thought, and it unnerved her. Jonas often came across as an open book to her—until now.

"What?" she growled, frustrated at her own curiosity and his utter lack of movement.

His thumb glided over her skin as he murmured, "Do you know how many times I've wanted to be in your home?" He glanced around. "It's nice."

"Nice? I have a passion for interior design and I've spent long, sweaty hours turning my house into my dream home. All you can say is 'nice'?"

He laughed. "It's stunning. Better?"

"A little," she conceded.

"And do you know how many times I've wanted to touch you like this?"

She quirked a brow. "You've fantasized about fondling my calf and icing my ankle?"

His lips twitched. "Ice can be damned erotic."

She couldn't have heard him right. "Ice? Erotic?"

He leaned forward and kissed the top of her foot, then looked up the length of her body. "Let me carry you to your bed and I'll demonstrate."

His bold words caused her to act impulsively. Taking advantage of his distracted mind, Deanna jerked her foot out of his grasp and stood, careful to keep most of her weight on her uninjured ankle. She placed her hands on the arms of his chair and leaned down to touch the thin line of his mouth with her lips. At first he remained perfectly still. As if too shocked to participate? Deanna didn't know, but when she tilted her head to the side, to better fit their mouths together, she felt Jonas's lips soften.

Strong, powerful arms came around her, tugging Deanna's body between Jonas's widespread thighs. In the next heartbeat, Jonas took over the kiss, forcing her mouth open, demanding entrance. His kiss, the furthest thing from gentle and coaxing, as he swept in and claimed. She should pull back and show him to the door. She'd only meant to prove to him that he wasn't dealing with a love-struck teenager who knew nothing about seduction. But she couldn't bring herself to break the kiss. To pretend the passion burning her alive was a figment of her imagination.

The frightening truth? Every time Jonas came near her, he had the unique ability to wrap her in a cocoon of lust. Lord help her, she wanted his swift, hard kisses. Deanna ached to feel the gentle caresses of his hands. She wanted him and had since the moment she'd spotted him at her family get-together all those years ago. She liked the wildness she'd glimpsed, as well as the tame parts she witnessed on the surface. No matter how hard she tried, she simply could not get him out of her head. He was dark and exciting, a little tortured, Deanna thought. So why did she constantly fight the attraction between them? To deny the pull of desire had proved futile. Dating other men hadn't worked. She wanted only Jonas. And he wanted her, too, but only for sex. She'd turned him down, and by doing so she'd become a challenge to Jonas. She wanted to be more to him. More than a conquest. More than a mark in his little black book, or whatever. To her surprise, Jonas pulled back, his heated midnight-blue gaze snaring hers.

"Do you know what you're doing?"

She didn't like the sweet tone in his voice. Too sweet. Jonas in sweet mode sent her heart into hiding. "What do you mean?"

He cupped her chin in his palm and stroked her lower lip with his thumb. "That wasn't a good night kiss, kitten," he whispered. "When you kiss a man the way you kissed me just now, it means you're giving him permission to do more. A hell of a lot more."

She jerked back, away from the teasing touches that drove

her body into overdrive. "A simple, friendly kiss. Don't read more into it than there is."

His head cocked to the side. "Are you so sure?"

She sat back down and crossed her arms over her breasts. It was annoying the way her nipples seemed to beg for Jonas's fingers and mouth. She wouldn't be swayed by her greedy breasts, damn it. "Just put the ice pack on my ankle and we'll call it a night, okay?"

Instead of growling at her as she'd expected, Jonas stood and stepped toward her. He leaned close, so close that Deanna could feel his hot breath against her lips. "You have it in your head that I'm a tame little puppy or something. Don't think for a second that you can pet me, then walk away. Whatever this is between us, Deanna, it's real, and it's hot enough to set us both on fire. So the next time you stroke me, I'm going to do more than sit here."

Deanna bit her lip and looked away. She hadn't really meant to tease him. Or had she? God, the man turned her inside out. Around him she did and said things that were totally out of character. As if another part of her, the evil part, took over, thrusting all rational thought into a lockbox.

"I'm sorry."

As Jonas stood over her, Deanna tried to calm her thundering pulse. When he reached out and caressed the cleft of her chin with his index finger, she gave up the fight.

"I want you," he growled, "more than I want my next breath. But I don't want to hurt you. I don't want you to have regrets."

Jonas's seductive voice and the gentle touch of his finger definitely sent her heart racing, but his cocky words were like a dash of ice water. "Don't confuse me for one of your mindless bimbos, Jonas. If I ever go to bed with you—and that's a very big 'if'—it won't be because I simply let my hormones run amok. Believe it or not, some women actually think before they act."

Jonas smiled and winked, as if he knew exactly how he affected her. "Good night, Deanna."

"Good night," she muttered. As he straightened and turned to leave, Deanna allowed her gaze to travel the length of him. Wow, the man had a nice ass. She couldn't help but stare at it each time she came into close proximity to the annoying man.

As Jonas opened the door, he gently ordered, "Lock up behind me."

"Gee, you think?" Deanna bit out as she stood. She tested her ankle by slowly putting most of her weight on it, but when no pain came, she let out a relieved breath.

Jonas turned and rolled his eyes. "That mouth of yours is going to cause you trouble one of these days."

As she reached the door, she planted her hands on her hips. "So I've been told." When he started to speak, she held a hand in the air. "Go home, Jonas."

He winked. "Sleep tight, kitten."

Deanna wanted to protest the ridiculous nickname, but Jonas quickly stepped through the door and shut it behind him. Deanna cursed as she locked and bolted the damn thing.

She dropped her forehead against the hard mahogany as an image of Jonas's ass sprang to her mind. "I am so freaking weak."

3

Pounding. On her front door. Maybe they'd go away? She waited, hoping it'd go away, but the infernal sound started right back up again. "Definitely not my head," she mumbled as she pried her eyes open and looked at the clock. Seven in the damn morning? Deanna stood and grabbed her robe. "Whoever it is better be half dead."

She slipped into the white terry cloth and tied it around her waist as she made her way out of her bedroom and down the stairs. By the time Deanna reached the front door, she'd worked herself into an angry fit. Pulling the curtains aside on the window to the left of the door, Deanna's anger turned into full-on rage when she spotted Jonas on her porch.

Unlocking and unbolting the door, she flung it open. "This better be important or I swear I'll pummel you, Jonas Phoenix."

To her satisfaction, Jonas actually flinched. "Ouch. You're definitely not a morning person, are you?"

"No. Now go away." She started to close the door in his face when a sweet aroma hit her nostrils. *Wait, was that doughnuts?*

She stopped mid-slam and raptly watched as Jonas rattled a bag in front of her face.

"Powdered doughnuts with chocolate cream filling just the way you like them."

Her mouth watered. Damn, he was good. She eyeballed the steaming cups. "And is that a mocha latte?"

Jonas grinned and Deanna's legs wobbled a little. Jonas's grins tended to have that effect on a woman. "Would I bring anything else to you this early?"

"Not if you want to live." She heaved a heavy sigh and stepped away from the door to allow him entrance. "No sense in letting perfectly good pastries go to waste."

He stepped over the threshold. "Figured you'd see it that way," he said, a little too cockily for her peace of mind, and headed toward her kitchen.

The sight of Jonas's ass encased in tight denim pleasantly distracted Deanna. Well, if she had to be awake at such an ungodly hour, at least a pleasant view and yummy treats awaited her. Or was that a yummy view and pleasant treats? She shrugged and followed the exquisite sight and smell. When she entered the kitchen, Jonas already had several napkins out of the bag and began to set a doughnut on top of one for her.

She licked her lips but didn't dig in. Not until she knew the real reason behind the kind gesture. "Is this like a bribe or something?"

Jonas chuckled and straddled a chair across from the table. "You are too suspicious. It's breakfast, Deanna, nothing more."

Drawn by the promise of sweet, chocolate filling, Deanna grabbed a chair and sat. *Okay, I'm weak.* Who wouldn't be when faced with chocolate cream filling? She picked up the doughnut and bit into it, then proceeded to moan. "These are the best doughnuts in the world."

"I knew you liked that little doughnut shop, but I've never actually been there until today."

"What made you go today?"

"I asked Wade about your favorite breakfast food. He told me you rarely eat breakfast, but if you do, then it comes from Donut World."

She swallowed before asking, "You're getting information about me from my brother now?"

"Whatever it takes, kitten." He picked up a doughnut and frowned. "And can you believe I've never had a chocolate-cream-filled doughnut before?"

She wanted to tell him to stop using the endearment with her, but she became distracted by Jonas's sensual mouth closing around the powdered treat. All too easily, she imagined those lips closing around her breast. Deanna had to clear the lump out of her throat in order to speak. "Well?"

Jonas took another bite, then one more to finish it off. A few seconds later, he sat back and swiped a napkin over his mouth. "I've seriously been missing out."

"Yep." They didn't say anything else. Simply sat and ate. By the time they were finished, Jonas had polished off three to her two.

"So, tell me the truth," Deanna said. "Why'd you really come over?"

Jonas crossed his arms over his chest. "Do I need a reason?"

She cocked her head to the side. "Yes, I think you do."

"Okay, there is something I want to ask you. But before I do, I want your word that you won't say no without at least giving it some thought."

Deanna stood and began cleaning up their mess. "Is this about decorating your apartment? I've already made up my mind about that." For months, Jonas had been attempting to get her to redecorate his apartment. She kept telling him no, but he still persisted.

"It's not about that, but now that you bring it up, *why* won't you decorate my apartment? I told you I'd pay you if money is the issue."

"That's not the problem." She couldn't possibly tell him the real reason: her very real fear of getting that close to Jonas's bed. Every time she thought of it, her insides turned to molten lava. "I just don't want to. Let it go."

"One of these days, I'm going to get you into my place. Mark my words."

She ignored that tantalizing thought. Or tried to. "Get to the point, Jonas."

"I want you to come to Miami with me."

She dropped the bag along with their used napkins into the trash before his words registered. No way had she heard him correctly. Deanna turned around and pinned him with an icy glare. "You want to take me to your little love shack? The one you and my brother own?"

Jonas stood and moved toward her. "It's not a love shack." Deanna gave him her best "yeah, right" expression. "Look, you told me last night that you think I'm nothing more than a play-boy. That all I want is sex."

"I know what I said, Jonas."

He glanced at her breasts, then quickly looked away. So brief that Deanna wouldn't have noticed if she hadn't been watching him so intently. "Come to Miami with me for the weekend and let me show you that I'm not the man you think I am. Let me prove to you that I want more than a few hot and sweaty moments between the sheets."

Deanna started to speak, but cool air against her upper chest stopped her. Looking down, she cringed at the way her robe had begun to gape. Geez, her breasts were barely covered. She could feel her cheeks heat with embarrassment as she drew the front closed.

"I'm not an idiot, Jonas," she said, picking up the conversation as she did her best to pretend she hadn't been about to flash him. "I know you and my brother use your place in Miami for weekend sex fests." She thought about her brother and how happy he'd been since meeting Gracie. "Well, not so much Wade now that he's met Gracie."

"I won't deny that we've brought women there in the past, but it's more to us than that. It's always been a place where we could get away from all the stress. To unwind."

She quirked a brow at him. "And how does bringing me there prove you're a relationship kind of guy, exactly?"

He moved closer, and Deanna soon found herself wedged between the counter and Jonas's big, hard body. Not a bad place to be, all in all. "Here you're constantly surrounded by your family and work," he murmured. "I can't get two words with you without one of your brothers interrupting. Especially now that Dean and Wade know how I feel about you. They've been hovering like a couple of mother hens. I want you alone, Deanna. Is that such a crime?"

She hadn't noticed her brothers coddling her, but now that she thought about it, she realized Jonas had a valid point. They had been coming around more, and calling daily too. Deanna suddenly felt like a coward. Hiding behind them to keep Jonas at bay? So not her style. Although, she *had* been avoiding him to save herself from potential heartache.

"I quit my nursing job," she blurted out. *Where had that come from?*

Jonas's eyes widened. "You did?"

She shrugged. "I've decided to do the interior design full-time."

"You have so many clients that you can afford to quit the day job?"

"I'm getting there. It's not easy. There is a lot of competition in this business, and you have to bid on jobs. I've lost a few, but I've been saving, so it didn't set me back. Nursing wasn't making me happy, and I figured if I'm ever going to do it, now is the time."

Jonas cupped her cheek in his palm. "I'm proud of you. Being self-employed is a tough choice to make."

With great effort, Deanna removed Jonas's calloused hand from her cheek. "Y-yeah, it is." She attempted to tamp down her reaction to his overwhelming nearness before continuing. "I hope I didn't make a horrible mistake."

"I think you'll do great, but why the subject change?"

Deanna looked down at the floor, uncertain how to respond. Uncertain how honest she wanted to be with him. Letting a man like Jonas into her private thoughts could prove dangerous. He struck her as the type of guy who would use every advantage he had with a woman to get what he wanted, and he'd already made it clear he wanted her.

Jonas tipped her chin up. "Is going to Miami with me so frightening, kitten?"

That nickname again. Damn if she wasn't starting to enjoy it too. "No, it's not. It's exciting, to tell the truth."

He moved then, pinning her against the counter. She could feel every hard, muscular inch of him. Her body stood up and took notice. Deanna had the wild urge to rub against him. To ease the ache he'd caused. With a lot of effort, she reminded her overheated feminine parts that she wasn't the type of woman normally ruled by her hormones. Right at that moment, her hormones seemed to have some really great ideas.

"Then what is it?" he asked, his voice softening. "You can tell me."

Deanna thought about the one real relationship she'd had with a man. Sadly, it hadn't been a good experience. Could she tell him about Gary? She looked into Jonas's eyes and realized the truth. He wasn't budging until he had an answer to her question.

Pushing a hand through her hair, Deanna said, "You might as well have a seat. It's sort of a long story."

Jonas hesitated a moment, and his intense gaze seemed to be searching for something in hers. Finally, he backed up, and she could finally breathe normally again. After he sat, she went to the other side of the table and took the chair she'd vacated earlier. "Gary Anderson."

"Huh?"

"He's a guy I dated while in college. I fell madly in love with him."

Deanna watched the way Jonas's entire body went rigid. "Okay, but what's he got to do with us?"

She rolled her eyes. "Well, if you'll hush, I'll tell you."

He sat back and crossed his arms over his chest. "Fine. I'm all ears."

"Dating Gary was a mistake, but I didn't know that at the time. I thought he was the one." She looked at the frayed cuff on her robe and started to pick at a loose thread. "I was young and stupid. Gary was self-centered, egotistical, a complete womanizer, and those were his better qualities."

He snorted. "Sounds like a real stand-up guy."

"I didn't know what he was really like, not at first. He completely swept me off my feet with his easy charm. And I guess I was at an age where I wanted guys to notice me. I had a wild streak. Gary took full advantage of it."

"The wild streak I can see, or at least I'd like to see it. But where did you meet this guy?"

"At a nightclub. I don't think it's even in business anymore. I was out with some friends from college. Gary was there. He asked me to dance when a slow song came on. He smiled and I caved. He was older, more confident. I suppose I let my heart overrule my head."

"He made you feel like Cinderella at the ball," Jonas surmised in a soft, understanding voice.

He hadn't phrased it as a question, but Deanna answered anyway. "Yeah. With his blond, wavy hair, blue eyes, and tall, muscled body, I let myself get carried away. Gary had a knack for making a woman feel special, cherished even."

"When did things change?"

"When a friend told me that she'd seen Gary out with another woman."

Jonas winced. "Ouch."

"Oh, I still couldn't bring myself to believe the truth. Gary seemed so sincere when he told me how much he cared about me. That he wanted to marry me after I finished nursing school. Everything came crashing down when a woman called to tell me she was pregnant with Gary's baby."

"Damn, seriously?"

"Yep. I still didn't want to believe it, but I met with the woman." Deanna thought back to the horrible day and cringed. "Girl, really. She was only eighteen, Jonas. It made me sick to my stomach. When I confronted Gary later, he came unglued. Turned the whole thing around on me. Told me I didn't trust him. That I had no right to sneak around behind his back and check up on him. That if I loved him, I'd have more faith."

Jonas shook his head. "Christ, what an ass."

"Exactly. Gary didn't know the meaning of commitment. His goal in life was to see just how much pleasure he could squeeze out of everything and everyone. He paid no attention to the people he hurt in his quest for fun. Unfortunately, Gary had a temper."

"A temper?"

Deanna nodded. "When I told him I wanted nothing to do with him anymore, he hit me."

Jonas cursed and shot to his feet, knocking the chair backward. "Bastard! I'll kill him," he gritted out, fists clenched at his sides.

Without thinking, Deanna stood and went to him. She didn't like seeing him angry. She wanted the playful Jonas back. In a gesture meant to soothe, Deanna placed her palm on his chest and smiled up at him. "This was years ago. It's over. But thank you for the offer."

He frowned down at her. "Where were your brothers during all this?"

"Wade was in the army at the time. Dean was busy with his construction business. It was still pretty new then." She smacked him on the arm before moving away. "Besides, I wasn't going to go running to my big brothers just because a guy made me cry."

She saw a muscle in his jaw jump. "You didn't tell them he hit you, did you?"

Give the man a cigar. "Of course I didn't. As far as they were concerned, Gary was a nice guy. When it ended, I told them we had different goals in life." She bit her lip and put a few more feet of linoleum between them. "Not entirely untrue."

Jonas didn't move. He simply stood there watching her, anger seeping from his pores. "The son of a bitch hit you, Deanna. He deserved a beating."

Deanna felt cool air against her chest again and tugged at the lapels of her robe. Darn thing seemed intent on giving Jonas a peep. As if her robe were on Jonas's side. "The point of the story is that I'm not a good judge of character. At least not when it comes to men I'm attracted to."

Before Deanna could blink, Jonas was in front of her with his hands wrapped around her upper arms. "Are you putting me in the same pot as that piece of shit?"

"No. Geez, Jonas."

He relaxed his hold. "Then explain, damn it."

"You go to my head, Jonas!" she shouted without thinking. "You're asking me to go away with you, and I'm afraid I'm going to make all the wrong choices. Again."

Jonas stilled, and Deanna knew she'd said too much. He had that look in his eyes. The one that made her think of a tiger about to have lunch—and she was lunch.

"You make me crazy, Deanna," he murmured. "For now, all I want you to do is think about my offer. Please. Take the week if you want. You can give me your answer next Saturday."

Jonas never begged. That he was doing so now cracked the wall she'd built around her heart. "I'll think about it," she hedged.

"Thank you. And maybe this will help a little." Jonas's head lowered, and Deanna sank against him, accepting the kiss. Hell, surrendered to it. When his lips touched hers, she tasted the sweet flavor of chocolate, but beneath that was the rich flavor of Jonas. And she was certain that last part was what kept her from pushing away and ending the kiss.

His lips were soft as they coasted back and forth, barely touching hers. As his tongue darted out, a shiver of excitement raced the length of her spine. He was doing it to her again. To be in his presence was to be a living, breathing flame of desire and need. When he pulled back and stared down at her, Deanna could see the wild hunger in those deep blue eyes of his. She well understood how he felt. Her entire body was screaming for more of his taste, his touch.

He slowly released her and growled, "No dating. For either of us. Not until you give me your answer. Agreed?"

Knowing Jonas wasn't going to be with another woman made her possessive side a very happy camper. Her answer was as easy as pie. "Agreed."

Without another word, Jonas walked out. After she heard the front door close, Deanna moved on wobbly legs to the nearest chair and collapsed into it. One week to decide whether she was going to spend a weekend in Miami with the intoxicating Jonas Phoenix. She'd have him all to herself. Experience him up close and personal. Every sexy inch of him. The juncture between her thighs dampened.

Covering her face with her hands, Deanna let out a loud moan. Yeah, like she was really going to say no. "I'm so freaking weak."

4

It was five o'clock on Friday, and Jonas had done everything he could to keep busy. To leave Deanna alone and let her think about his offer was killing him. But he'd promised not to push. Damn it, he was going insane. He wanted to swat her bottom for being so distant too. He hadn't heard a word from her. Not a peep. At the same time, he was very tempted to just show up on her doorstep and beg her to put him out of his misery.

Hell, he used to love his job. When he and Wade had opened Phoenix-Wade Investigations, it'd been a proud day for both of them. It had seemed like a natural progression from their Special Forces days. Now, three years later, they had a steady stream of clients. They'd even toyed with the idea of bringing in another investigator to take some of the pressure off. And yet, Jonas couldn't give a flying fuck about the business, the clients, the damn tax document he should've had finished days ago. The only thing on his mind was Deanna.

"You're doing it again."

At the sound of another voice in the empty office, Jonas tore his attention away from the tax document he'd been going over and swiveled his chair around. Wade was leaning against the doorjamb. He had that determined look in his eyes. Jonas hated that look. "What?"

"Snarling. You've been doing it all week. What's going on?"

Jonas shook his head. "You aren't going to like it."

Wade frowned. "Is this about the Emerson case?"

Leo Emerson had hired them to find out if his wife was cheating on him. They'd watched the woman for the past two weeks with no sign of another man, which was good. But Emerson hadn't been convinced, so he'd asked them to keep at it.

Grateful for the distraction, Jonas said, "It's almost as if the guy wants her to cheat. What the hell is wrong with people?"

"Hell if I know." Wade tossed his keys onto his desk. "I just got back from another boring trip around town. I've followed that woman to the dry cleaner, the grocery store, and yoga class so many times I think I could make the trip blindfolded. From what I can tell, she's completely devoted to her husband. I'm calling Emerson today and telling him we're done."

"Good deal."

"Now, onto the real issue here." Wade pulled his chair out and sat, facing him. "What's got you all pissy?"

"Your sister," Jonas bit out. Wade cursed. Jonas held a hand up in the air and rushed to say, "Before you start in on me about your sweet, innocent baby sis, I might as well tell you that I asked Deanna to go to Miami with me for the weekend."

Wade slammed his fist against the desk. "Christ, Jonas. She's my sister!"

"Yeah, I'm aware." Jonas rubbed his forehead. Ah, hell, he was getting a headache. Wasn't that just the icing on the cake? "But it doesn't change the fact that I'm attracted to her. Besides, you told me you were okay with me pursuing her. Have you changed your mind?"

"No, I haven't changed my mind," he gritted out. "But I also don't want to think about you taking her to the beach house either." Wade paused; then, in a calmer voice, he asked, "Did she say yes?"

Jonas tapped his foot against the hardwood floor as he answered Wade's question. "She hasn't given me an answer yet. I didn't want to rush her. I told her to think it over and let me know." And it was driving him mad. He wanted to get her alone. He ached to see her naked. To bury his cock inside her sweet, hot pussy. Shit, if he didn't hear from her soon, he was going to self-combust.

"Jonas?"

"Huh?"

"Quit thinking about her!"

Jonas winced. "Right. Sorry."

"Have you two even been on a date?"

"Nope, and that's half the problem. She's too damn good at avoiding me." His gaze shot to Wade as he ground out, "And with you and Dean always around, it's hard as hell trying to get some alone time with her."

"If you want an apology, it's not going to happen. She's our sister and we will always look out for her."

The hell of it was he understood Wade's feelings. "I'd be the same way if I had a sister," he admitted. For a second, Jonas thought of telling Wade about Gary, but he nixed the idea. That was Deanna's business. Besides, if anyone was going hunting for the asshole, it was going to be Jonas. It didn't matter that the whole thing had occurred years ago. He never should've hit Deanna.

"Hell, you'd be worse." Wade looked over at the blank tax document. "I see you've been hard at work."

Jonas picked up the paper. "This should've been done days ago."

"I'll work on it—don't worry about it." Wade took the paper from him. "I owe you for everything you did for Gracie anyway."

"You don't owe me, but thanks." Jonas had done whatever he could to help Gracie with her stalker situation because Wade was his friend and Gracie belonged to Wade. End of story. "I'll try to get my shit together."

"While you're doing that, consider calling Deanna."

"I can't." Jonas stood and grabbed his keys from the desk drawer. "I promised not to push."

Wade tossed the paper onto his own desk, then crossed his arms over his chest. "And if she never gives you an answer?"

"She will. She might be as stubborn as a mule, but she won't leave me hanging." He just hoped like hell she gave him an answer soon.

Wade's cell phone rang, and judging by the grin when his friend looked at the number on the screen, Jonas had to conclude Gracie was on the other end. He left him to talk with his woman in private, only marginally jealous of the pair of love-birds.

Half an hour later, Jonas pulled into a parking spot in front of his apartment complex. As he shut off the engine and got out, he scanned the lot and tried to remember the trip there. He'd just spent the entire drive home thinking of Deanna. "If I don't get that woman out of my head soon, I'm going to end up wrapped around a freaking tree."

Once inside his apartment, Jonas headed straight for the fridge. A cold beer was a poor substitute for Deanna's warm smile, but it was his only option at the moment. He popped the top and took a long drink before setting it on the counter. As he opened the cabinet and took out a box of spaghetti, he sighed. "Another Friday night spent at home alone. Yippee."

As he was getting out a pot to cook the pasta, his phone rang. He grabbed it from the cradle on the counter and answered on the second ring, hoping it was Deanna. "Hello?"

"Jonas, it's Mom."

Jonas frowned. The only time his mother called was on holidays or when she was going out of town. "Hi, Mom."

"I hope I didn't disturb you."

Jesus, did the woman always have to sound so formal? "No, Mom, I was just getting ready to make dinner. What's up?"

"I wanted to let you know that your father and I are going to spend a few months at our place in London."

Jonas picked up the large pot and ran water in it. "Do you need me to check on the house or anything?"

"No, thank you. It's all arranged."

Having had this conversation a hundred times before, Jonas's next response came with practiced ease. "Sounds good. Take care, then."

"You, too, Jonas."

After they hung up, Jonas placed the phone back in the holder, then shook his head in disgust. Each time the woman called, he got a little more sick to his stomach. She was so cold he could practically get frostbite just talking to her.

He couldn't help but compare how different his family was from the Harrisons. Wade's mother, with her warm, friendly nature, was the polar opposite of his mom. Hell, from the day he'd met Mrs. Harrison, she'd treated him as if he were one of her own.

On the other hand, Jonas couldn't remember a single time his mom had told him she loved him. It was always "take care." He wondered if she was even capable of loving someone. Money, she loved. Adored it, even. People were expendable, though. Even her own husband slept in a different room. No, what his parents had was the exact opposite of what he wanted in a marriage.

Jonas knew if he ever tied the knot, his wife wouldn't be sleeping in a room down the hall. Nor would his children go to bed at night wondering if their parents loved them. Laughter and joy and love, that's what he wanted in a marriage. That's what his children would know. He would go to every single one of his kids' games too. And he wouldn't make excuses about being in important business meetings.

As Jonas placed the pot of water on the stove and started to turn on the burner, his doorbell rang. Could it be that Deanna had finally decided to put him out of his misery? Jonas turned the burner off and headed for the living room. He tried to tell himself that the unexpected visitor could be anyone. An ex-girlfriend. Wade. The annoying woman down the hall who kept trying to flirt with him, even though she was married.

It rang again and Jonas tore himself out of his thoughts and sprinted toward the front door. His entire body went from zero to sixty as he glanced through the peephole. It seemed to take a shitload of time to unlock the door and get it open. When he did, Jonas nearly swallowed his tongue at the sight that greeted him.

Deanna stood in the hallway wearing a short black dress and a pair of the sexiest black pumps he'd ever seen on a woman. *Attractive* didn't begin to describe her. Long legs, silky dark hair spilling down over her shoulders, and curves in all the right places. His hands itched to reach out and touch.

"Deanna," he said by way of greeting.

She planted one hand on her hip and clutched a small black purse in the other. "Are you going to let me in or what?"

Jonas grinned at her sullen expression and stepped back to give her room to enter. After she was inside, he shut and locked the door. Deanna looked around the room; no doubt the interior designer in her was hard at work measuring up his furnishings. He, on the other hand, was busy measuring *her* up. Such a sweet ass. What he'd love to do to that delicious body part alone. Yum.

"Uh, I told you I needed a decorator, so don't complain if it's not up to par."

She turned, halting his little fantasy. "It's not so bad."

"It's ugly as hell and we both know it."

Their gazes clashed. "I didn't come here to talk about your couch."

Jonas moved closer, noticing the way her spine stiffened. "I was hoping not," he murmured. "And?"

"I'll come to Miami with you."

She said it so fast, Jonas had to take a second before the full meaning of her words hit him. "Be sure, Deanna. Be damn sure."

She nodded and placed her palms against his chest. "I am. I'm through denying myself."

He kept his hands at his sides and willed himself to stay calm. "I won't hurt you, kitten. I'm not Gary."

"I know you aren't, but I'm not the fling type of woman, Jonas. I don't do casual sex."

"Good," he growled. "There's nothing casual about what I feel for you."

Jonas wrapped his arms around her and pulled her against him, needing to feel her curves and valleys; then he tasted her as if he had all night. He licked her lips, and they parted for him. He thrust his tongue in and fucked her hot mouth. Her soft, pliable flesh against his hard body made him crazy with need. She was a drug to him. At that moment, Jonas knew he would do anything, say anything, to be inside of her sweet heat. The idea that she had so much control over him pissed him off.

Jonas lifted his head and stared down at her closed eyes and flushed face. He took in the scoop neckline of her dress and the tops of her heaving mounds of flesh that were exposed. Christ, what he wouldn't give to tug the material a few inches south, to see her tits all plump and soft and ready to be suckled. He ached to wrap his lips around her nipples and nibble on them with his teeth. Bending his knees, Jonas lifted her into his arms and strode toward the couch.

Her eyes shot open when he sat her down in the center. He

saw realization dawn in their pretty depths. "W-what are you doing?"

"Giving you a taste of what you'll get in Miami."

"Jonas, please."

He wasn't certain whether she was pleading for him to continue or let her get up and leave. Jonas bent down and kissed her again, tasting her sweetness. He lifted an inch and asked, "Please what, Deanna?"

She buried her fingers in his hair and tugged him forward. "Please kiss me again."

"Mmm, my pleasure, kitten." He tilted her head back, forcing her to look at him as he covered her mouth with his. She let out a little whimper. "You've been driving me crazy," he whispered between kisses. "I've been a pain in the ass all week because I couldn't stop thinking about you." He kissed his way over her chin and lower. When his lips found the jumpy vein in her neck, he licked and sucked. Deanna's fingers tightened, pulling almost painfully at his hair. "Soon I'm going to kiss every inch of you. I'm going to fill you up." Jonas went to his knees in front of her and took hold of the hem of her dress. "Until then, until Miami, there's this . . ."

"Jonas, what are you doing to me?" she asked in a voice gone husky with her arousal.

"I've been dying to taste you," he answered. Deanna's eyes rounded and fire sparked to life in their brown depths. "Lift up a little for me. Prove to me that you want this."

When she quickly complied, Jonas's dick hardened. He slipped her dress upward a few inches, not quite exposing her panties. The satin of her lightly tanned skin beckoned him. Lowering his head, Jonas kissed a little mole high on her inner thigh. "Jesus, you have the sexiest legs I've ever seen." When he pushed the dress up to her waist, exposing a black, silky thong, Jonas's dick wept with joy. "Goddamn, that's hot."

She started to protest, and he could see the way her cheeks

bloomed pink at his erotic words. He didn't know how experienced Deanna was, but he suspected she was way too innocent for the likes of him. Not that it mattered, because he wasn't going anywhere.

Jonas fingered the leg band of the thong and hummed his approval. "Did you wear this for me, Deanna?" She licked her lips and stayed silent. Her gaze ate him up, though. If she only knew what that look was doing to his self-control, she'd get up and run.

Not willing to give her too much time to rethink her decision, Jonas tugged the little black scrap of material to one side, baring her pussy for the first time. The neatly trimmed, soft, dark curls glistened in the light from the table lamp. It was the single most delicious thing he'd ever seen. Jonas was suddenly starving. Staring at the beauty of her most intimate flesh, Jonas murmured, "So hot. Hot and wet and all mine."

"Oh, God."

"Put your legs over my shoulders," he instructed. Deanna lifted both legs at once and positioned them exactly the way he wanted. Her cunt was an inch from his mouth now. Fucking perfect.

"Lick me, Jonas."

Hearing the husky little demand from Deanna turned him inside out. His cock swelled painfully inside his jeans. He grasped her hips and pulled her to him, then placed a soft kiss against her damp pussy lips. "Oh, hell yeah. Now that's what I've been missing. I'm going to swallow every last drop of your cream, kitten." Then, using only his thumbs, Jonas spread her open, exposing her clitoris. He sucked the little bud into his greedy mouth.

His balls drew up tight as he imagined filling her with his cock. She'd squeeze him like a loving fist, he just knew. His tongue moved inside her succulent channel, and his hands clasped onto her bottom, bringing her closer, delving deeper and giving her everything he had to give. He hissed as Deanna raked her fingers through his hair and clutched onto him as if for dear life. Then she cried out as he flicked his tongue over and around her clit. Time after time, he toyed with her. Suddenly, he could feel her thighs beginning to quiver. Her hips moved against his face as she began fucking his mouth. Her heels dug into his back, but he barely noticed. The taste, sight, and feel of Deanna's hot, silky heat filled all his senses.

Without warning, she screamed his name and came into his mouth, her thighs tightening around his head for a moment before she slumped against the couch. Jonas swallowed her tangy juice, taking his time to linger over her as if she were his very own luscious dessert. "I could become addicted to you," he acknowledged aloud. "You taste like warm honey." And he'd never forget her flavor, not as long as he lived. Watching her lie there, so open and trusting, it pulled at something inside Jonas. Something he couldn't quite put his finger on.

Careful not to break the spell around them, Jonas kissed her swollen nub one more time, then slowly lifted his head. He cupped her throbbing pussy in his palm and watched as her eyelids lifted. She smiled down at him, and damn if he didn't want to see that look on her face again and again. That look was for him alone.

"If that's a taste of what's to come," she whispered, "then I think I'm really going to enjoy this trip."

The words were so unexpected, Jonas couldn't help but laugh. "Damn straight, kitten."

5

It was Saturday afternoon, and Deanna was still a little wobbly from the encounter with Jonas the night before. And because she hadn't slept worth a crap, thanks to her mind wandering to the man's oh-so-talented mouth, she'd gotten up early and gone straight to the gym in the hopes of working off some of her sexual frustration. It hadn't worked for crap. The sad truth was, now that she'd had a sampling of what Jonas had to offer, she wanted more. Deanna desperately wanted to see him strip out of his clothes and bare that perfect male body to her. And she wanted to taste him, the way he'd tasted her. She longed to feel his cock against her tongue and suck him dry.

It was going to be a damn long week.

He'd called earlier to let her know he'd purchased the plane tickets. They would leave around one in the afternoon on Friday and get back late Sunday. Luckily, her weekend was clear because her newest client was out of town on business and wouldn't be ready to start the face-lift on his living room until he returned. Still, that meant she'd have to wait an entire week before she could have Jonas all to herself.

A cold shower. That's what she needed. Deanna headed for her bedroom, but on the way to the stairs, she glanced around the living room and her chest filled with pride. Her home had been a labor of love. She'd enjoyed making it her own. The interior designer in her couldn't help mentally comparing it to Jonas's apartment. In the short amount of time she'd been inside the place, two things had stood out the most: the lack of family pictures and the starkness of the living room. There hadn't been any real signs of Jonas, just plain white walls and dull furniture. No warmth. She realized then that she didn't really know that much about Jonas's life before he'd met Wade in the army. She knew he was an only child and that he wasn't terribly close to his parents, but she didn't know why. Miami was going to be her chance to find out more about the man who made her heart race like a greyhound chasing a rabbit.

Deanna thought again about Jonas's plea to have her redecorate his apartment. Now that she'd seen it for herself, she just might. He needed a home, not just a place to sleep and eat, for crying out loud.

Thinking of her own house, she knew she'd gotten lucky when she'd stumbled onto the FOR SALE sign. Like many of the houses in her neighborhood, it was older but it had character. She'd fallen in love with the oddly shaped rooms and arched doorways.

She'd done the living room in country blue, with her mother's handmade accents decorating the walls. The plush blue furniture and yellow walls were cheerful and inviting. She'd really lucked out when she'd found the square oak end tables and large trunk that doubled as a coffee table at a garage sale. The floors were polished oak that matched the tables perfectly. The large, oval area rug that her mother had purchased years ago pulled the room together beautifully. It had been the rug that gave her the idea for the décor, because she'd instantly fallen in love with the blue and yellow tones.

The kitchen still wasn't finished. She wasn't sure what was wrong with the room, but it certainly wasn't the kitchen table. The large, rectangular oak table seated six comfortably. She'd vowed that someday she'd have the husband and children to fill it. An image of Jonas sprang to mind. No, she chided herself; he is not the marrying type. Going away with a man for the weekend and marrying him were two totally different things and not to be confused.

Through another doorway was the family room. Being a fan of football, Deanna had enjoyed buying the large flat-screen television to watch her games. The twin black leather recliners and couch always seemed to be where Dean and Wade headed whenever they came over for a visit. She could all too easily imagine spending a lazy Sunday with Jonas in there, cuddled up together. Damn, there she went again.

Taking the stairs up to her bedroom, Deanna was more than a little desperate to shower and hopefully clear her head, but she stopped when she caught sight of her workroom. Situated across from her bedroom, it was easily her favorite room in the house. It didn't just have her sewing machine and yards and yards of material and tools, but it also contained her heart and soul. She took pleasure in all the hours she'd spent in there creating things for clients. When she stepped inside her bedroom, Deanna imagined inviting Jonas over. It was entirely too easy to picture what they could be doing in her big, lonely bed. One phone call and they could be filling the entire upstairs with moans of satisfaction. No, she wouldn't cave. Heck, if Jonas could wait, then so could she.

Deanna quickly shed her clothes and stepped into the shower. She braced herself and turned the water to cold. "Holy hell that's cold!" Okay, the cold shower thing was totally bogus. At least for women. Quickly washing and rinsing, lest she end up with hypothermia, Deanna stepped out and dried off. Geez, she was still shivering. At least slipping into her favorite pair of plum-colored lounging pants and a short-sleeved white T-shirt took some of the chill off.

As Deanna looked at the green neon numbers on the clock, she remembered her mom was supposed to come over for a visit very soon. They were going to talk about her mom's new job working at the women's shelter. Gracie, Wade's new lady love, had suggested it. Deanna was thrilled her mother had found something to do that she enjoyed, but Deanna still worried about her safety. The shelter wasn't on the best end of town. Plus, she knew that with battered women came angry husbands spoiling for a fight.

Heading down the stairs and entering the kitchen, Deanna filled her teapot and set it on the stove to boil. When she looked over at her kitchen table, she remembered Jonas sitting there last Saturday. He'd looked so damn good with his long, muscular legs spread wide as he devoured his doughnuts. Of course, he'd looked even better devouring her the previous night. "Okay, he's not just handsome. The man is also hot and demanding and everything my libido craves." And, she mentally added, he happened to have the softest hair she'd ever touched. Thick enough to bury her fingers into. It was a little long by today's standards, but Deanna loved it. And his hands. Oh, wow. When he had cupped her sex after giving her that glorious orgasm, Deanna had melted into a puddle. She'd always had an obsession for a man's strong, calloused hands, and Jonas's were grade A. He wasn't overly gentle, but he didn't manhandle her either.

And before their weekend was over, she vowed those talented hands would caress every inch of her body.

The teapot started to whistle, forcing Deanna back to reality. She flipped the burner off and used a pot holder to move the teapot to a cooling pad. While she grabbed a couple of cups from the cabinet and a box of her mom's favorite Earl Grey tea, her mind inexorably went back over Friday night, when she'd come home to find Jonas on her porch. He'd asked why she hadn't invited her date inside, and Deanna couldn't bring herself to admit the truth. That her date had been a disaster. He'd been like all the other men before him, which meant he'd taken one look at her and fallen in lust with her body. Completely oblivious to the fact that there were other parts besides her ass and breasts. He hadn't cared about her job or her hobbies. She'd even tried to talk about her interior design business, but he'd somehow managed to turn the topic right back to sex. It'd been another disappointing date.

And her real fear, the one Deanna barely admitted even to herself, was that she was terribly afraid Jonas would turn out to be the same. He'd get his fill of her body in Miami, then be ready to move on once they arrived back home. It would crush her. She didn't understand why, but she knew beyond a shadow of a doubt that it wouldn't be so easy to shrug it off.

"No, I'm not backing out," she said aloud. "Besides, if he does see only the surface stuff, I'll damn well give up on men completely."

As Deanna began pouring the steaming water into her cup, she heard a faint but cheerful, "Hello? Deanna?"

"In the kitchen, Mom," she called back. "The tea is nearly ready." Deanna was already pouring the second cup when her mom walked into the room carrying two bags of groceries. "Mom," she muttered, "you do not have to buy me food every time you come over."

As her mother placed the bags down on the counter, Deanna carried the cups to the table. She watched as her mom pulled out a chair and sat. "It's just a few things I picked up at the store. Those cookies you love and that new romantic suspense book you and I've been waiting to read."

Sweat beaded her mother's brow, and she was panting slightly. "Are you okay, Mom?" Deanna leaned down to kiss her mom's cheek before sitting adjacent to her. "I told you before not to overdo it."

"Don't fuss, young lady," she admonished, grabbing a napkin out of the holder from the center of the table. After swiping it over her brow, she wadded it up and placed it on the table next to her cup. In a stronger voice, she added, "I'm not that old yet."

Deanna snorted. With her soft skin, very few wrinkles and dark brown hair—that now came from a bottle—Audrey Harrison was still quite a catch. "You look great for your age and you know it, but why do you appear as if you've just run a marathon?"

Her mother's eyes brightened. "It's this new class I'm taking. One of the ladies down at the shelter recommended it. It's tai chi. Great for flexibility." She bit her lip and shook her head. "Or so they say. Today was my first class, and I feel about as flexible as a steel pipe."

Deanna sipped her tea and tried not to laugh as an image of her mom doing the deep lung movement "snake creeps down" sprang to mind. "Sounds like a real blast."

Her mom grinned. "You should've seen me trying to do some of those moves. I'm pretty sure the instructor thought I was going to pass out at any moment."

They both laughed. "So, besides attempting to throw your back out, what else has been going on?"

"Things are going great down at the shelter. I'm still trying to get the hang of things, but I'm really enjoying talking to all the ladies. One woman is around my age. She's been married to this guy, a real loser, for twenty-five years. He's used her as a punching bag. Poor thing." She finished off her tea, then sat back. "It's nice to get out of the house. I didn't know how much I needed it until now. I guess I was lonelier than I thought. I'm grateful to Gracie for suggesting it, honestly."

Mention of the house gave Deanna the opening to try, again, to convince her mom to sell the family home. It'd become too big for her to live in alone. "Mom, you need to seriously consider selling the house and moving into an apartment. Dean called the other day and said he found a great place. And it's right in town, so you wouldn't have to drive as far to the shelter every day."

"I don't mind the drive, sweetie. It gives me time to think."

Deanna couldn't count the amount of times they'd had this conversation. "This isn't really about the drive, Mom. You don't want to sell because of Dad." After Deanna's dad had died from a brain aneurysm two years earlier, her mom had clung to the house. All their memories, the good and the bad, were tied to it. Deanna understood her mom too well. She wasn't all that crazy about selling their family home either.

"We'll talk about the house later. For now, let's dig into those cookies I bought you."

Well, I lost that round. "Fine, but someday soon we need to do something about the house. It's too much for you to keep up, and it's not safe for you to live alone and so far from Dean, Wade, and me."

As Deanna stood to get the box of cookies out of the bag her mom had brought over, she heard an incoherent curse from behind. After setting the box onto the table, Deanna stopped short at the glare of disapproval on her mother's face. "Er, what did I say?"

"I am perfectly safe in that house," her mother said, all but daring her to disagree. "I don't need my three children worrying over me, you hear?"

"Loud and clear." Deanna opened the box of cookies—mmm, chocolate chunk, Deanna's favorite—handed her mom one, then smiled in an attempt at a truce. To her relief, her mom smiled back and took the cookie.

"You always could get around me with that pretty smile of yours," her mom said. "So, dear, what have you been up to these last few days?" She placed the cookie on a napkin, untouched.

An image of Jonas's head buried between her legs sprang to mind. "Uh, nothing much. Working on some new things for a client. I went to the gym this morning." She paused and realized she'd have to tell her mom about her upcoming trip. "By the way, I'm going out of town next weekend."

Her mother stood and brought her cup to the sink. "Oh? Business or pleasure?" she asked over her shoulder.

And here we go, Deanna thought, wishing the floor would swallow her up. "Pleasure," she blurted out.

Her mom rinsed the cup and began to wipe down the counter. "I see." She turned around and gave her that I-can-see-right-through-you look that only a mother seemed to possess. "Is there a man involved?"

And now for the grand finale! "Yeah. Jonas."

God, she so did not want to get on the subject of Jonas Phoenix. Her mom was much too astute; she'd notice right off if Deanna appeared overly interested in the man. Yet, she could never bring herself to hold out on her mom.

With dismay, Deanna noticed she now had her mother's undivided attention. "Our Jonas?" her mom asked. "Wade's army friend?"

"The one and only."

After returning to her seat, her mom said, "Hmm, a weekend away with Jonas. I think I need to hear the rest of that story." The mischievous smile playing at the corners of her lips didn't bode well for Deanna.

"It's no big deal, so don't go reading too much into it. He asked me to go to that beach house he co-owns with Wade. I said yes. The end."

"You must like him, though, or you wouldn't have said yes," she surmised as she continued to nibble on her cookie.

Deanna picked at her own chocolate chip treat, not really interested in eating it anymore. "He's a nice guy, good-looking in a rugged sort of way. He's been trying to get me to go out with him forever." She shrugged as if it meant little to her. "I decided to put the guy out of his misery." *Does one go to hell for downplaying the truth?* Deanna would definitely have to give that one some serious thought later.

Her mom reached across the table and covered her hand. "It's more than that. You like him, don't you?"

"I'm attracted to him, yes. Is there something besides physical attraction, though? I don't know. I'm hoping to find out in Miami."

"You know, Susan down at the Shop n Bag didn't use words like *good-looking* and *nice* when she talked about Jonas. The way she described him made me think more along the lines of a strawberry cheesecake. She kept using the word *delicious.*"

Deanna saw red. "Susan Lyttle is too young to be checking out men like Jonas. Is she even twenty years old yet? And how does she know Jonas anyway?" Ew, was that the little green monster of jealousy in her voice? Not the least bit pretty.

Her mom laughed. "She's twenty-five, which is a very legal age, and since it's no big deal, why do you care?"

Too late, Deanna realized she had revealed more than what she had intended. This was why she never told her mother lies. She ended up trapped like a blasted lobster. Time to come clean. "Maybe I care a little. Maybe I've always cared a little," Deanna admitted with no small amount of fear in her voice.

"I thought as much," her mom replied with a gentle smile. "You've always been a little too sarcastic to him. I wondered if maybe you had a crush on him."

"Sarcasm isn't flirting, Mom," Deanna said, confused.

"For you it most certainly is. There are little things you do and say whenever you like a guy. Sarcasm is one of them. You also stammer a little."

Her cheeks heated in mortification. "I do not!"

Her mother nodded. "Yes, you do. But don't worry, sweetie, I don't think Jonas caught on."

Lord, she hoped not. "Can we change the subject now?"

"One more question first. Have you told Dean and Wade about your weekend with Jonas?" Deanna shook her head. "Well, I can tell you right now your brothers aren't going to like it."

"I'm a big girl now, Mom. They don't run my personal life."

"I agree, but they might see it differently."

"It's not my problem. What Jonas and I do is not their business."

Her mom tsked. "Don't be snide, Deanna. Your brothers can't help it if they love you and want the best for you. It's in their DNA. Besides, you'd be the same with the two of them."

Deanna laughed. "Yeah, you're right. I guess I can't fault them for caring, can I?"

Her mother sat up a little straighter, her eyes a little too watery for Deanna's peace of mind. "Since I've been working at that shelter, I'm beginning to realize that what we have is a whole lot more than what a lot of people have. We shouldn't take it for granted."

"You're right. I'm pretty lucky to have such a loving family," she replied, meaning every word. "Speaking of family, Jonas never talks about his. Why do you think that is?"

"He talked to me about them once."

Now that, Deanna hadn't expected. She leaned closer. "He did?"

Her mother let out a deep breath and tucked her hair behind her ear. "It was at Wade's birthday party one year. Jonas mentioned never having had a party for his birthday."

Deanna frowned. "He's an only child and his parents never celebrated his birthday?"

She shook her head. "No. At first, I didn't think I'd heard him correctly. After he told me a little more about his mom and dad, I realized just how different his upbringing had been from the way your father and I raised you three."

"What do you mean?"

"His parents are very rigid people. Wealthy too. They don't have family get-togethers, no parties with streamers hanging from the ceiling. He said when he turned ten, his mother took him to his first piano lesson. That was his present, even though he'd asked for a basketball hoop and had zero interest in learning to play the piano."

Deanna immediately hated Jonas's mother. "I take it he never got the hoop?"

"No, his parents explained that it would look trashy attached to the house."

"Wow." Her heart ached for the little boy Jonas had been. "No wonder he always looks a little baffled at our family functions."

Her mother nodded. "Like a fish out of water. And it's also why Wade's opinion is so important to him. He's like a brother to Jonas."

She instantly felt guilty for giving Jonas such a hard time for getting Wade's approval before asking her out. "He basically asked Wade for permission to . . . you know."

Her mother smiled and pride lit her eyes. "I imagine he did. Jonas might not have much experience with family, but he understands honor."

"I wonder, though, what if Wade had said no." That question had nagged at her mercilessly.

Her mother winked and placed her hand on top of hers. "Jonas doesn't strike me as the type of guy to give up so easily, sweetie."

A zing of pleasure ran through her as she thought of how incredibly persistent Jonas had been. "Definitely not."

"So, next weekend when you're off having fun with that big cutie, just remember one thing."

"What's that?"

"There are no do-overs in life. You have to grab it while you can and enjoy every second of it, because you never know when it'll be snatched away."

Deanna heard the little catch in her mom's voice and knew she missed her husband. They'd been so in love; it broke Deanna's heart to see her sad. "I'll remember, Mom. I promise."

"Good." She stood and said, "Now, how about you show me what you've been working on for that new client."

That quickly, Deanna's mind switched into designer mode, but then she remembered there was something else she'd wanted to discuss with her mom. "Before I do that, I wanted to ask you something."

"Anything, dear."

"Are you sure you're okay with me quitting nursing?" Deanna bit her lip, afraid she'd disappointed her mother when she'd quit her day job in favor of the design work.

"Of course I am. I want my kids happy, and nursing wasn't doing that for you." She frowned. "Why do you ask?"

Deanna shrugged. "Because you were a nurse and, I don't know, I thought maybe you'd be a little upset that I wasn't following in your footsteps."

"Oh, don't be silly. It's true I enjoyed being a nurse. I found it quite rewarding. I want my kids to get the same sort of pleasure from their jobs, no matter what that is. Interior design has always been your passion, Deanna. I'm proud to see you turning that passion into a successful business."

Deanna's throat closed with emotion. "Thanks, Mom."

"You're welcome," she said, kissing her on the cheek.

They spent the rest of the day talking about various types of material and the Asian-inspired design her client had in mind for his home. It wasn't until she lay in bed later that night that Deanna let herself think of Jonas. His mouth. His hands. It was crazy to want a man as badly as she wanted Jonas. Friday seemed light-years away.

6

"I only came here to talk to my brother. To tell him about the trip. Go away, Jonas."

Jonas had been heading to his car when he'd spotted Deanna's little red coupe pulling up to Phoenix-Wade Investigations. When she'd parked and gotten out, he'd all but swallowed his damn tongue. Today she was wearing a tight pair of dark blue jeans, knee-high leather boots, a black leather jacket, and her hair was up in a high ponytail. She looked like a kick-ass chick in an action movie.

It'd taken him only a few seconds to alter his course.

As he cupped her cheek now, Jonas decided to taunt her a little. "Wade and I are business partners. You knew I'd tell him I was going away this weekend. So why are you really at our office, Deanna?"

"There are other things I wanted to discuss with him too."

"It's Wednesday and we haven't spoken since I called on Saturday about our flight time." He winked and cocked his head to the side. "You sure you weren't missing me?"

"I-I'm sure."

The little stammer in her voice belied her words. Taking hold of her shoulders, Jonas maneuvered their bodies so that she was pinned between him and her car. It was already dark out, even though it was only six-thirty in the evening, and the street was all but deserted. Jonas put his hands on the roof of the car, caging her in and effectively keeping her from escaping. "I told you once not to lie to me, kitten."

He noted the way Deanna took in their surroundings, as if to confirm that they were alone. Apparently satisfied, her attention landed back on him once more. "It's not a lie," she murmured.

Jonas leaned close and whispered, "Then why are you turning red?"

She slapped his arm. "Because I'm being suffocated by a big, annoying guy!"

"Do you want me to let you go?" Jonas pressed his erection into the softness of her belly and just barely contained a groan. "And be honest, Deanna."

She was so silent and still, Jonas wasn't sure she'd heard his question. Finally, she shook her head.

"Always so stubborn," he gently chided as he placed a quick kiss to her lips. She moaned and wrapped her arms around his neck. Shit, he loved the way she responded to him. He couldn't wait to get her to Miami. "I want to ask you something. Something intimate. May I?"

She shut her eyes tight and mumbled, "Yes."

"Have you ever . . . thought about me?"

Her eyes shot wide open and Jonas watched her swallow several times. "You mean, like, fantasized?"

Jonas nodded.

"Yes," she answered, with a bluntness that Jonas admired. When Deanna lowered her head, as if unwilling to meet his gaze, he knew the admission had been embarrassing for her. It'd cost her. Bold yet shy, the woman was such a contradiction.

"I've thought of you too. So damn many times."

She lifted her head and smiled. "I sort of figured, considering you've made no secret about wanting me."

"You don't have to be a rocket scientist, that's for sure," Jonas acknowledged. "So, what do you do when you think about me, Deanna?"

The intimate question seemed to bring her shyness right back, because she didn't answer. Jonas wouldn't let her retreat from him. He moved his hips lower so that he was pushing and stroking the tempting juncture between her legs. She whimpered and thrust her lower body against him.

"Tell me, kitten," Jonas softly demanded as he began to give her little butterfly kisses along her lips and cheeks. When he reached the shell of her ear, he growled, "Do you touch yourself? Do your hands caress and your fingers stroke?"

She buried her head in his chest and whimpered. A few seconds later, she lifted her head and met his gaze, searing Jonas to the bone with the fire of her desire. "Sometimes," she stated in a low whisper.

Deanna's simple answer made him nearly insane with need. She innocently brought the most erotic picture to his mind. Christ, did she have any idea of the dangerous effect she had on him? He ached for her in a way that he'd never ached for a woman. He could wait a few more days, he reminded himself. For now, he'd settle for details of her pleasuring herself.

"I want you to tell me exactly what you do, kitten."

She shook her head. "We're in public, Jonas. Wade could be watching us even as we speak."

Jonas moved his hands, burying them beneath Deanna's leather jacket. Her cotton-covered breasts resting in his palms were nothing short of heaven. "Wade and Gracie went out to eat. They won't be back for another hour, at least. And it's too dark for anyone to see more than a couple embracing." He plied her nipples through the soft fabric of her T-shirt.

"You might've told me he wasn't here."

Jonas dipped his head and licked her lower lip before asking, "Would it have mattered?"

"Probably not," she murmured, moving her hands to his head.

He felt delicate fingers delving into his hair, and Jonas knew a new kind of torment. Having Deanna turned on and not being able to do anything about it sucked raw eggs.

"Details, Deanna," he chided. "Give me something. I'm dying here."

His hands squeezed and massaged Deanna's supple breasts. God, how he resented clothes. Naked, that's what they should be. Naked and in a king-sized bed.

"I touch my breasts first," she confessed. "But it doesn't feel nearly as good as what you're doing right now."

Hell if that little tidbit didn't have his dick harder than ever. "You like the way my hands feel on you, huh?"

"Oh, God, yes."

"Mmm, you have perfect tits, kitten. You fill my hands as if you were made for me." Jonas continued his pleasurable torture for another minute; then he slid his hands down her sides and heard her whimper. "Shhh, let me make you feel good," he crooned.

"N-not here."

"My body is providing cover, I promise." He placed his lips against hers, desperate for a taste of her. His tongue swiped over her bottom lip, and he felt her shudder against him. "Trust me, kitten," he insisted.

When she didn't protest, Jonas took his hands out of her jacket and brought them around to cup her ass. "When you're alone in the dark, do you finger yourself?" He moved his hips up and down. Shit, even through the denim, Jonas swore he could feel the heat of her pussy. "Do you slide those pretty fingers in deep and play?" he asked, needing to know if she was as crazy for him as he was for her. "Do you wish it were my cock instead, kitten?"

Deanna moaned and arched her neck. Jonas's blood heated as he stared at the regal line of Deanna's neck exposed to him. He touched her vein with his tongue and laved her. "Tell me what you do to yourself. Tell me now, girl." He hadn't meant to sound so demanding, but he was beyond reasoning.

"Yes, I use my fingers and I . . . imagine it's you."

"Christ, that's a pretty visual." Jonas reached between them and went to work on the front of her jeans. In seconds, he had them open and his hand inside. His thumb grazed her clit through the silky panties she wore. He was tempted to look down to see what color she wore today, but he didn't want to break the spell around them.

"Look at me, Deanna." Her eyes fluttered open, and Jonas felt triumphant when her warm mocha gaze landed on him. He pinched her clit, then used two fingers to caress her slit. Her panties were already damp, and his mouth watered for another taste of her cream. "You're wet, kitten. Did this hot, little pussy miss me?"

"I can't believe we're doing this," she said, her breathing labored. "My Lord, anyone could come along."

Jonas continued to slide his fingers up and down, touching and teasing her through the soaked material. "Yeah, they could. But isn't that part of the thrill?"

Deanna's gaze filled with wicked intent as she moved one hand out of his hair and slid it down the front of his chest and to his abs. She didn't stop until she'd reached his cock. When she cupped him through his jeans, Jonas cursed. "Jesus, girl, don't push me. I swear I'll fuck you right where you stand."

"Not until Miami, remember?"

He widened his stance to give her better access. When her hand moved up and down, massaging his length, he lost all reason. "Damn it," he bit out before slamming his mouth down over hers. His tongue coaxed the seam of her lips until she surrendered and gave him entrance. Ah, now that's what he needed. Deanna's unique brand of sweet, innocent passion.

At the first easy touch of his tongue to hers, Jonas felt her legs quiver, as if she could barely hold herself upright. He wrapped one arm around her waist and held her steady while he plundered and explored. He flicked her clit, then stroked her pussy with his fingers. Deanna's small hand squeezed his cock. Goddamn that felt good. Jonas had to grit his teeth against the need to shove his pants down to his knees and give her free rein—to hell with public indecency laws.

When he plucked at her clit, he felt the throbbing of her body's hungry response to his ministrations. Something inside him shifted as he watched her climb higher and higher, her hand on his dick pumping faster. He knew then that no other man could ever touch her in the same way and live. The desire she kept hidden from the world was for him.

Without hesitation, Jonas delved beneath the waistband of Deanna's panties and encountered wet, silky skin. His nostrils flared to life as he picked up her succulent scent. "Mmm, such a sweet kitty," he murmured as he fondled and toyed with the little nub of her desire. Dipping two fingers deep, he fingerfucked her. Without warning, her inner muscles tightened.

"Jonas," she pleaded, removing the hand she had cupped around his dick in favor of clutching onto his shoulders instead, as if desperately needing the support.

"That's it, Deanna, let it go. I've got you," he soothed.

As if she'd simply been waiting for his permission, Deanna exploded all around his fingers. Jonas quickly covered her mouth and swallowed her screams. The feel of Deanna coming undone in his hands was the sweetest thing in the world.

As he lifted his head, his fingers still buried deep, Jonas

caught her watching him, a sexy little smile playing at the corners of her mouth. He kissed her cheek. "What are you thinking?"

"I'm thinking that once again you got shortchanged. And I'm starting to think that where you're concerned, I'm way too easy."

Jonas slowly removed his fingers and brought them to his mouth. "That's not the way I see it," he replied in a voice gone raw with desire as he sucked each digit clean. "Licking your juices will keep me satisfied until Friday, believe me." Then he cupped her chin in his palm. "And as long as I'm the only man you're easy with, then I don't see the problem."

Deanna remained silent, unmoving. Her eyes, those deep brown pools of chocolate, seemed to see clear into his soul. After a few seconds, she said, "I also think that I have a lot of making up to do when we reach Miami."

He grinned in anticipation. "And I think I'm seriously going to enjoy every second of it too."

Jonas kissed her, keeping it brief so as not to get distracted, then went about buttoning and zipping her jeans. When she removed her hands from his shoulders and stepped back, Jonas missed the connection instantly. "Soon we're going to be in a bed doing this, and there won't be any of this dressing and leaving afterward either."

"At this point, I'm not sure Miami is all that necessary." She crossed her arms over her chest and looked down at the pavement. "We could just, you know, go back to your place."

Hell of an idea, Jonas thought. Then he remembered why he wanted her out of the state to begin with. He took her head between his hands and urged her to look at him. With her gaze on him once more, Jonas gave her the unvarnished truth. "We could find a bed if that's what you really want. But I don't want a quick lay. I want more from you than that."

"You want to prove that you aren't a player."

He nodded. "I won't stand here and tell you that sex isn't on my mind. Where you're concerned, it's pretty much always on my mind. But in my gut I know we can have more than that."

"And what if—"

Jonas placed a finger against her lips and cut her off. "No what-ifs. Give me a chance, Deanna. That's all I ask."

After she nodded, he removed his finger. When Deanna reached inside a pocket on her leather jacket and pulled out a set of keys, Jonas hummed his approval. "You look damn good in leather, kitten."

She frowned and planted a hand on her hip. "Okay, I have to know. Why do you call me 'kitten'?"

He leaned close and whispered, "Because every time I see you, I have this wild urge to pet you until you purr."

"Oh."

He chuckled at her short, one-word reply. "Now scooch, before I lose what little control I have left."

She rolled her eyes and walked around to the driver's side. "You're a very bad influence on me, Jonas Phoenix."

He bobbed his eyebrows and shot right back, "You have no idea, *kitten*."

7

"Our flight leaves at one-fifteen, Deanna!"

"I'm aware," Deanna shouted back. Jonas's deep voice coming from the bottom of her stairs flustered her, and she banged her foot into the leg of her bed. "Ow, crap!"

She ruthlessly ignored the pain and went back to tossing stuff into her suitcase. Sandals, bathing suit, summer clothes, and nighties. She didn't much care if they wrinkled, either, not with Jonas alone in her living room. He was looking at her things. Knowing him, he'd be touching her shelves and picking up picture frames. He was too curious for his own good. He was probably dissecting her while she piddled around. What had she been thinking to agree to meet at her place? She should have told him she'd meet him at the airport instead. She hadn't been thinking. Heck, her brain was still muddled from the orgasm he'd given her on Wednesday.

They hadn't even made it to Miami and the man had managed to give her not one, but two orgasms. She felt a tad selfish, actually. Not once had she been able to get beneath his clothes. She'd wanted to, though. Criminy, she'd all but ached to unzip his fly and hold his rock-hard cock in her hands. He'd distracted her; that's what he'd done. How was a woman supposed to think when a guy as hot as Jonas had his fingers and lips all over her? Impossible.

She rushed into her bathroom and grabbed her deodorant and makeup, birth control pills, and a myriad of other very important items she couldn't live without. Now all she needed was to get him out the door and away from her things.

As Deanna lugged the suitcase and toiletry bag into the living room, she was shocked to see Jonas sitting on her couch, legs spread out in front of him, reading one of her books. She moved closer and read the title, then felt her face burn. He seemed to sense her presence in the room because he glanced over the top of the hardback.

"Fascinating stuff," Jonas said, waving the book in the air as he read the title aloud. " *'Everything You Need to Know to Satisfy Your Man.'* " He grinned. "Damn catchy title too."

Deanna dropped the suitcases and went to take her book back, but Jonas dodged her. Anger welled to the surface. She held out a hand. "Don't be a jerk. Give me the book."

"I will, but first I want to know if you've read the section on oral pleasure."

"None of your business." Dang it, she hadn't meant him to see the bloody thing.

"Now, see," he said, "that's where you're wrong."

"I don't need instructions, Jonas. I'm not a virgin."

"Then why the book, Deanna?"

Because I want to blow your mind in Miami and figure a few tips couldn't hurt. No way was she about to tell him that little nugget of truth. "I was curious."

"S'that why you're turning red?"

Crap, he had her there. Deanna swiveled on her heel and walked out of the room. She needed a cold drink, that's all. She grabbed a bottle of water from the fridge and unscrewed the cap. After several sips, Deanna went back into the living room. Jonas still had his nose buried in the book. She stopped in the middle of the room. "The way you're reading that, I'm starting to think you need tips on satisfying *your* man. Is there something you want to tell me, Jonas?"

Jonas tossed the book onto the coffee table, then stood and walked toward her. "What I want to know is, do you have any intention of getting a tongue ring?"

She snorted. "Not in this lifetime. Pain and I do not get along."

His lips kicked up sideways. Damn, he was cute when he did that. "Well, there goes that fantasy."

Too late, his words registered and Deanna's anger shot to the surface. "You're welcome to go find another woman willing to fulfill it."

He reached out and stroked her hair. "The only woman starring in my fantasies is you."

"Good," she ground out, unwilling to admit how much that knowledge pleased her.

Without warning, he kissed her. His soft lips lingered a few seconds, drawing a moan from her, before he lifted and whispered, "Why can't I keep my mouth off you, kitten?"

To Deanna, Jonas sounded truly baffled by his own reaction to her. Before she could attempt a witty comeback, he muttered, "Let's go, before I forget my good intentions."

She snorted and picked up her toiletry bag. "You have good intentions, huh?"

Jonas only shook his head and picked up her suitcase. Deanna surreptitiously eyeballed the strength of his bicep. She was very tempted to wrap both of her hands around his upper arm and give a little squeeze. Resisting wasn't easy, but if she started touching the man, she wouldn't stop at his bicep.

"If you don't scoot, I *intend* to strip you naked and tie you to the bed."

For once, Deanna decided to err on the side of caution.

* * *

As the plane started to take off, Deanna's heart lodged in her throat. She gripped the arms of her seat and began to silently recite the Lord's Prayer. When the plane shook a little, she gave up the prayer in favor of cursing. "Crap," she muttered.

Jonas sent her a questioning look. "What's wrong?"

"Uh, I'm not real fond of flying," she admitted, clenching her eyes closed tight.

A hand covered hers, and curiosity forced Deanna to open her eyes. When she spied Jonas's fingers slowly entwining with hers, she bit her lip and looked down at her lap. "Thank you."

He leaned close and whispered, "Are you going to pass out? Throw up?"

The questions made her feel stupid, even though that hadn't been his intention. "No," she gritted out. "It's not that bad. Just like my feet on the ground is all."

"I'm sorry, kitten. I didn't know."

His gentle voice calmed her a bit. "It's not something I'm good at owning up to."

His thumb stroked over her knuckles. "Fear, you mean?"

"No," she answered with complete honesty. "Weakness."

Jonas laid his head against the back of the seat and closed his eyes. "We all have our weaknesses, Deanna."

Caught by his relaxed pose, Deanna took a moment to look her fill. The word *strength* described Jonas wonderfully. In fact, his picture probably sat next to it in the dictionary. As her gaze landed on his fly, Deanna had to swallow down the urge to reach out and cup the luscious bulge she spied there.

"Uh, even you?" she asked, picking back up on the conversation.

"I'm not made of stone," he said. His voice sounded a little drowsy, and it was all the sexier for it too. "I have my weaknesses."

"Name one," she demanded in disbelief.

He opened his eyes and looked over at her. "Promise not to laugh?"

"I'm gripping on to your hand for dear life because I'm terrified we're going to crash. Trust me, I'm incapable of laughter at the moment."

"Okay, but if you laugh, it'll hurt my feelings."

Deanna made a cross over her heart. "Swear to God and hope to die."

"Ants."

Sure her brain had processed something wrong, Deanna asked, "Huh?"

"I hate ants. Don't like to look at them, don't like them crawling on me." He gave a mock shudder. "Can't stand the little buggers."

It was such a normal thing, Deanna couldn't respond for a few minutes. "So, is this something you've always been afraid of?"

"No, it started when I turned twelve."

"Something happened," she surmised. "What?"

"I'll tell you, but if you ever breathe a word of it to anyone, especially Wade, I'll—"

She let go of his hand, then smacked his thigh. "Stop threatening me and tell me what happened."

Jonas smiled and placed his palm on her knee. "I grew up in a wealthy neighborhood. No skateboarding ramps in the driveways. No tree houses in the backyards." Jonas rolled his eyes. "Those things are for the lower class, my mother used to say."

Deanna's heart ached all over again as she thought of how lonely that sort of life would be for a boy. Especially a boy like Jonas. "That sounds like a very boring childhood."

He nodded. "I wanted more. I wanted adventure. It used to make me wonder why I was so different from the other kids. Most seemed content with their parents' rules, but I always pushed the boundaries." His hand skated a little higher on her leg, until he massaged her thigh. "Anyway, I had it in my head that I was going to break the cycle of boredom."

She chuckled. "I'm afraid to ask what you came up with."

He smacked her thigh in reprimand. "No laughing, remember?"

Deanna made a zipping motion over her mouth. "Sorry. Go on."

"Flashlight tag."

"Oh!" she exclaimed. "I used to love that game. Wade, Dean, and I used to play that all the time. I rarely won, but it was fun all the same." Deanna realized she'd interrupted him again and felt her cheeks heat.

Jonas's hand smoothed over the spot he'd swatted as he continued with his story. "It was summertime and my parents were out of the country. I had a nanny. Mrs. Chadwick." He shuddered. "She had this mole—"

Deanna cleared her throat. "The point, Jonas?"

"Right, sorry." His hand slipped up her leg another inch, and Deanna had to suppress a moan. "Mrs. Chadwick always fell asleep by nine. Every night like clockwork. A twelve-year-old boy can get into a lot of trouble after dark."

Deanna snorted. "I know. I have brothers, remember?"

He looked over at her. "I—"

The flight attendant came down the aisle then, interrupting Jonas's story. "Can I get you a drink or a snack?" she asked, but the way the petite redhead looked at Jonas, as if she wanted to eat him up, made Deanna want to smack her.

Before Jonas could say anything, Deanna answered for them both. "We're fine, thank you."

The woman walked away, but not before glaring daggers at Deanna. Jonas quirked a brow. "What was that about?"

"I don't know what you mean," Deanna lied.

"I was thirsty," he said after a beat of silence.

"So was she," Deanna blurted out. Too late she realized what she'd admitted to.

Jonas grinned, and it was just a hair too ornery for Deanna's peace of mind. "Oh, yeah? I hadn't noticed."

Deanna rolled her eyes. "Then you must be blind, because she wants you. Bad."

Jonas leaned across the armrest separating them. "I'm not available," he whispered against her ear.

Deanna couldn't respond to that tantalizing statement, didn't dare. "Finish the story."

His hand moved another inch higher. Now his fingers were so close to her crotch that Deanna instinctively placed her palm over them in an effort to keep Jonas from venturing any farther.

Jonas winked and continued. "I decided to get some of the kids in the neighborhood together to play a game of flashlight tag. Only three were willing. Most were too afraid of defying their parents." He smiled. "Jimmy, Steve, and Ryan. Jimmy and Steve were brothers. I could always count on the two of them to say yes to an adventure."

"You were the instigator." She shook her head, reluctantly charmed by him. "Now why doesn't that surprise me?"

He laughed. "Hey, Jimmy and Steve weren't too bad at coming up with ideas either."

"Boys of a feather?" Deanna asked.

His hand slid out from beneath hers, then without warning, it covered her mound. "You could say that, yeah."

"Jonas," she warned.

He leaned close. "Do you really want me to stop, kitten?"

No, she didn't. "Someone will see," she said by way of an answer.

His index finger pushed down, hitting her clit with unerring accuracy. Deanna felt the touch clear through her jeans. "I wouldn't let that happen."

"The flight attendant . . ."

"They've finished their rounds for now." She started to protest, but he made a shushing sound. "Do you want me to tell you about my issue with ants or not?"

"Yes," she mumbled, unable to deny the delicious torture of having Jonas so close to where she needed him.

"Where was I?" He thought for a second, then answered his own question. "Right. So, the four of us sneaked out after dark and met behind my house. Things were going pretty good, too, until I decided to hide underneath a neighbor's boat. Seemed like the perfect spot. Several minutes went by, and I thought I'd about won. Then I felt something crawling on me. I didn't think anything of it at first. Bugs never bothered me much. Then I felt more of them. Pretty soon they were up my pants, underneath my T-shirt. Even in my hair."

Deanna shuddered, momentarily forgetting about Jonas's hand between her legs. "Ew, what'd you do?"

"Ryan shined the light on me, all excited that he'd found me. Then his eyes got really big. When I looked down, I saw why. I'd lain right on top of an anthill. A big mother."

"Oh my God, I would've freaked."

Jonas curled his lip. "After I swatted the crap out of the little suckers, Ryan and I both ran home. Neither of us said a word about it to Jimmy and Steve."

"Did you ever play flashlight tag after that?"

"Hell no. We also stayed away from that boat." Jonas rubbed his jaw. "I wonder whatever happened to those guys."

"What do you mean?"

"We moved out of that neighborhood a few years later. Lost touch."

"Oh," Deanna mused. "So, that's why you're afraid of ants, but you've been all over the world during your army days. Surely you've come across bigger, scarier bugs."

"Yep, but I've never been covered in them, so they don't bother me."

She frowned, wondering if he was being straight with her. "Is that a true story?"

He laughed as he resumed stroking her. "Why would I lie about something that ridiculous?"

"To take my mind off the flight," she answered, curious if that had been his plan all along.

"Deanna, I've told a few fibs in my day, but my fear of ants is very real."

His fingers traced the seam of her jeans, and Deanna nearly moaned aloud. "Jonas, you have to stop."

"Soon, you're going to be begging me to continue."

She wrapped her hand around his, then picked it up and moved it to the armrest. "Maybe, but until then, take a nap or something."

"Spoilsport," he murmured.

When the flight attendant showed up out of nowhere, Deanna yearned to tell her where she could stick her nuts. Instead Jonas said, "Thanks, but I already have everything I need."

Deanna's stomach did a little flip at his words. The eager little redhead might not be a happy camper, but Deanna was sure buzzing.

8
_____

During the rest of the flight, Deanna and Jonas had only exchanged small talk; she suspected that was because they were both too wound up for any real conversation. Now, as she stood inside the entrance of the beach house and watched Jonas take her suitcase and toiletry bag upstairs, her nerves went a little haywire. There was no going back now. She knew it in her bones. Would she even be able to undress in front of him without shaking? With her luck, she'd end up tripping over her own feet or doing something else equally as embarrassing.

Deanna tried to get her mind off the evening to come and instead took in the room around her. The furnishings, she noted, were very manly. Stainless steel and shiny black surfaces. Not for the first time, Deanna wondered just how many women Jonas had brought here with the sole purpose of seducing and conquering.

"I can see those wheels turning, Deanna," Jonas said as he returned.

She looked him over and felt the same girlish desire as the first time she'd spotted him at their family picnic years ago.

God, she never should have come to Miami. What did she know about a man like Jonas? He had *expert lover* stamped all over his delicious body. She'd be lucky to escape with even an ounce of her feminine pride left.

"I know just the thing to take the edge off," Jonas said as he walked to the far side of the room. For the first time, Deanna noticed the fully stocked wet bar. Jonas turned over two short glasses, then poured some amber liquid into each. When he brought one to her and murmured, "Try it," Deanna immediately shook her head. "I don't care for alcohol unless there's an umbrella sticking out of the top of the glass."

He chuckled. "Come on, kitten. Give it a try. A little sip, that's all I ask."

Deanna thought a glass of Diet Coke and a bag of chocolate chip cookies would soothe her frazzled nerves much better, but she didn't think that would sound too sophisticated. Hesitant, she took the proffered glass and gave it a sniff. Jonas stopped her with a hand covering the rim.

"You don't have to try it if you don't want to. I won't be offended, Deanna."

Suddenly it seemed imperative to try the drink. "No, it's fine. Besides, you're right. I could use something to relax me." After Jonas removed his hand, Deanna brought the glass to her lips. She did as he'd suggested and took a small sip. The smooth liquid flowed over her tongue and down her throat, surprising her with its delicate flavor. It had a sweet, cherry flavor.

"Mmm, it's good."

Jonas tipped his head to the side, scrutinizing her. "Just good?"

"Well, I do like the warm cherry flavor, but it's no margarita."

Jonas chuckled. "How about you go get freshened up or whatever it is women do, so I can get you a margarita?"

"And food. I'm hungry."

"Mexican sound good to you?"

"I love Mexican." Deanna swirled the liquid around and took another sip before handing the glass back to Jonas. "I'll just be a minute."

"Take your time," he said as he unclipped his cell phone from his belt. "I'm going to check in with Wade anyway. Let him know we arrived safely."

Deanna nodded. "Good idea. Otherwise he'll start calling both our cell phones."

"Exactly." Jonas winked. "And I really don't want any interruptions while we're here."

No way was she going down that tempting road. "Where's the bathroom?"

"Up the stairs and to the left."

She clutched her purse in a tight fist and started toward the stairs. When she heard Jonas call her name, Deanna stopped and shot him a questioning look over her shoulder.

"The bedroom is on the right."

"*The* bedroom?" she asked as butterflies began to flutter to life inside her stomach. An image of Jonas curled around her as they slept sprang to mind.

"There are three bedrooms, kitten, but do you really want your own room?"

Instead of answering, Deanna pointed to the phone Jonas clutched in one fist. "Call Wade."

"Yes, ma'am."

The hot look Jonas shot Deanna's way practically sent her running up the stairs. She didn't stop to catch her breath until she'd reached the upstairs landing. Curiosity got the better of her, and she gave in to the need to peek at the bedroom. Holy smokes, the room was big. A king-sized bed sat along one wall. A lightweight white blanket, trimmed with delicate blue flowers, covered it. The beautiful light pine sleigh bed gave Deanna plenty of ideas too. Naughty ideas. Of course, the panoramic view of the ocean directly across from it was pretty damn gorgeous too. All too easily, Deanna could imagine waking up to the warm Florida sun filtering through the gauzy white curtains, with Jonas's nude body draped all over her. There she went again, thinking of the man. Lordy, he was more addicting than cupcakes. Deanna ruthlessly pushed the big lug out of her head and headed toward the bathroom. Food and a margarita, that's what she needed. Once she had those two cravings satisfied, she could see about sating other hungers.

"You're making me nervous," Deanna growled, then proceeded to kick his shin.

Jonas winced at the sharp pain. "Ow, and why?"

"Because you seem utterly mortified by my choice of dinner entrées. They're flautas, not snakes, Jonas."

He dug into his beef enchiladas. With any luck, he'd need the energy later. "You fascinate me," he replied after swallowing a large bite. "Besides, I've never seen a woman so small eat something so big."

"Rude and insulting all at the same time. You're seriously multitalented."

Jonas took a long swig of his beer. "I don't mean it that way. I'm just glad you aren't the type to consider a few pieces of lettuce dinner."

"I've always had a healthy appetite." She shrugged. "Mom told me once that when I was little, I could eat nearly as much as Dean. It used to boggle her mind."

Jonas pushed his plate away and leaned forward. "I like your mom."

"Most people do." Deanna looked around the restaurant. "This place is fabulous, by the way. I love the vibrant colors.

And the cascading waterfall." She pointed to the middle of the room. "Nice touch."

"I can't take credit for finding this restaurant. Wade discovered it."

Deanna nodded and scooped up the last of her flauta. "Wade loves good food. Actually, Mom made sure all three of us knew our way around a kitchen."

"Your mom is pretty terrific." Compared to his mother, Jonas thought, Mrs. Harrison was a freaking saint, but he kept that sentiment to himself. "I remember the first time I met her. She hugged the stuffing out of me."

"The family picnic, right?"

He winked at her. "And here I thought you'd forgotten that day." Deanna remained silent, leaving Jonas to wonder. "So quiet all of a sudden. What thoughts are skittering through that beautiful head?"

She finished chewing before dabbing at her lips and sitting back in her chair. "Do you remember what you said to me that day?"

Remember? Jonas had all but branded his brain with the memory; he'd played it over and over so many times. It felt like yesterday instead of years ago. "I remember everything. Why?"

"You told me that meeting me had been the highlight of your summer. You couldn't have meant that, so why'd you say it?"

"I meant every word, Deanna."

She frowned and looked down at the table, then started to fiddle with her napkin. "But we rarely talked after that. It wasn't until recently that you'd started on your relentless campaign to get me to go out with you."

"You were too young then." Jonas reached across the table and placed his hand over hers, gaining her full attention. "I had no business anywhere near you."

Deanna rolled her eyes and pulled her hand away. "We're only two years apart in age, you and I. And besides, I was hardly a sweet, little virgin when we met."

"True, but don't forget that I'd already been to hell and back," he explained. "Wade and I have been to some of the worst places in the world. I've killed, Deanna. Trust me—you weren't ready for what I wanted from you. Not then."

"And what is it you want from me, Jonas?"

He grinned. "Naughty things, kitten. Very naughty things."

Deanna's lips twitched, as if attempting to hold back a laugh. "Behave, we're in public."

The waiter came around then and asked if either of them wanted dessert or a refill. Never one to drink much, Jonas had ordered a light beer. One was enough. When Deanna declined another margarita, the waiter left to get their check. Jonas pointed to her empty glass. "Why not order another? Live a little."

"I've never quite mastered the art of holding my liquor," she replied. He watched her root around in her purse a moment, before pulling out a tube of lip balm.

As Jonas watched her apply it, he nearly got distracted from her answer. Leaning forward, Jonas murmured, "Can't hold your liquor, huh?"

She replaced the cap and dropped it back into her purse. "Not so much. I tend to get a bit too happy."

His eyebrows shot up and his cock came to full-alert status. *Happy*—he liked the sound of that. "And that's a bad thing?"

To his utter shock, Deanna blushed. "In my case it is."

Curiosity got the better of him. "Care to explain?"

The waiter returned with the check, forcing Jonas to drop the conversation while he fished out his credit card. Once they were alone again, Jonas waited, hoping Deanna would go into more detail. She didn't disappoint him. "All my inhibitions disappear. It's not a comfortable feeling for me."

She was killing him. An immediate picture of a carefree Deanna sprang to mind. He liked it a hell of a lot. "Most people enjoy letting it all hang out every once in a while. Taking life too seriously leads to an early grave."

"Maybe, but if I suddenly develop the urge, I'd rather be coherent."

"You don't like to give up control," he surmised.

She cocked her head to the side, as if unsure how to respond at first. "It's not that," she said. "I guess if I'm in the mood to go romping naked through a forest, for example, then I don't want alcohol to blur the memorable event for me." She laughed. "I mean, I'd want to remember a crazy moment like that. Wouldn't you?"

No doubt about it, Jonas liked the way the lady's mind worked. "You had me at 'running naked'."

Deanna snorted. "You need serious help."

The waiter returned with his card and Jonas filled in the tip and signed the check. He stood and held out his hand. "Come on, you can tell me all about these forest fantasies back at the house."

When Deanna reached out and placed her hand in his, a wicked smile kicking up the corners of her glossy lips, Jonas's blood heated and his cock strained the fly of his jeans. Great. Walking through a crowded restaurant with a hard-on wasn't his idea of fun. He leaned close and whispered against the shell of her ear, "Save that look for when we're alone, kitten."

Instead of moving as Jonas had intended, Deanna lifted her head and caressed his lips with hers, barely grazing. The kiss left him wanting more, which was no doubt her intention. When she pulled back, there was a clear challenge in her dark brown gaze.

Jonas took her face in his large hands and ground out, "If you don't turn around and start walking, I'm going to forget we're in a public place and lay you across that table."

She squinted, and a hint of uncertainty slipped across her face. "You're all talk, Jonas."

He released her and smiled. "Keep it up. I never did get dessert."

To his relief, Deanna stayed silent and started walking out of the restaurant. Thank God, because being arrested for indecent exposure would sure as hell put a kink in his plans.

The cab drive had been quick and uneventful. Now, as Deanna watched Jonas unlock the door to the beach house, a little thrill ran the length of her spine. She had the sexy, dark-haired Jonas all to herself in the gorgeous city of Miami. Yowza. When he opened the door and let her enter first, she realized for the first time that he actually did that a lot. Held her chair, paid for dinner, opened doors for her. She wondered if he was a little old-fashioned. Deciding to find out, Deanna said, "I forgot to pay you my half of the dinner bill."

Jonas closed and locked the door, then switched on the lamp next to the black leather sofa. The soft, intimate light sent butterflies to flight inside her belly. "Your half?" he asked.

Unless Deanna missed her guess, Jonas sounded distinctly annoyed. She had to look away to keep him from seeing her grin. "Yeah," she answered, pretending an interest in the generic, store-bought black-and-white photo of a beach hanging on the wall beside the door. "There's no reason for you to pay for the both of us."

He took hold of her shoulders and slowly turned her to face him. "If you were a dude and we were going to see a ballgame together, then I'd expect you to pay half the check. You're the furthest thing from a dude."

Oh, wow, he was old-fashioned. At the new knowledge, Deanna's heart did a little backflip. Stepping closer, Deanna murmured, "Careful, Jonas, or I'll start to think you're a nice guy."

His hands slid down her arms in a gentle caress. "I've been trying to tell you that for months. It's about time you wake up and smell the latte."

Deanna started to speak, but instead yawned. She quickly covered her mouth and muttered, "Oops, sorry."

"You're tired?"

"A little. I didn't get a lot of sleep this week." *Because I was awake thinking of you.*

"Me neither."

At his quiet, two-word reply, bells went off in Deanna's head, waking her up in an instant. "W-why is that?"

"I couldn't stop thinking about you," he admitted. "About this . . ." His mouth swooped down and took hers in a wild show of possession. Deanna's temperature shot right into the red zone, and her blood began to race. Without conscious thought, her arms wound around his neck, tugging him closer. He groaned against her lips and ran his tongue along the seam. Unable to resist temptation, Deanna parted them and felt his rumbling growl of approval. As he dipped inside, Deanna tasted the uniquely spicy flavor of Jonas Phoenix.

Jonas wrapped one arm around her back and the other behind her knees, lifting her easily into his powerful arms. The rippling of muscles beneath his black pocket T devastated Deanna's senses.

He broke the kiss when he reached the stairs. "Do you want this, Deanna? Do you want me?"

"Oh, God, yes."

"Are you still tired?"

"Not even a little." The answer practically flew from her mouth. She could be embarrassed later over her enthusiasm. For now, she just wanted Jonas.

Jonas let out a breath. "Good, because sleeping next to you all night and not being able to touch would've been a whole new kind of hell for me."

It should've been enough to hear his words, but she still needed to know she wasn't just any warm body. "You want *me* that much?"

"Yes, you," he ground out. "I'm dying for you here, kitten. This week seriously sucked."

Without another word, Jonas took her up the stairs and to the bedroom. He strode to the bed and placed her carefully atop the cool blanket. An odd thought struck her as she realized the house wasn't just Jonas's but Wade's as well. "Wait, Wade doesn't use this room, does he?"

He chuckled. "No, his room is at the end of the hall."

"Just checking." It was still weird to realize she wasn't just in Jonas's beach house, but also her brother's. Knowing Wade had never used the bed she was about to make love to Jonas in made it less weird.

Jonas put one knee on the bed, then the other, before straddling her. He kissed her gently and drifted his mouth down over her chin to her neck, teasing her beyond measure. He lifted and muttered, "The shirt."

"Needs to go," she breathed out. "I agree."

Jonas sat back, then took the hem of her T-shirt between his fists and tugged upward. "I love you in red, kitten. Bet you didn't know it was my favorite color, did ya?"

Deanna tried to concentrate on his praise, but as cool air hit her belly, she began to lose track. "Red is my favorite color too."

"It's going to be so much prettier on the floor, trust me." He pulled it up and over her head, then tossed it aside. "Shit."

"What?"

"You like lingerie, don't you?"

She looked down at the red lacy bra, which was completely see-through, and blushed. "It's sort of a secret indulgence of mine."

"I'll buy you some, then. Pinks, blues, purples. All the colors of the rainbow."

"It sounds lovely, but for now can you just please kiss me again?"

"Don't rush me. I plan to savor you." He zeroed in on the little triangle cutout between her breasts. His tongue dipped in and tasted her there. She arched off the bed, desperate for more, so hungry for his touch all over.

Jonas nuzzled her overheated skin, then stopped long enough to murmur, "Easy, kitten. Slow and easy."

Deanna didn't much care for that idea, and her body wasn't real thrilled with it either. "I don't want easy, Jonas. I want hard."

Jonas abruptly stopped his playful touches. As his captivating blue gaze sought out hers in the room dimly lit by the light filtering in from the hallway, Deanna wanted to scream. Instead of moving him along faster, she'd killed the mood completely. Great.

Jonas reached over and touched a lamp next to the bed. The soft glow brought everything into view. Including Jonas's big, gorgeous body perched atop hers. She had the insane urge to simply lick him from head to toe, like a great big ice-cream cone.

"You want to be fucked hard?"

Well, dang. She hadn't exactly figured on him wanting to examine her statement. "I was sort of hoping, yes."

"There's definitely something to be said about hard and fast, but not this first time, Deanna."

"Why not?"

"Because I could hurt you. I'm not a small man, kitten."

"Bragging? Really?"

"No. I'm not."

"Just how big? Like, scary big?" *Did I really just ask that?* Deanna clenched her eyes shut. Maybe he didn't hear the question.

Jonas's lips against her forehead forced her to open her eyes. He was looking down at her with such tenderness that her anxiety seemed to melt away. "I'm not freakishly large, if that's what you mean. But I happen to know how tight you are. My fingers were inside you. Trust me, we need to go slow."

"I want to see you, Jonas. Take your clothes off. Please?"

"Your wish . . ." he murmured as he moved off her and stood beside the bed. First, he yanked his T-shirt over his head and dropped it to the floor. Next, he started on the fly of his jeans. Before she even had a chance to enjoy the show, Jonas was naked. Curious *and* turned on, Deanna devoured the sight of Jonas's muscular chest sprinkled with dark curly hair. The six-pack abs had her practically drooling too. The tantalizing trail of hair that led to his crotch caught her eye, and there is where she lingered. His cock jutted out from his body, full and pulsing with vitality. It was long and thick, and she was desperate to wrap her lips around the bulbous head already dripping with precum. No, Jonas was most definitely not your average Joe, she thought with equal amounts of anticipation and nervousness.

"You're staring, but I can't tell if it's in a good way or not."

"Every part of you is magnificent," she said, unable to pull her eyes away from the heavy weight of his erection. "Yes, I think maybe you're right. Slow might be a good idea."

He grinned and let his gaze travel over her torso. "You're a vision in my bed, you know. I can't tell you how many times I've wanted to see you like this."

Deanna reached out a hand. "I'm lonely."

Jonas entwined their fingers and crawled across the bed. "You're overdressed, kitten."

"Do something about it, then." She admired the man's efficiency because within seconds she was lying against the cool blanket as naked as he was. When he looked her over and let loose a low growl, she knew the time for words was over. Jonas brushed his lips to the pulse in her neck and Deanna moaned.

"Jonas." She dug her fingers into his mass of dark hair to hold him firm while he suckled her skin. She ached to feel those lips and that tongue lower. So much lower.

As if she'd spoken the thought aloud, Jonas inched downward, touching off several little sparks of desire as he went. When his tongue flicked over one erect nipple, Deanna nearly shot off the bed. She forgot her misgivings. Her body craved Jonas's touch. It'd been so long since she'd derived any real pleasure from a man, because the only one she'd wanted, the only one who could possibly fill her, was the one lying on top of her.

As if afraid to bruise her, Jonas carefully ran his tongue back and forth over her areola, then sucked her nipple into his warm mouth. She felt the vibration of his hum of satisfaction and the raspy feel of his five-o'clock shadow. The sensations tormented her oversensitive skin and fueled the blaze raging inside her. His hands on either side of her body effectively pinned her to the bed. Deanna reveled in the intoxicating feel of Jonas surrounding her with his lethal strength.

While he switched to the other breast, Deanna marveled at his patience. He appeared to have nothing but time to play and tease. Like he was a king settling in for a great feast with the way he laved at her skin and toyed with all her erogenous zones.

Deanna urged him lower with a tug on his hair, and her excitement soared when he obliged, moving his loving torture south. Her body reacted with a flow of moisture to her center. Every inch of her was ready for him to take her.

"Please, Jonas."

A grunt was her only indication that he'd even heard her plea. He sat back on his haunches and stared down at her naked body. "This body deserves to be worshipped. For hours. Days, even."

She could barely breathe, let alone speak, but she attempted to answer. "Uh, thanks?"

"All night you sat at that booth, and all I could think of was fucking you." He passed a hand over his face and grumbled, "Damn, Deanna."

"Such a poet, Jonas."

He reached down and cupped her mound. "Such a little smart-ass."

She tried to maintain her cool composure, but when his middle finger found its way through her curls and sank all the way to the knuckle inside her heat, she gave up any pretense of control over her own body.

"Mmm, just look at you. Your slippery little cunt is so ripe. I think I'm going to really enjoy making you scream with pleasure."

When a second finger joined the first, her hips began to move, matching his pumping rhythm. After thrusting several times, Jonas brought both fingers all the way out. She wanted to beg him to come back, but her words died on her tongue as she watched him suck her juices off.

"Tangy," he whispered. "Rich and warm and so addicting."

He spread her wide and dipped his head between her thighs, sweeping his tongue over her swollen clit. She arched upward and he was there, holding her down with an arm over her stomach. She moaned and writhed under his assault. His tongue dipped in and out, laving and sending her into a different realm. She went wild when he sucked her clit between his lips and nibbled it. Once. Twice. Suddenly, Deanna burst apart, shouting his name and flowing into his greedy mouth.

10

Jonas stayed in place for several seconds after her orgasm ended, as if relishing the little aftershocks. Then he lifted his head.

"You are so fucking beautiful when you come," he murmured.

Amen, was all Deanna could think as she let her eyes drift closed. Then his weight lifted and Deanna opened them again. She watched him stand beside the bed, staring down at her with some unnamed emotion on his face.

"Why are you looking at me like that?"

He crooked his finger and grinned wolfishly at her. "Come over here, kitten."

Deanna rolled to her side and sat up. When she stood and went to him, Jonas placed his hand on the small of her back and directed her across the room. He stopped her when she reached the dresser. The mirror. As she stared at her reflection, heat flooded her cheeks. Her gaze shot to his. His guttural words turned her legs to jelly.

"I'm going to make you come again. Only this time, you'll see what I see."

"I'm not sure I can, not like this."

"You can," he whispered; then he dipped his head to the side and kissed her nape. As if he'd pulled a string, Deanna began to climb that same cliff all over again.

Jonas slid his hands up and down her arms, teasing goose bumps to the surface. Deanna forgot her trepidation and simply sank into the moment. With her eyes open, she watched Jonas move his lips lower, until he was behind her. He was totally out of view now, but she felt his mouth against her shoulder blades. Deanna's body hummed to life as he kissed and licked. "God, I had no idea."

"Mmm, what?"

"That shoulders could be such a hot spot."

"Only with *my* mouth," he growled. "No other."

Deanna let the possessive statement go for one reason only—because she knew deep down that if any woman chose to put her mouth on any part of Jonas's body, Deanna would go postal.

Her body jolted when Jonas's mouth came into contact with her bottom. She could only assume he was on his knees as he stroked the seam of her buttocks with his tongue. His talented hands massaged and fondled her ass cheeks. Deanna leaned forward and braced her hands on the top of the dresser, then shuddered when he parted her.

"Spread your legs for me. Nice and wide."

Deanna did as he bid, but only barely. She just wasn't as open, as uninhibited, as he was.

Thankfully, Jonas seemed to understand her nervousness, because he didn't press the issue. His tongue caressed her again, moving slowly between her thighs to her swollen labia. He separated her and dipped in, piercing her entrance in fast, stabbing motions. So much sensation; it'd never been this way. He made her feel alive with a few clever touches.

"Such a pretty ass and pussy. Let me see more, kitten. I won't hurt you. Please, for me."

That's when Deanna knew the scary truth. That she'd do anything for him. Giving up all sense of modesty, she widened her stance. He hummed his approval and was there again, sucking at her clitoris and taking her over that jagged edge. She happily soared higher and higher as his tongue probed and his lips brushed and tormented. Deanna shouted Jonas's name as he tugged her nubbin with his teeth. She went up in flames, pushing backward against his face, achingly aware of his hard, calloused hands holding her hips still. As he kissed her pussy and licked her tight, pink anus, her legs nearly buckled.

In an instant, he was standing again, his body molding to the length of hers as he stared at her in the mirror. "You tear me up, Deanna. Goddamn, I want you."

"Then take me, Jonas," she choked out.

"Mmm," he murmured as he leaned over and opened a drawer. She watched him pull out a condom, his body pressing against her, keeping her pinned as if he were afraid she'd vanish if he gave her an inch of space. She wiggled her ass and he cursed. "Hurry, Jonas."

His eyes shot to hers in the reflection. "Don't rush me, girl. I'm already on a hair trigger here."

The idea that he was that anxious for her pleased her beyond measure. It made her feel as if she weren't the only one so affected.

She watched him move back a few feet, and instantly Deanna missed his heat and scent surrounding her. Although, when she got a good eyeful of his muscled chest, she forgave him for leaving her. Jonas was deliciously male; his pectorals were solid rock, and he had a wide rib cage and ripped abs that Deanna ached to caress. She thought maybe she might start drooling at any moment. And *big* didn't even begin to describe his erection. He was huge. She hadn't been with a lot of men, but Jonas definitely put them all to shame. When he ripped the condom packet open, Deanna turned around. "Wait."

He quirked a brow. "Wait?"

She stepped closer, then slowly lowered to her knees in front of him. "I've wanted to taste you a thousand times. Would you really deny me this chance, Jonas?"

"Hell no." He wrapped a fist around his cock and held it out for her. "Come and get it."

Deanna leaned in and took the swollen head into her mouth. She tasted his sticky fluid and lapped it up. He groaned and wrapped both hands in her hair and guided her. His hands shook and he was rougher than she expected. When she took the first few inches inside her mouth, his cock seemed to thicken even more. He praised her, and she took another inch, then felt him touch the back of her throat. Deanna gagged.

"Easy, kitten," he crooned as he pushed her head off him to give her a breath, then pulled her forward again. This time Deanna prepared herself for his size by relaxing her throat. She took him deep, and suddenly Jonas was fucking her mouth, his movements alternating between fast and out of control, and slow and gentle. When she reached down and cupped his balls in her palm, Jonas pulled her head off him, then praised her with a kiss.

"Too much of that and you'll get a mouthful of cream."

"I wouldn't mind," she admitted as she imagined drinking his cum.

"Later," he said, his voice rough and low. "First I want this pussy. Are you going to give it to me?"

She smiled and stood, then moved back into her position in front of the mirror. Jonas grinned as he rolled the condom on. As he stepped forward, bringing their bodies into contact again, Deanna's breath caught in her throat. His heavy erection slipped between her buttocks, and Deanna wiggled her hips, hoping to move him along faster. Jonas positioned his cock at her entrance, aligning their bodies but not penetrating. She sighed in contentment and closed her eyes to better savor the moment. All that power and sleek grace snuggled against her. She could die happy now; Deanna was sure of it.

"Give me your hands," Jonas softly demanded.

Yeah, okay, that had her eyes popping open. "Huh?"

He ran the bulbous head up and down her pussy lips, and Deanna's mind went blank. He was so close to where she needed him to be and yet so very far away.

"Put your hands behind your back."

She did and when he took hold of both wrists in one of his large hands, Deanna's nervous jitters returned. "Uh, Jonas, I think it's probably fair to warn you that I've never done anything all that wild during sex."

"Let me show you a few things, kitten. Nothing crazy, I swear."

"What sort of things?"

"Shhh, don't get all wide-eyed. I would never hurt you."

Very carefully, as if afraid of her bolting at any second, Jonas squeezed her wrists slightly. "I want you bound, but until then, this will have to do."

Deanna watched him in the mirror; his eyes were on her throat. She could see how arousing it was for him to have her at his mercy. She tested her hands by tugging a little. Nope, she wasn't budging. This was all so new to her. "I know you wouldn't deliberately hurt me," she hedged.

With his free hand, he stroked her cheek. "Never, kitten. I take care of what's mine."

There it was again, possessiveness. "Mine?" she asked as their gazes met in the mirror.

He cupped her chin and ground out, "You have a problem with that, Deanna?"

"I don't know. I'll think about it later." Then passion took over. She widened her stance and pushed her buttocks into his groin in a silent, feminine request. He obliged and slipped inside an inch. He'd only just barely entered her, but it was enough to stretch her beyond what she'd ever experienced. As she stared at him in the mirror, it was like seeing a predator ready to devour his meal yet content to take his time and enjoy the tasty morsel.

He pushed a little more, and Deanna squirmed at the fullness of him. "Jonas."

"Shhh, it's going to be okay."

"I'm not so sure. I don't think I'm made to handle you."

His gorgeous blue eyes roamed tenderly over her reflection. "Of course you are. It'll just be a little slower than I'd anticipated."

His free hand went to her torso, and he lightly brushed her nipple with the backs of his fingers. She leaned her head back and closed her eyes. "You have beautiful tits," he praised as his hold on her wrists tightened. When he inched inside her tight channel a little more, Deanna's inner muscles stretched to accommodate him. Jonas's fingers moved down her belly to her mound, and he cupped her gently as he slid his cock in a little more. He took her clit between his index finger and thumb and squeezed. She moaned and circled her hips, intent on feeling his warm hands against her slick flesh.

"Oh, hell yeah," Jonas whispered against the shell of her ear. He pumped at the swollen bit of flesh. "Play, little kitty," he urged.

Deanna watched him in the mirror as he began to slide his fingers up and down until soon he was massaging her clit in slow circles. So many sensations bombarded her at once, and Deanna didn't know if she was coming or going. When he slipped his cock all the way out, then pushed inward, nearly balls-deep, she shouted his name.

"Fuck, you're so damn hot. I'm going to make you come, Deanna. All over my dick."

"Yes!"

His fingers plucked and tugged at her clitoris. Jonas appeared to lose control, thrusting hard and deep. Suddenly he stopped and she could feel him so solid and full inside her hot pussy, filling her to the core.

"Christ, you're tight."

She couldn't speak. A few more massaging circles knocked Deanna right off her axis.

"That's it," he breathed against her neck, "bathe my cock, kitten."

And as if he had so much command over her, she did. This time he pulled his cock all the way out, then slammed into her. Deanna shuddered and screamed as her orgasm rushed over her. She tried to move her hands, but she couldn't. He had her quite effectively bound. Once she settled, he released her wrists.

"Hold on to the dresser," he demanded.

She clutched the edges in a tight grip; then Jonas drove into her, hard and fast. "Son of a bitch," he muttered as his hips flexed. The palm of his hand pushed against her upper back, forcing her down against the cool, wood top as he pounded into her from behind. Deeper and harder with each stroke, until his balls slapped against her clit and elicited another series of moans from her.

Jonas leaned over her, covering her body with his as he pushed forward one more time. "Mine," he ground out as he came, filling the condom with hot liquid.

He was sweating and breathing as if he'd run a marathon, their bodies sticking together with the heat of their passion. If it weren't for the dresser digging into her hips, Deanna could have happily stayed that way forever.

She wiggled a little and Jonas let out a sigh. He stood up and pulled his cock free. Deanna desperately wanted him back. He helped her stand upright and turned her around to face him. Her legs were a little wobbly, she realized. He stared down at her, and the expression on his face was so intense it sent a rush of warmth through her. It hadn't just been sex for him; she was sure of it.

"You're amazing."

Heat crept into her face. "Well, you're not bad either."

Jonas laughed. "You're a mouthy little thing."

She bit her lip and looked away. "One of my charms."

He flicked her nose. "I'll treasure the sight of you like this, you know."

Curious, her gaze came back to his. "Like what?"

"Drowsy eyes, breasts a little red from my mouth." His gaze traveled over her. "You look well loved, Deanna, and it's the sexiest sight I've ever seen."

Not willing to let things get too weird between them, Deanna brought the conversation away from sex and onto cleanliness. "Um, thank you, but I think I'm in need of a shower."

He nodded and grabbed her hand, then started to walk to the far side of the room. She saw him open a door and flip on a light. This room, like the bedroom and living area, was also all manly and modern. "You and Wade need a decorator."

He snorted. "Don't like the décor?"

"It's nice, but there's too much black and steel."

When he went to the shower, turned the knobs, and tested the water, she began to get a little antsy. He moved to dispose of the condom—which she hadn't even remembered him putting on—then stepped into the tub and held out a hand to her.

Deanna let him entwine their fingers and stepped under the hot spray. As she closed her eyes and savored the feel of the hot water and big, hard man, Deanna felt fingers against her ass, cupping and stroking. She opened her eyes and glanced over her shoulder. "You can't possibly be ready to go again."

"Your ass is a thing of beauty. I'm thinking of building a shrine for it."

She laughed. "You like my butt that much, huh?"

"I've stared at it about a million times. Still, I have to admit, I like it a hell of a lot better without anything obstructing my view."

The praise, since it came from Jonas, went straight to her heart. "Going around naked could get me into trouble, though, don't you think?"

"Yes, because then other men would see it and I'd have to kill them. That'd suck."

"It'd put a real crimp in my plans for you."

"Plans?"

"Oh, I have plans."

He wrapped his arms around her middle and pulled her back against him. The hot, steamy water cascading over their bodies sent Deanna into another, more carefree plane of existence with Jonas.

"Mmm, wicked plans?" he asked against the wet skin of her neck.

"Definitely wicked."

"Ah, I can't wait, kitten," he whispered as he began to smooth his palms over her body, massaging her aches and effectively bringing her body back to life.

For the first time that Deanna could remember, she stopped trying to analyze Jonas's intentions in favor of the dark-haired hunk loving her instead. When he moved away and poured soap into his hands, Deanna shuddered. As he started to wash her arms, shoulders, and all the parts in between, Deanna's body stirred to life all over again.

Their shower took much longer than she'd anticipated.

11

It was the middle of the night—or super early in the morning, rather—and they were sitting at the kitchen table eating cheese puffs. The only thing she wore was one of Jonas's old T-shirts, and all he'd pulled on was a pair of black boxers.

They'd both had the munchies after their shower, but Jonas hadn't wanted to take the time for a meal, so he'd grabbed the first bag of snacks he'd come to when they'd entered the kitchen. Since Deanna was as anxious as he was to get back to the bedroom, she hadn't complained. But the minute she'd told Jonas about her newest client, Terrance Valdez, Jonas had stopped eating, and she noticed his smile had turned into a dark, nasty frown.

"Is that supposed to be a joke, Deanna?"

She crossed her arms over her chest, beyond confused by his attitude. "What's the problem? Why is that a big deal?"

Jonas pushed a hand through his hair and let out a heavy sigh. "Valdez is a known drug dealer. He's bad news. Real bad news."

No way were they talking about the same man. "Terrance is a businessman. He buys companies, not drugs." Deanna thought of the little, gray-haired man with the kind eyes and shook her head. "Jonas, I really don't think we're talking about the same person here."

Jonas was on his feet so fast the chair fell backward. Deanna stiffened. "Trust me, Deanna. We're talking about the same guy. There's only one man with that name, and he's not even close to being a legitimate businessman. Christ, what the hell were you thinking taking him on as a client?"

Deanna's good mood vanished. "Wait just a damn minute here." She got to her feet and moved around the table to better confront him. "My clients are none of your business, Jonas Phoenix. Just who do you think you are to speak to me like this anyway?" He started to say something, but she poked him in the chest and shot right over him. "You do not have a say in it. This isn't the Dark Ages, you dork. Women don't have to ask their . . . whatever you are, for permission."

He took hold of her shoulders and pulled her close. "You and I are together, Deanna. That makes it my business. Especially when it comes to your safety. And trust me, you aren't safe if you're anywhere near Valdez." He leaned down until they were nose to nose. "When we get back to Ohio, you'll tell him to find a new decorator for his goddamn mansion."

Her eyes shot wide. "Are you even listening to yourself?"

He dropped his hands and looked at her as if she'd grown two heads. "What?"

"Get this straight. I decide who my clients are, not you. If Terrance turns out to be a drug dealer, which I highly doubt, then I'll tell him to get lost. Until then, back off!"

"You honestly believe there is more than one rich man named Terrance Valdez who lives in Zanesville, Ohio?"

Deanna rose up on her tiptoes and bit out, "Maybe, maybe not. All I know for sure is that I've spent a great deal of time

and worked a lot of hours to build this business of mine. Don't
even think that you can come in and start making decisions for
me just because we slept together."

"It's not because we slept together," he ground out. "It's because I care about what happens to you. I fucking care if you
get shot!"

Deanna closed her eyes and counted to ten. When she
opened them again and saw Jonas's worry, she knew he wasn't
trying to dictate her life. He was genuinely concerned. "I get
that you're worried, I do, but you're being unreasonable. I've
had to deal with overprotective men my entire life, and it makes
me crazy. Please, don't treat me like some silly piece of fluff
who needs to be coddled and looked after. I'm begging you,
Jonas."

Jonas's arms came around her and he pulled her in close. He
was stiff and unyielding, as if afraid to let her go. "I'm sorry."
He spoke against the top of her head. "I don't mean to treat
you that way. But the guy is a criminal, Deanna. There's no
telling what all he's done."

"*If* he's a criminal," she reminded him as she pushed back
and looked up at him. "We don't even know if it's the same
guy."

"It's my business to know these things, remember?"

"Yes, I remember. But how would you feel if I suddenly
started telling you how to run your PI business? Which cases
you could take and all that. You'd be okay with me walking in
and taking over?"

"Of course not, but I'm an ex-soldier. You're a decorator,
Deanna. You aren't trained to deal with guys like Valdez."

"I'm not trained to deal with criminals, that's true. But don't
cheapen what I do. I'm proud of being an interior decorator. It
gives me pleasure. It's hard and demanding, but I love it."

Jonas plucked her right off her feet and held her at eye level.
"I know and I'm sorry."

Well, that sure took the air right out of her sails. "You don't play fair," she complained.

"No, I don't," he said with total sincerity. "It would be smart to remember that, kitten."

She squinted at him. "Put me down."

"Nope. Not until you accept my apology."

She kicked his shin. "This is not a comfortable position, darn it."

Jonas looked around, seemed to notice his chair knocked over, then stepped around the table and took hers instead. He plopped her onto his lap and took her face between his palms. "Say you forgive me."

She merely picked up another cheese puff and popped it into her mouth. Crap, it might've been cardboard for all she noticed. Honestly, how was a woman supposed to concentrate on food with so much hard, male flesh beneath her butt?

Jonas kissed the side of her neck, turning her insides to mush with the little gesture. "Pretty please, forgive me?"

When he licked her pulse, Deanna caved. "I forgive you."

She felt his lips curving upward and wanted to punch him, but he kissed the tender spot behind her ear, and her hands decided there were better things to do. She opened her legs to give herself access to the erection poking into her backside, then cupped him through his boxers. Jonas made a deep, gravelly sound in his chest and kept on teasing her with little tiny kisses. His hands came up and cupped her breasts through the thin T-shirt he'd given her to wear. All the sexy lingerie she'd brought along with her and he wanted to see her in one of his T-shirts. The man was constantly confusing her. Deanna no longer knew which end was up.

She forced herself to stop fondling him, then batted his hands away. "Wait, did we come to an agreement or not?"

Jonas coasted one hand down her belly until he cupped her mound protectively. "We'll figure it out later." He littered little kisses over her collarbone and nibbled on her neck. "Why can I never get enough of you? It's never been this way for me."

Deanna understood all too well. "I know what you mean. There's some serious chemistry between us, I guess."

"It's more than that," he admonished as he picked up a cheese puff and fed it to her. "It's your strength. Your intelligence. Your feisty attitude. You're the whole package, Deanna."

She liked hearing that. And for some crazy reason, she liked him feeding her too. A man had never treated her with such care. "You know, after I found out about Gary cheating on me, I thought maybe there was something wrong with me. Like I wasn't woman enough or something."

Jonas cupped the back of her head and forced her to look at him. "And do you still feel this way? Even after last night?"

"No. You make me feel sexy and treasured. You've discovered a side of me that no other man even took the time to find."

"I like that, Deanna. You can't know how much that pleases me."

She smiled and wrapped her arms around his neck. "You do?"

His arms came around her middle, holding her tight. "I love knowing that no man has ever touched you the way I do."

She rolled her eyes. "I can see I'm going to have to be careful what I say. Otherwise you'll get a big head."

He chuckled and grabbed a cheese puff. "Open up, kitten."

Deanna obeyed, letting Jonas pop the tasty treat into her mouth. As her lips closed around it, he muttered something unintelligible, and she felt his cock harden beneath her buttocks.

"Thirsty?" he asked in a rough voice.

"Yes."

Jonas picked up the bottle of water he'd retrieved from the refrigerator earlier and handed it to her. Deanna took several drinks before handing it back to him. He gulped down the rest and placed the empty bottle on the table. That's when it dawned on her that the house had been ready for them when they arrived. Curious, Deanna asked, "How is it that this place is all spick-and-span and so well stocked?"

"Our neighbor, Mrs. Grimly. We pay her to come in and take care of the place when we're not using it. She's real sweet. I called her ahead of time to let her know I was coming for the weekend and asked if she'd pick up a few things from the store."

"Oh. I'm surprised Wade never mentioned her."

"I'm surprised you've never used the house before. I mean, didn't you ever ask Wade if you could come down here for a vacation?"

She shook her head. "I knew Wade came here with women."

"Ah, that's right. You said we used the beach house for our *sex fests*. You know, Wade usually spent time alone here. Well, that is until he met Gracie."

"And you?"

"I've been here with women before," he answered in a soft voice, "but it's been a long time—and none of them were you, Deanna."

Jealousy sparked to life inside her as she imagined Jonas with another woman in the bed they'd so recently made love in. Had he taken other women in front of the mirror, the way he had her? She suddenly felt sick. *Don't even go there*, she chided herself. *You'll only make yourself crazy.* To keep from dwelling, Deanna slid off his lap and grabbed the empty water bottle.

"I'm not sure why I asked you that," she lied, taking the empty bottle to the recycling bin. "It's really none of my business."

Deanna pasted on a chipper smile and was about to turn around when she felt Jonas behind her, caging her in. "If it makes any difference, it sends me into an ugly rage whenever I think of you with other men."

"Neither of us are virgins," she stated, as if by saying it aloud it would somehow make her feel better. It didn't.

"True," he admitted, "but that doesn't mean we have to think about each other's exes with fondness."

"No, definitely not."

Jonas nestled his semierect cock against her bottom, letting her feel the full brunt of his arousal. "So, how about I take you back to bed."

"To sleep," she admonished. "I want to go to the beach and shopping tomorrow." She glanced at the clock on the wall. "Later today, I mean."

"Later. Much later."

"Jonas, if you start that thing up, we'll never get to sleep."

He chuckled. "Start that thing up? It's a dick, not an engine, kitten."

Deanna pushed against him, and Jonas got the hint, stepping back a few feet to give her room. When she turned around and saw the hunger in his eyes, she nearly gave in.

"It was a long flight, and we both used up a lot of energy earlier. We need sleep." Was she attempting to convince him or herself? Deanna wondered.

"Fine," he growled as he steered her out of the kitchen. "But after we're both rested and you've had your shopping fix, I've got plans for that hot little body of yours."

Deanna could well imagine what sort of plans Jonas had in his oh-so-clever mind. Crazy as it seemed, she was becoming pretty darned fond of said mind. In fact, if she wasn't careful, she was going to end up falling in love with the clever, sexy, possessive, somewhat bossy man. And that would definitely be the craziest thing of all.

_____

12

"Oh, come on. Guys go in this store all the time." Deanna tugged on his arm, but he wasn't budging.

"No way, Deanna." Okay, maybe he was being a pussy, but ladies' lingerie? Really? "And you're full of crap. Guys don't go into those stores. They order online."

She rolled her eyes. "Surely you can handle a few pairs of panties and bras."

Jonas peered into the window. All he saw was rack after rack of frilly lace and colorful satins. "I didn't say I couldn't handle it, but there isn't a single dude in there. Only women."

After waking in the middle of the afternoon, Deanna had fixed them both a quick breakfast of scrambled eggs and toast. Then they'd put on their swimsuits and headed to the beach.

They'd laid out a couple of towels, then Jonas grabbed a bottle of sunblock. "Come on, kitten, I don't want you to burn."

She rolled her eyes and sat down on one of the towels. "I can put on my own sunscreen, Jonas." She plucked it out of his hand and said, "I'm not helpless."

He swatted her gently on the hand. "Don't be so contrary and give me the lotion."

She slapped it into his palm. "Do you always have to have your own way?"

He flicked her nose. "Only when it comes to getting my hands on you."

She laughed. "You're perverted."

He pushed on her back. "Lie down so I can rub my hands all over that hot, siren's body of yours."

Deanna moved to her side, then lay out flat on the colorful beach towel. She wore a white one-piece that came up high on her hips. Like any red-blooded male's, his gaze went straight to her long, lean legs and the round globes of her ass. Jonas clamped his jaw tight against the need to lean down and bite the creamy flesh, swimsuit and all.

He liked that her body wasn't darkly tanned, but more the color of honey with a slight redness at the tops of her shoulders from the little bit of sun exposure. Her hair, swept up into a messy pile of curls on top of her head, tempted him to reach out and play with a few of the dark strands that had escaped. They were scattered around her nape and sticking to her skin. But that wasn't what had him as hard as a damn spike. It was the barely there suit she'd chosen to torment him with. It had those little ties around her neck, all but daring a man to pull the string and find the treasures beneath. Jonas stopped his survey, wishing like hell he could tamp down his raging boner, and cleared his throat.

Popping the top, he squirted some of the thick, white cream into his hands, then started on her back. It took only a few seconds before she relaxed and closed her eyes.

Leaning close to her ear, Jonas whispered, "You're the most beautiful woman I've ever seen."

Deanna's eyelids fluttered and her gaze caught his. "We're in Miami, Jonas. There are tanned, blond beauties all over this beach. Every one of them sexier than me by far. And that's not me putting myself down. It's just a fact."

"You don't understand, Deanna," he said as he squirted more lotion onto his hands before starting on her shoulders and arms. "There's more to beauty than a pretty package."

She closed her eyes once more. "What's your idea of beauty, then?"

"My idea of beauty is the way your warm, brown eyes fill with mischief whenever you think you've managed to get a dig in."

She laughed. "I don't think. I know."

With her arms coated, Jonas moved to her legs, working from her feet up. "Beauty is when your pretty, ruby lips curve upward whenever I'm lucky enough to get you to smile or laugh." He drizzled lotion over her calves and worked it into her skin. "Beauty is that big, mushy heart of yours that you too often wear on your sleeve."

She lifted her head and squinted at him. "Are you saying I'm a pushover?"

He shrugged. "Maybe a little."

As he massaged her thighs, Deanna moaned and dropped her head to the blanket. "I'll be mad at you later. Right now I feel too good to be anything other than content."

Jonas let his fingers drift between her legs, just barely grazing her pussy through the swimsuit. Deanna went rigid. He patted her bottom and stretched out next to her. "You want to know what else I find beautiful about you?"

"W-what?"

"The way your body responds to mine. A single touch and you're ready for me, aren't you, kitten?"

"Don't be smug," she admonished. "Smugness isn't attractive."

"True, but you have the same effect on me, you know. All you have to do is look at me and I'm putty in your hands," Jonas admitted as he glared at a man walking by. He stared at Deanna as if he wanted to snack on her. When the jerk's gaze traveled over Deanna's body, Jonas had the urge to trip him. After the guy was gone, Jonas growled, "I'm not the only one on this beach who finds you attractive."

Deanna's eyes shot open and she looked around. Her gaze came back to his and she frowned. "Seems I'm not the only woman who finds you attractive either. Guess that makes us even."

He kissed her sun-warmed cheek and murmured, "As long as I'm the only one spreading cream on your sexy curves, I'm fine with it."

"Ditto," she said as she sat up and took hold of the bottle. When she poured some of the lotion into her palm and smoothed it between her hands, Jonas groaned.

By the time Deanna finished, they'd both gotten a little too overheated. It'd taken all Jonas's strength not to give in to his dick's demands to take Deanna right there in the sand. In fact, if she hadn't reminded him that part of the reason for the trip was to prove they could have more than good sex together, he would've.

Now, as they stood at the entrance to Christy's Boutique, Deanna all but laughing at him, he knew he should've just gone with his first instinct—sex.

"You are the same man who defended his country from ter-rorists, right?"

"Yes, but—"

"And after the steamy sex we shared last night, I would've thought you'd be the last guy to blush at a few pairs of under-wear."

Christ, she was good at manipulation. Jonas hated shopping. Damn it. Come to think of it, what man enjoyed it? Still, he'd insisted that he wasn't an oversexed playboy, hadn't he? That he wanted to get to know her on this trip. And wasn't this something a regular couple would do?

He was about to give in when Deanna shimmied up against

him and rose on her toes. Jonas braced himself, wondering what she'd do next. "I thought you said you wanted to buy me some lingerie," she whispered. "I was sort of hoping to have something that would always remind me of this trip."

Right away, Jonas had an image in his head of Deanna in nothing but a lacy red thong. His dick hardened, and since the only thing he wore was a pair of flimsy black swim trunks, a hard-on was the last thing he wanted. "You'd better watch it, kitten," he warned, "or you're liable to find your pretty ass up against a wall."

Deanna bit her lip and started to speak, but he slammed his mouth down onto hers, effectively cutting her off. When he lifted away, they were both breathing a little heavy and people were staring. Shit. Without saying a word, Jonas grabbed her hand and walked into the store. Deanna stayed silent, too, he noticed with no small amount of satisfaction.

As Jonas maneuvered around racks of silky teddies and satiny nightgowns, taking in the colorful array of fabrics, bits of silk, and scraps of nothing, he realized he did want to buy Deanna something. Something sexy. Something that would make her think of him every time she wore it against her soft skin. He only had to pick that perfect something. He remembered the red lace she'd worn the night before. She'd said her favorite color was red, but he knew she'd look beautiful in any color. Jonas glanced around, and his gaze caught on a walled-off section at the back of the store. Curious, he tugged her in that direction.

The back of the store was set up like a separate room that stored a collection of items with a more wicked slant and a naughtier scheme. Ah, yes, he found just what he was looking for on a hook jutting out from the back wall. It was a minuscule pair of black and red striped satin thong panties, with a matching bra. Jonas picked the set up and turned them around. He pictured Deanna wearing them and his hard-on grew to a painful length inside his trunks.

Jonas shoved them at her. "Here, try this on."

"Uh, Jonas, they're probably not even the right size." She checked the tag. "Good Lord, that's a lot of money for something so tiny."

He looked at the bits of material and asked, "Are they the right size?"

"Yes, but—"

"Then try them on."

"They're expensive," she said in a hushed voice.

"I'm buying them, remember?" When she started to protest, he stopped her with a finger to her lips. "You dragged me into this bloody store, and if you know what's good for you, then you'll get your cute ass into the fitting room."

"You're being bossy again," she muttered as she continued to glare at him.

"I'm barely restraining myself from jumping your lovely bones." He looked around, spotted a line of fitting rooms on the far wall, and pushed her toward them. "Go, kitten, and don't even think of not letting me see them when you get them on."

Deanna walked, but Jonas noticed her back was a little too rigid. She was pissed at his high-handedness, no doubt. What was it about the woman that tore away all the layers of his civility? She got to him. Turned him into a damn Neanderthal. It was friggin' annoying.

As she moved, Jonas's gaze unerringly went to her ass. She still wore her white one-piece bathing suit, but she'd pulled a black mesh cover-up over it. It hindered his view, but not by much. When her bottom jiggled a little, his heart kicked into overdrive. As she slipped through the curtain and disappeared, Jonas took a moment to calm down. Going at her like a deer during rut was not the way to the woman's heart, he told himself. If he could just remember that later, once they were alone, maybe he'd be able to save a sliver of his dignity, but he wasn't holding his breath.

When his cell phone started to vibrate, Jonas pulled it out of the pocket on his white T-shirt and checked the caller ID. Wade. Christ, he was probably checking to see if he'd turned Deanna into a mindless sex slave yet. When it vibrated again, Jonas knew he'd have to answer it or the entire cavalry would converge on them. He took a deep, fortifying breath, then flipped it open.

Deanna couldn't figure out why she was letting Jonas have the upper hand. Okay, that wasn't entirely true. Part of her knew exactly why she was giving in to him. It was Jonas's lack of control around her that had caused Deanna to hold her tongue. Jonas was always so charming. Joking and flirting. Not so much today, though, and she had a feeling it was because he wanted her so badly. It helped to know she wasn't the only one aching.

Deanna slipped her cover-up over her head, then tugged at the straps of her bathing suit. Soon she was naked. As she stared at her body in the mirror, she was shocked to see the little love bites on her breasts and belly. She turned around and saw a few on her bottom as well. The slight purplish bruises around her hips where Jonas had grasped on to her were all signs of his loss of control. And even as gentle and easy as he had been, his desire had still left its marks. Her body flushed when she realized just how thoroughly he'd made love to her. It was that thought alone that had her putting on the sexy thong and bra with total confidence.

Deanna wiggled and adjusted until she had the two pieces in place. As she looked at herself in the mirror, she wondered what Jonas would think. The shiny stripes looked good against her ivory skin tone, she thought, but would Jonas like it? Only one way to find out.

Deanna pulled the curtain aside a few inches and peeked out. Jonas quickly appeared, taking hold of the curtain and moving it out of the way. She noticed the way he used his body to block the entrance, effectively keeping the other customers from seeing her in the skimpy outfit. His gaze took a slow route over her body. Down, then up. Then he repeated the process two more times.

"Damn." He closed his eyes for a few seconds and took a deep breath before opening them again. "Turn around."

He hadn't said *please,* but Deanna obeyed all the same. As she gave Jonas her back, Deanna watched him in the mirror. His gaze appeared glued to her butt. It never wavered, and for a long time she feared he didn't like the striped set. She was about to tell him they could skip the whole idea, but then he looked up. Their gazes met in the mirror, and Deanna felt singed by the wild, out-of-control blaze in Jonas's eyes.

"You're stunning," he said finally.

Deanna felt her cheeks heat at his unabashed praise. She was about to thank him when he lowered his head and kissed her neck. She bent her head to one side to give him better access, and whimpered when he bit her. He settled his lower body against hers, and Deanna could feel the evidence of his arousal pushing into the cleft of her buttocks. He rotated his hips, rubbing himself against her while he licked at the place he'd bitten.

"Jonas," she moaned.

He kept his hands in balled fists at his sides as he raised his head. "You need to get dressed." Deanna nodded, unable to speak past the lump in her throat. "If I stay here another second, I'll be inside of you, kitten." Without waiting for a reply, Jonas stepped back and closed the curtain, leaving Deanna utterly breathless.

After Jonas paid for the racy bra and panty set, they left the store. The walk back to the house ended up being an extremely quiet trip. Neither of them spoke. Words weren't necessary, though. They wanted each other; it was that simple.

13

Jonas had kept his damned hands to himself in the store, but kissing her had been a matter of necessity. He'd been so hungry for her that he'd had to have a little something to tide him over. Still, he knew that if he had put his hands against that luscious ass of hers, he would have to be inside of her. No way would he have had the self-control to keep from sliding his cock deep.

Christ, when had he become so greedy? Hell, he never allowed his cock to rule the show. Of course, that was before he'd sampled Deanna. Before he'd seen her eyes go dark with passion. Before he'd watched her shout out her pleasure. All other women paled compared to her. He'd always known that if he ever got her into his bed, he'd never be the same again.

In his gut, Jonas had known for years that Deanna was the only woman for him. When he'd teased her, she'd all but ignored him. When he'd tried to charm his way into her good graces, she'd practically given him the finger. She'd been a challenge from the beginning, but now it was more. Far more. She'd somehow wiggled her way into his heart, and damn if he didn't like her there.

Jonas slid the key into the lock on the front door and turned the knob, letting her in ahead of him. Once they were both inside, he closed and locked them in before placing his wallet, keys, and cell phone on the entryway table. Deanna turned around, and Jonas watched as she put her purse next to his things, then dropped her packages onto the floor. She didn't bend to pick them up, only stood there quietly watching him. So eager, yet willing to let him lead. The knowledge turned him on something fierce. Christ, to hell with the bed. To hell with the couch, even. He moved, pinning her against the door.

She lifted her head and their lips found each other. Deanna opened her mouth, and Jonas took advantage and delved inside. His tongue tangled with hers. She tasted sweet, but he wanted more. He wanted all of her. He gripped the hem of her cover-up and hiked it up. Soon, their clothes were littering the floor and he was pushing his cock inside her tight heat. God, she felt good. Tight and hot, and so fucking slick with her juices. Then he remembered. No condom. He pulled out instantly.

"Christ, I can't believe I forgot."

"What?"

"A condom."

"I'm on the pill, Jonas," she said, her voice husky with her passion. "And I'm clean."

"I got a clean bill of health last month, and I haven't been with anyone in longer than that, but are you sure?"

"I'm sure. Please, I need you."

"I'm here, kitten." He wrapped his arms around her and cupped her ass. "Guide me in," he urged. When she took his cock in her small fist, it was all he could do to keep from coming. Deanna brought him to her entrance and he thrust forward. His cock pushed between her pussy lips, but it wasn't enough. He needed the fast, hard loving she'd talked about the night before.

Jonas lifted her off the floor and sucked in a breath as

Deanna wrapped her long, lean legs around his waist. Her arms came around his neck next, and Jonas heard her moan his name. He held her tight as he impaled her with his hard cock.

"Ride me."

When Deanna's lower body began a slow, torturous rhythm, Jonas felt his balls drawing up tight. "Fast," he coaxed, "like you wanted. Fuck me good, Deanna."

"Thought you'd never ask," Deanna murmured as she slammed her pussy onto his dick.

"Ah, God," he gritted out. His fingers dug into her ass cheeks. Jonas let loose a string of curses as her inner muscles clutched and held him tight. Then she lifted up once more, until he was barely seated inside her an inch. As the bulbous head kissed her pussy lips, Deanna thrust onto him again. Their mouths met, and Jonas gently bit her lower, plumper lip. He suckled, then dipped his tongue inside, teasing a moan from her.

Deanna pulled almost painfully at fistfuls of his hair, then rode his cock hard, forcing him clear to the hilt. Jonas almost lost his balance, but he swiftly pumped back at her, and the pace was on. They took from each other, demanding—hell, almost punishing. He sucked at her tongue; then he felt her mash her breasts against his chest, and he pulled his mouth off her so he could watch her pretty tits bouncing with each rapid movement.

"Jesus, you're a sight," he crooned.

She was out of control, thrusting up and down. Suddenly, she screamed and flung her head back against the door as her orgasm bathed his cock. Jonas erupted, filling her with jets of hot cum.

Deanna slumped against him, boneless, completely done in. Both of them breathed heavy, their chests rising and falling in fast, shallow pants. She'd thoroughly worked him over.

"Well, that should hold me over for at least an hour."

She lifted her head and eyed him as if he had a swarm of spiders crawling all over him. "Are you kidding? I'm dead. You killed me."

As he released her thighs, she slowly slid to the floor. Jonas waited until he was sure she wasn't going to fall before he stepped away. "You're the one doing all the pounding, kitten. All I did was stand here."

She laughed and started toward the stairs. "Shower, or are you hungry?"

"Shower, but only if I get to be your loofah," he teased.

When her feet hit the first step, Jonas's gaze drifted down her body. That's when he saw marks on her buttocks. Bruises? He drew closer. Christ, he'd hurt her. He'd been too rough.

"Deanna," he called out.

She stopped her ascent and looked over her shoulder at him. Jonas closed the gap, then knelt down behind her and kissed the bruises forming on the soft skin of each cheek. One by one, he touched his lips to each mark he'd left on her perfect skin. "I should be tied up and beaten."

"Jonas, maybe you weren't paying attention just now, but I was the one going all cavewoman." Deanna cupped his cheek, caressing his jaw. "I like the stubbles on you, by the way. You should let it grow out a little."

He looked up at her from his position, her tender expression and sweet smile tugging at his heart. She was so delicate. From her big, caring heart to her soft, creamy skin. "I could do a little bit of a beard. For you."

She cocked her head to the side. "Really?"

"Mmm, really." As he stood back up and took her into his arms, cradling her against his chest, he said, "I'm sorry, kitten. I should have been easier with you."

"Jonas, please don't be sorry for needing me as much as I do you. I never want you to be anything other than what you are. You are a passionate lover, but you're also an incredibly gentle man."

"If that's true, then why do you have marks on your ass?"

"Love marks," she said softly, "and I sort of like seeing them there."

"You like them, huh?"

"Mmm."

Her whispered answer drifted over Jonas's skin. To have his mark on her was a sign of possession in Jonas's eyes. Knowing she liked it gave him a small measure of hope. He wanted her emotionally involved with him. With all his might, Jonas clung to the small kernel Deanna unwittingly offered. Damn, how he ached to hear Deanna say that she wanted him to make love to her, and not just sate her lust. If he had anything to say about it, she'd give him something before their weekend was over. Some sign that he meant more to her than merely a fun weekend.

As he took her up the stairs to the bathroom, he flicked on the light, then put her on her feet. He went about the task of getting the water in the tub the right temperature before he asked, "How about a bubble bath instead?"

She nodded and crossed her arms over her breasts. "I love bubble baths."

He pointed to a shelf next to the mirror. "Hand me the bottle on the top shelf."

She moved to grab it but had to stand on her tiptoes to reach the top. The move put her ass in direct line with his mouth. He grinned and leaned forward, then dropped a kiss directly above her ass cheeks. She yelped and swiveled around, nearly dropping the bottle on his head. He quickly grabbed it and cupped her hip to steady her. She batted his hand away, and Jonas had to turn around to hide his grin. As he dumped a good portion of the creamy liquid into the warm water, he heard Deanna mumble something from behind. He turned his head and quirked a brow.

"I said, you're entirely too fascinated with my butt."

He shrugged, totally unrepentant. "It's a very nice butt."

"Just nice?"

He chuckled at her disgruntled tone. "It's the best butt I've ever kissed."

She stood straighter and shot her nose into the air. "That's better."

He gestured to the tub. "Your bath awaits, my lady."

She smiled and got into the foamy water. Jonas waited for her to relax before stepping in behind her and sitting down. Pulling her against his chest, he ground out, "Ah, yeah, that's good."

"I agree one hundred percent."

They sat there for a few minutes, enjoying the hot water and fragrant bubbles. It was Deanna who broke the silence. "Tell me about your parents."

Jonas scowled. "Why?"

She tilted her head back to look him in the eye. "Because I want to know more about you."

"There isn't much to tell." He stroked her cheek with the backs of his knuckles. "My mother gave birth to me and so they raised me. That's about it."

She slapped his thigh beneath the water. "That's a fairly cold, short story, Jonas."

He picked up a sponge and squirted some bath gel onto it. "My parents are fairly cold people." He started on her shoulders, rubbing the sponge up and down her arms. "They derive pleasure from money. The more they have, the happier they are and the more they want."

Deanna relaxed against him, her hands drifting up and down his thighs on either side of her body. He wasn't certain she even knew she was doing it. "They don't sound like very nice people," she said in a faraway voice.

"They weren't cruel." He worked his way over her chest, paying special attention to each of her breasts. "Just not parent material. My mom told me once that she'd miscalculated and missed taking one of her birth-control pills. That's how I was conceived. In her mind, she made a mistake and rectified it by raising me instead of aborting me."

She clutched his thighs in her hands, her short nails digging into his skin. "God, that's awful, Jonas. Babies are a gift. A blessing."

He nuzzled the top of her head as he drifted the sponge beneath the water to her belly, and beyond. "I knew you felt that way. I've watched the way you are around your little cousins a time or two, Deanna."

"You have?"

"Yeah. You're a natural with kids."

Her exploring hands moved higher, coming precariously close to his cock. "Okay, your parents are robots, but what about cousins, aunts, and uncles?"

Jonas caressed the sponge over her pussy, and he felt her shudder from the gentle abrasion. "I have one uncle on my dad's side, but he's single and a workaholic. I've seen him a handful of times."

"So, I guess Wade's approval when you asked to date me was sort of important because he's like a brother to you?"

"It's more than that." He paused and tried to put his feelings into words, something he seriously sucked at. "When you depend on someone to have your back in a war-torn country like Afghanistan, it forges a bond."

When her fingers barely grazed his balls, Jonas had to force himself to stay on track. "I always knew I could count on Wade when we went into an op together, and vice versa. I wasn't about to flip my finger up at that relationship by dating his baby sister. At least, not without talking to him first."

"And if he'd said no?"

"Then I would've figured out a way to get him to say yes."

"Why?"

Jonas dropped the sponge and cupped her chin. He tugged until she was looking at him. "Are you looking for me to say that I care about you? That you matter to me? Because I do, Deanna."

Several seconds drifted by as she stared up at him, not speaking. Finally she looked away and said, "Do you know why I was hurt that day at Gracie's apartment? When you backed down to Wade?"

"Damn it, girl. I told you I was sorry about that. Will you never let it go?"

She swatted at him from beneath the water, and Jonas sucked in a breath at just how close she'd come to smacking his balls. "Shush and listen," she chided him. "It wasn't for the reason you think. It wasn't because you didn't stand up for me. I know you thought that. It hurt me because it felt like you saw me as Wade's kid sister. I didn't want to be that, not to you. I wanted you to see me as a desirable woman. Not an extension of Wade."

Jonas snorted. "Kitten, I stopped seeing you as Wade's sweet, little sister the first time I met you. You wore that black one-piece and I about swallowed my damn tongue. I wanted to eat you up that day."

"I wanted you too. Like crazy."

"If I'd known that then, I wouldn't have left, at least not without you. And as much as that thought is appealing, it would've damaged my friendship with Wade."

"I understand. You don't have to explain. I wouldn't appreciate it if someone stuck me in the position of choosing between my family. It would be awful."

"Deanna, you need to know something."

She went back to rubbing his thighs. "Hmm?"

"Now that we're here, now that our relationship has moved past friendship, I won't let anyone keep you from me. Not ever again. Do you understand?"

She tilted her head to look into his eyes. "Are you saying we're a couple?"

He kissed her forehead and murmured, "Do you want to be?"

"Maybe." She looked forward again. "It feels rushed, though. I don't want to jump into anything."

"No jumping, then." He dropped the sponge and used his hands to stroke her wet curves. Ah, much better. "But can we at least agree that we're exclusive?"

She nodded vehemently, which pleased the hell out of him. "Yes, I think that's a safe assumption."

"Good, because if some guy made the mistake of touching you, I'd probably gut the bastard. And then I'd end up in prison, which would shoot my five-year plan to shit."

"Gut? That's gross and violent." Deanna shuddered. "Too violent."

"Yeah, well, I'm real good with a knife. I'll show you sometime."

Deanna pushed herself upright and turned around. "Really?" she asked, with excitement in her dark chocolate eyes. "Could you teach me?"

"Sure, if you want." He clutched her around the waist and pulled her close for a kiss. Jonas kept it brief, knowing he'd take her again if he didn't, and she probably needed a break after the encounter against the door. "I'll buy you one too. One that'll fit your hand just right."

"I'd like that very much. Thank you."

"Hmm, I think we'd better get out. The water's getting

cold." He lifted her to her feet, then waited for her to leave the tub before he got out and started to dry off.

She patted herself dry, then wrapped the towel around her body and looked up at him. "Jonas?"

Jonas used a towel to dry his hair. "Yeah?"

"I want to taste you."

Jonas froze. Now, that was a damn nice visual. "Taste me?"

"Yes." She reached out, wrapped her hand around the base of his cock, and pumped. "I want you in my mouth."

Jonas dropped the towel. "Are you talking about my cum?"

She nodded and went to her knees before him. "I didn't get to yet and I've been dying for it."

"Take what you want, kitten," Jonas said softly. "Slide that dick into your mouth. Take me to heaven."

14

Deanna bent her head and took Jonas's cock into her mouth. Deep, or as deep as his thickness and length would allow. As she'd found out already, the man was well built. She hollowed her cheeks and sucked hard on his engorged flesh.

"That's so fucking good," Jonas praised. "Love that cock real sweet for me, kitty."

With his intense, coarse words, a barrier inside of Deanna seemed to break away. For the first time, she felt as if she were truly free to explore him. To take what she wanted. She cupped his balls and squeezed as she swirled her tongue over and around the bulbous head of his shaft. Jonas's deep voice rumbled low in his chest as he pulled her hair. The sting at her scalp sent little arcs of pleasure skating down her spine. The pleasure-pain had her pussy dripping with need.

As she slipped his cock from between her lips and licked down the underside to his balls, she looked up and noticed his blue gaze watching her every move. It turned her on to have his eyes on her. With Jonas she wasn't shy. She only felt hot, womanly desire around him.

Intent on drawing out his pleasure, Deanna sucked one of his balls into her mouth.

"Oh, hell, Deanna," Jonas gritted out. He tried to pull her backward. "My cock," he explained, his voice rough and so low she barely heard him.

She released his sac. "My turn."

"Little tease." He gentled his hold and widened his stance, as if surrendering to her ministrations.

Deanna felt triumphant as she went back to nuzzling and playing with his balls. His musky male scent filled her senses. Teasing her way over his cock with her tongue, Deanna didn't stop until she had his throbbing, swollen head in between her lips. He moaned and a pearl of moisture hit her tongue. "Mmm, I like your flavor, Jonas," she confessed, hungry for more. Only when he shot his cum onto her tongue and down her throat would Deanna be satisfied.

"There's a lot more where that came from."

Not willing to wait another second, Deanna stuffed her mouth full of his cock in eager anticipation. Her clit swelled and her pussy ached to have Jonas filling her. She suckled and laved, and when her hand squeezed his sac gently, Jonas shut his eyes and threw his head back on a groan. Deanna took him deeper, so deep the engorged head nearly set off her gag reflex.

Jonas's hold on her hair tightened. "Deanna."

Suddenly he took control, pumping her mouth and sending them both mindless with pleasure. When his cock slid out, Deanna tightened her lips and hummed around the thick length. The vibrations had his cock flexing inside her mouth and his entire body stiffened. He cursed and tensed a heartbeat before his hot cum flooded her mouth. Deanna moaned as she swallowed the creamy fluid, drinking every salty drop. She pulled her mouth free and delivered a gentle kiss to the tip.

"Tasty," she whispered as she sat back on her heels and stared up at him. The savage look in his eyes struck Deanna directly in the heart. A muscle in his jaw jumped angrily. She flushed from head to toe as she thought of how many times he must have had a woman go down on him. Had Deanna pleased him? She couldn't deep-throat Jonas; he was simply too big. Maybe other women could, though.

"Was it okay?" she asked, feeling unaccountably shy and unsure.

"Okay? Hell, you just rocked my world, Deanna."

The intensity behind the words effectively shredded her worries. She held up her hands, but instead of taking them, he dipped at the knees and grasped her around the waist, lifting her into his arms.

"All others pale compared to you, Deanna," he told her, as if reading her thoughts. "Every other woman was forgotten the moment I kissed you on your front porch. Didn't you know that?" She shook her head, unable to put into words what she'd been thinking, that she might not have pleased him. "Your warm, giving nature is as precious as gold to me. You so easily make me feel . . . happy. Do you know what a gift that is? How much I cherish it?"

He placed her on the bed and came down on top of her. "When you lie so beautifully pliant beneath me, totally trusting, placing yourself in my care, it humbles me."

"Jonas." At his honest confession, emotion clogged Deanna's throat and tears threatened to spill over.

"That you would even give me, of all people, the time of day, makes me feel like the luckiest son of a bitch in the world."

His description had her frowning. "What do you mean, you of all people?"

"I'm not exactly a prize, Deanna. I grew up in an unemotional, frigid household. I joined the military the first chance I got so that I could fuel my need for danger. I was an adrenaline junkie. I've done some pretty horrible things. On a good day,

I'm a bloodthirsty bastard. Hell, it's no wonder Wade wanted to keep me away from you."

"Bloodthirsty I can see. But you're a good man, Jonas. An honorable man."

"Honorable and good are qualities I'm not sure I'll ever possess, but I'm just enough of an ass to be glad you think I do."

As if unable to wait another second, Jonas bent his head and kissed her waiting mouth. She felt a quiver of anticipation cruise through her body, tasted the heat of eager breath as his tongue tangled with hers. She wanted to stroke him to a fever pitch all over again. To send him soaring with anxious desire.

His mouth went on a journey over her torso even as his hands moved slowly over her curves. Deanna arched her back, enjoying the feel of his rough palms coasting over her skin. His fingers delved into her dark curls. At once he located her soft puff of skin, and he skillfully began stroking and squeezing, teasing little sounds from her throat. Deanna stopped thinking at that point and instead let Jonas explore her in the most erotic way possible.

Jonas watched as Deanna slowly surrendered. It was in the way her muscles relaxed and her legs fell open. He pushed them apart even more, making room for the width of his shoulders between. He filled his hands with the firm globes of her ass and knew he should take time to praise the beauty of the soft pink folds of her pussy and the tempting little pearl nestled there, but he didn't. Instead, he simply lowered his head and dined on her creamy heat, sliding his tongue deep, tasting her hot channel. Deanna's fingers tunneled into his hair as she pushed him against her pelvis, forcing his tongue a little deeper. Flicking her little nub several times, Jonas watched as Deanna flung her head back and screamed out her climax, drenching him in her juices.

Jonas wasn't done; he wouldn't stop until he'd wrung every

last drop from her. Nibbling and kissing her swollen lips and sensitive clit, Jonas heard her pleasure-filled cries. She slammed her hips against his face as wave after wave of her orgasm crashed over her.

When she collapsed, her hands falling to the mattress, Jonas lifted his mouth off her and stared at the sexy picture she made. Her hair was a wild tangle of dark strands, and her body glistened with perspiration. Damn, she took his breath away.

Jonas moved to his knees, then grabbed a pillow. He lifted her hips and pushed it beneath, propping up her lower half. Deanna's eyes flew open. "What are you doing?"

"Stay put while I grab a few things." He pressed a hand against her stomach and ordered, "Don't move, understand?"

Deanna nodded. "Okay, but if you come back with something kinky, I'm running."

He laughed as he left the bed. "Don't be a prude, kitten."

"The fact that you didn't rush to reassure me is even more frightening, Jonas."

He winked and left the room. After he located the things he needed, he came back to find Deanna nearly snoring.

Jonas placed the items on the bedside table and moved carefully back onto the bed. Deanna stirred but didn't wake. He reached over and picked up one of the items, a cup of ice. As he fished out a cube, Jonas smiled and touched the tip of the rapidly melting chunk to her belly button. Deanna jolted upright.

"Do I have your attention?"

"You did *not* just do that."

"Ah, but I did." She tried to sit up, but he easily held her down. "I told you before that ice can be damned erotic, remember?"

Deanna attempted to bat his hands away, but he wouldn't be denied. "Yes," she blurted out, "but I didn't expect you to demonstrate while I was asleep!"

He chuckled. "You can get me back later if you want."

"Oh, trust me, I'll want."

"Will you, kitten?" Jonas asked as he skimmed the ice cube over one puffy nipple, fascinated when the berry tip hardened. Deanna gasped and tried unsuccessfully to push the cube away. Jonas was bigger and stronger, and he wasn't about to be denied the treat of watching the heat of her passion melt the ice.

Jonas tossed the ice onto the floor and picked up one of the other items he'd gone in search of—a small length of rope. "I want to tie you up."

She snorted. "Not a chance in hell."

He quirked a brow and dropped the rope onto the mattress beside her body. "Because of the ice?"

"Because of the ice."

"I thought you trusted me. The ice is for your pleasure, not your torment."

"I do trust you," she explained slowly and clearly, as if talking to an imbecile. "It's you combined with a cup full of ice that I don't trust."

"Hmm, unless I'm mistaken, that sounds suspiciously like a challenge, and you know how much I love a challenge, kitten." Jonas grabbed both of Deanna's wrists in one of his hands, then held them above her head.

"Paybacks are hell, Jonas," she gritted out as she struggled to get loose.

Jonas picked up another cube of ice and slid it between her full, lovely tits, captivated by the little bounce as she struggled and pleaded with him to stop.

Jonas took the cold square away and rushed to reassure her. "Shhh, Deanna. It'll feel good, I promise."

She stilled. "You swear?"

"If it doesn't have you moaning soon, I'll let you tie me down and tickle-torture me. I'm that confident."

Deanna squinted, clearly suspicious. "You're ticklish?"

Ah, that got her attention. "Behind my knees and my feet. Especially my feet."

"Okay, you can use the ice."

"And the rope?"

"As long as you don't fall asleep and leave me . . . hanging."

He laughed at her pun. "Girl, with you naked in my bed, I highly doubt I'm going to drift off into la-la land." Jonas released her wrists and tossed the rapidly melting cube away, then picked up the rope. Within seconds, he had her bound.

"Okay?"

She wiggled her hands, as if checking the knot. "So far."

It was obvious her calm, tentative reply was all he was going to get out of her. He moved between her legs, positioning his body so her thighs draped over his. Jonas spread her open so that he could see all of her sweetly hidden secrets. As he plucked out another cube from the cup and gently glided it over her concave belly, Deanna relaxed completely. When he drew the ice over her pussy lips, her breath caught. She didn't try to push him away, he noticed. With her brown eyes filled with desire and watching his every move, Jonas knew he'd remember this moment forever.

Careful not to cause even an ounce of discomfort, Jonas stroked Deanna's little bud with the melting bit of ice. She rotated her hips, and his name escaped her mouth. Jonas's dick thickened as all the blood in his body seemed to travel south. As he dipped the ice between her swollen folds, Deanna's hips thrust upward.

"Jonas, that feels . . . oh, God." As Jonas drew the sliver down her slit to the pink pucker of her ass, Deanna stiffened. "Jonas?"

"I want to fuck your ass, Deanna."

He sketched her smooth skin with the cube, then watched as it finally turned to liquid and disappeared. He left the cup of ice alone in favor of the last item—a bottle of cherry-scented body oil. He grabbed the bottle and popped the top. After soaking his index and middle fingers, Jonas slid them over her tight pucker. Deanna's eyes shot wide, her face flushed with arousal.

"I want to make love to every inch of you."

"But *there?*"

"Yes, there. Have you ever been loved like that, Deanna?" Jonas asked as he kept his fingers poised at her entrance.

"Yes, but you're bigger than most guys, Jonas. Much bigger."

"I'll prepare you," he promised. "It won't hurt, kitten. I'd never hurt you." He slid one finger inside the tight opening. It was barely an inch and already she writhed and moaned. He'd wanted to be gentle and civilized with Deanna, but the primitive side of him demanded that he make love to every part of her body.

He dipped his finger in a little more. "Are you in pain?"

"N-no."

"Another finger, sweeting," Jonas explained as he let his middle finger join the fun. He stretched and prepared her for the more intense invasion of his cock. Her breath hitched and he stilled. "Deanna?"

"Deeper, please."

"Ah, hell, kitten. You're killing me." He'd been prepared for her to tell him to stop, and instead she'd urged him on. Jonas wiggled his fingers, and they slid a little deeper. She moaned, and Jonas desperately wanted to feel that tight, hot fist around his dick. She tried to move her hips, as if to push him farther in, but he held her secure with a hand against her lower belly. "No, Deanna," he said in a firm voice. "You need to be ready or I could hurt you."

Deanna lifted her head and Jonas witnessed the fire in her expressive brown gaze. He pulled his fingers free, and Deanna pleaded with him, begging him to fill her again. This time he squeezed three fingers inside and buried them clear to the knuckles. He pumped in and out, and Deanna thrust against him, fucking his fingers.

"Now," he growled as he brought his fingers out.

"Yes."

He grabbed the bottle and squirted the sweet liquid onto his cock in preparation of the tight fist of Deanna's ass. As Jonas moved to his knees between her thighs and wrapped a hand around his heavy length, Deanna bit her lip and watched with a mix of eager passion and tense fear.

Jonas rubbed the bulbous head over her sweet little pucker. "No pain, Deanna."

She gasped as Jonas pressed inside. He was barely over the rim and already his cock felt strangled. "You're tight," he uttered. "Like a hot, little glove holding my cock captive."

Jonas stretched out on top of her, bracing his arms on either side of her head, and showered her with kisses. Her bound arms came around his neck, and her legs lifted and wrapped around his hips as she submitted to him. Jonas felt her inner muscles relax, and he took full advantage, thrusting inward all the way, filling her completely.

15

Deanna couldn't take her eyes off Jonas. His feral expression turned her on. Up to this moment, he'd been gentle and sweet in his loving. Now it was as if he'd opened the cage and let his inner beast free. She liked him like this, she realized, rough and a little aggressive.

"Your big brown eyes are devouring me, kitten." His right hand made a slow journey down her rib cage to her mound, and there he stayed. As his fingers danced over her clitoris, Deanna's pussy flooded with liquid need, and pleasure spiked anew. "Do you like it, Deanna? Do you like my dick in your ass?"

"Yes," she blurted out, giving him the unvarnished truth. "It hurts a little, but it feels good too."

"Yeah, you're so damn snug," he ground out as he continued to torment her clit. "If I move too fast, I'll come."

He slid in and out, slow and gentle, his thick length stroking nerve endings she'd never known existed. With each erotic glide, Jonas appeared to turn a little wilder, a little more out of control. His fingers flicked and toyed with her pussy, and

Deanna's body climbed higher and higher. Her legs clamped around Jonas's hips, holding him close, as if he'd disappear if she let go.

"You'll think of this, Deanna," he whispered against her ear. "Of my cock taking your tight little asshole." He pulled out nearly all the way, then slammed forward, burying his cock inside the snug entrance. Deanna cried out at the forbidden pleasure of it.

"You're going to need it again and again, and I'm going to give it to you," he vowed.

Deanna couldn't concentrate, could barely breathe. Jonas fucked her harder, faster, all the while pumping her clit with his finger and thumb.

"Deanna." Her name was a rumble of sound against her cheek, and the heat of his breath seemed to fan the flames of her desire.

Jonas wrapped a fist in her hair and forced her to look at him. "This ass belongs to me. Your pussy, your mouth, they're for me to touch and taste and love."

Deanna made a desperate attempt to deny his claim, to let him know what she thought of his declaration of ownership, but when he pulled out of her and thrust in hard and deep, the words died in her throat. His fingers played with her little nub as if she were an instrument and he the skilled musician. A caress, a pinch, and she knew the frightening truth. Only Jonas could make her so utterly weak; only he had the power to make her burn this hot. He worked her body as if he'd been doing it for years.

"Jonas," she whimpered.

"You want to come, kitty?"

"Yes!" Deanna shouted as she gripped the back of his head.

"Then tell me this ass is mine. Say it," he softly urged.

He may as well have been asking her to jump off a building without a safety net below. To give him so much power over her sent a bolt of fear through Deanna. "Don't ask that of me, Jonas."

He shocked her to the core when he pulled his dick free, leaving her staring up at him. Suddenly he had her on her stomach with her arms stretched out above her head and her bottom raised in the air from the pillow he'd placed beneath her earlier. Jonas leaned down and murmured, "We belong together, Deanna."

She tried to sit up, but his palm on her back held her prisoner. "Easy," he soothed. "Is it so terrible to belong to me, kitten?"

"It's not as simple as that, Jonas."

"Yes, it is," he snarled. His palm coasted down her back, then over her buttocks. He squeezed and shaped, and Deanna squirmed as fire licked up her spine. She needed him to fill her, to take them both to that place only he seemed capable of seeking out.

"We fit, Deanna. All you have to do is be a good girl and admit it."

"No." She was tempting the beast and she knew it, but Deanna couldn't seem to stop herself.

A sudden gust of air swept over her seconds before Jonas's palm connected with her ass. She stiffened. "You spanked me!"

"Bad girls get spankings, Deanna," he said by way of explanation. "Now tell me what I want to hear."

She tried to break free, but the rope around her wrists made it impossible. When he swatted her again, this time the other cheek, Deanna's flesh started to sting. Three more swats and Deanna wasn't sure she wanted him to stop at all. Her skin tingled and her pussy dripped with her juices. Jonas petted her. "Fuck, your ass is turning pink. Say the words, Deanna, before I shoot my cum all over that pretty flesh."

Deanna heard the ache in Jonas's voice and instantly surrendered. "We fit." She said it so quiet, but she knew he heard.

Jonas leaned down and kissed her buttocks before stretching

his body out on top of her. He used his knee to push her legs apart, and when the head of his cock touched her tight pucker, Deanna moaned, needing him to chase away the cold emptiness. Jonas pushed inside, one slow, torturous inch at a time, until finally he filled her completely.

He caressed her neck with his lips. "So stubborn."

"Just make love to me, Jonas."

"My pleasure," he murmured as he began to pump in and out of her. His fingers found her clit again, only this time he didn't stop his sweet torment until she'd reached that dizzying summit. Her body tightened as waves of pleasure threw her into another dimension. She screamed his name and succumbed to the orgasm splintering her mind.

The instant she came, Jonas went wild, driving and grinding his cock deep. With his arms surrounding her, keeping her beneath him, he gave his passion freedom.

Deanna flexed her ass, and her muscles clamped down on Jonas's cock.

"Jesus," he said in a strangled voice. Three more hard thrusts and he erupted. Hot spurts of cum filled her ass.

When he collapsed on top of her, both of them exhausted and sweating, Deanna sighed, utterly content with Jonas's big, hard body wrapped around her, his cock still seated deep. She didn't want the moment to end.

"I spanked you."

Deanna laughed. "I noticed."

Jonas lifted up and pulled out of her. Instantly, Deanna missed the deep connection. He turned her over and took her chin in his palm, forcing her to look at him. "Did you like it?"

"Maybe."

Jonas's ornery grin had her heart skipping a beat. "Uh-uh. I swatted your cute, little ass and you nearly came. Tell the truth."

"Fine, I liked it. But not the reason behind it."

He cocked his head to the side. "Forcing you to admit we belong together, you mean?"

"Yes. You manipulated me."

He dragged his knuckles down her cheek. "I told you I don't play fair."

Deanna rolled her eyes. "Is that supposed to be an apology? Because it sucks."

"I'll apologize for being an arrogant, overprotective, uncivilized ass. But I won't apologize for wanting to call you mine. Never."

"You forced it out of me. That's the part that frustrates me. Not the actual belonging part." She wiggled her fingers and asked, "Will you untie me, please?"

Jonas leaned down and kissed her. His mouth crushed hers, claiming her all over again. He broke away and went to work on the knot. When it came free, Deanna brought her arms down in front of her and rubbed her wrists.

"Let me see," he demanded. When she held them out and Jonas saw the red welts on her skin from where the rope had rubbed back and forth, he cursed. "Shit. I should've used something softer. I'm so sorry, kitten." He began a gentle massage on both of them at once and Deanna laughed. "What's so funny?"

"I'm pretty sure my butt hurts more."

He wagged his eyebrows. "I'll massage that too."

"I think I'd rather grab a quick shower so we can get some dinner. I'm hungry."

Jonas stood and helped her to her feet. He glanced at the clock next to the bed. "It's late, but there should still be at least a pizza place open. If you want, I can check and see. Maybe get a large delivered?"

As they walked together to the bathroom, Deanna surreptitiously looked him over. He was still semihard. Geez, his cock was larger than any other guy she'd known, and he wasn't even fully aroused! As Jonas flipped on the light, she thought about the well-stocked refrigerator downstairs. "Your neighbor went to a lot of trouble to make sure we had something to eat. Seems a shame to let it go to waste."

He nodded as he turned on the shower. "Good point."

"I saw lunch meat and cheese in your fridge. Sandwiches?"

He took her hand and kissed a mark on her wrist before helping her into the shower. "Works for me."

They both went silent, as if unwilling to ruin the moment. Jonas went about washing her, and as every curve and valley ended up thoroughly soaped and rinsed, Deanna felt like a goddess. He paid special attention to her bottom, and by the time they were through, the water was barely warm.

She wondered what it was going to be like tomorrow, when their time in Miami came to an end. How would she ever manage to shower or eat or sleep without him? It scared her to think that she was falling for him. Or maybe she'd always been halfway in love with Jonas. The trip had just helped her cross the last few hundred feet to the finish line.

Jonas couldn't seem to stop staring long enough to eat his sandwich, and it wasn't because he wasn't hungry. He was starving, in fact. Watching Deanna devour her own ham and Swiss took top priority, though. Not that he had a fetish about women and food. It was just that Deanna happened to be naked. And he sure as shit had a fetish about a naked Deanna.

"I've never known a woman so completely at ease with her body," he revealed, a little baffled by her lack of modesty.

She finished off the last of her sandwich before replying, "Does it bother you?"

"Hell no. If I had my way, you wouldn't own a stitch of clothing."

She dusted off her breasts where a few crumbs had landed, and Jonas had to reach beneath the table to readjust things.

"You haven't eaten more than a few bites, Jonas. I thought you were hungry."

"Famished," he admitted.

"Then eat," she instructed as she dabbed at her lips with a napkin.

Jonas pushed his plate away and crossed his arms over his chest. "I'm a little distracted at the moment."

She stood and took her plate to the sink. "That's a shame, because that lunch meat is really good."

Jonas's gaze followed her every move. With her ass facing him, he could see how red her cheeks were from his spanking. Ah, Christ, there went his dick again. When she leaned forward, he assumed to rinse her plate, he had a sneaking suspicion he was being played.

"Deanna."

"Yes?"

"Turn around," he demanded.

Deanna put the plate in the drainer and slowly swiveled around. Her laughing brown eyes and upturned lips greeted him. "Is there a problem?"

"You're purposely tormenting me," he concluded. "I just don't know why."

She walked across the room and placed both hands on his chair, then leaned in close. "That ice was cold, darling."

Jonas plucked her off her feet and sat her on his lap so that she was straddling him. "Your hot body melted it quicker than a microwave, kitten."

She smacked his chest and glared daggers at him. "I still think I should get to tie you up and torture *you* for a while. It's only fair."

Jonas wrapped an arm around her, more because he couldn't seem to keep from touching her than anything else. "Later you can have your fun. For now I want you to tell me something."

She pulled the plate closer and pointed to it in a silent gesture for him to eat. "What do you want to know?"

Jonas let his hand drift south until he was cupping her ass. "I want to know about you."

Her breathing sped up. "Uh, just random things or do you have something specific in mind?"

"Start with random stuff. Pet peeves?"

"Okay, let me think." She was quiet a moment. When he picked up his sandwich and bit off a mouthful, she began. "I hate when I go to the store and find carts all over the parking lot. It's lazy not to put them in the cart corral."

He swallowed. "I agree. Drives me crazy. Next?"

"It's annoying when people talk really loud on their cell phones in public." She rolled her eyes. "I don't want to know about so-and-so's new hairstyle."

"Definitely annoying." Jonas ate another bite and waited for her to tick off another peeve.

"It bugs me when I see a mother yell at her child. I know discipline is important, but screaming like you've lost all the sense God gave you is abuse, plain and simple."

"Pisses me off. So far we have a lot in common." He ate the last bite of his sandwich before asking, "What about favorite things?"

"Hmm." She paused. "Daisies are my favorite flower. You already know my favorite color. My favorite author is Robert Louis Stevenson. Oh, and my favorite scent is the smell of my mom's oatmeal raisin cookies, fresh from the oven."

"Mmm, those are good."

Her brows shot up. "You've had them?"

He nodded. "She's stopped by the office and dropped off a dozen for Wade and me a few times."

"I didn't know she ever did that." She brushed at the corner of his mouth with her thumb. "Okay, so what else do you want to know?"

"Tell me about your relationship with your brother. I've always wondered about you and Dean."

"The twin thing?"

Now that he wasn't hungry, he was able to devote all his concentration on Deanna. Her breasts were all but in his face. Unable to deny the tempting treat, Jonas dipped his head and kissed the tip of one, then the other. "Yeah, the twin thing," he replied. "You two are so different, especially considering you're all soft and curvy and sweet and he's . . . not."

Deanna's hands went to his hair, and she started to sift her fingers through the short strands. It felt good. Good enough he could almost fall asleep—if not for the sexy body on his lap. "Dean can be quite sweet. He's just more guarded than Wade or me."

Curious about Deanna's quiet, brooding twin, Jonas pushed for details. "Why?"

Deanna's fingers continued to massage his scalp as she answered. "He was in love once, and the woman broke his heart. It was tough on Dean."

"Ouch, that sucks."

"He hasn't been serious with a woman since. I'm starting to worry he'll never let himself fall in love again."

Jonas reached up and smoothed his hand down the length of Deanna's hair. It was soft and shiny and lay in natural waves all around her shoulders. He liked it that way. With her face free of makeup, Deanna looked like a sweet, innocent teenager. So, what did that make him? A dirty, rotten scoundrel? Jesus, probably.

"You and Dean are pretty close, huh?" he asked, picking back up on the conversation and ruthlessly ignoring the idea that maybe she was too good for him.

"Very. We've always known what the other was thinking."

Deanna dropped her hands from his head and snuggled up against him, as if content to let him stroke her. "Did you ever have one of those moments when one of you knew something was wrong before anyone else?"

She nodded. "We were in the seventh grade. He was staying at a friend's house overnight when he broke his arm falling off a bike. A few minutes before the boy's mother called, I knew the phone would ring. I knew something was wrong with Dean. I could just feel it."

"Damn, I bet that freaked out your mom."

"Mom doesn't get worked up easily. She's always been able to take things in stride."

Jonas could see that about Deanna's mom. He'd never heard the woman so much as raise her voice, and yet she always seemed to get her way with her three kids. "So, has Dean always coddled you?"

"Yes. Well, that's not entirely true. Dean could be somewhat tough on me, especially if he thought it was for my own good. Back in high school, he'd challenge me to arm-wrestling matches and he never *let* me win."

Jonas tensed at the visual that brought to mind. "Arm wrestling? That's not even close to a fair fight, Deanna. Your brother is a big man. I have to assume he was big in high school."

"He's always been muscular. But Dean taught me self-defense. He's shown me all sorts of little tricks to use against a guy."

"Have you ever had to use them?"

She snorted. "I should've used them on Gary, but my heart was involved then. Not so easy to hurt someone you think you love."

He kissed the top of her head. "No, it's not," he murmured. "So, what'd Dean say about you taking this trip with me? He couldn't have been happy."

"Uh, I didn't exactly tell him."

"He doesn't know?"

"By now he does. Mom or Wade would've told him."

Jonas cupped her chin in his palm and urged her to look at him. "Are you ashamed to be here with me, Deanna?"

Deanna rolled her eyes. "Don't be ridiculous. Of course I'm not ashamed. It's just that Dean is more protective of me than Wade. It's like he can't bring himself to believe I'm all grown up and allowed to have sex. I think if I'd become a nun, he would've been thrilled."

Enticed by the temptation of Deanna's taste, Jonas brushed his lips back and forth over hers. "I wouldn't have been happy if you'd become a nun," he confided in a hushed tone.

Deanna laughed. "I'll just bet."

Jonas started to ask if she was going to talk to Dean when they returned to Ohio, but his cell phone rang, shattering the moment. He picked it up from the table and looked at the time on the clock on the wall. "It's midnight. What the hell?"

It rang again. "Answer it," she urged him. "Maybe it's an emergency."

Jonas flipped it open, not bothering to check the caller ID. "Hello?"

"What the hell do you think you're doing taking *my* sister to that beach house, you motherfucker?"

Jonas's gaze shot to Deanna. "Dean," he said, and watched as Deanna's eyes grew round with shock. "What a pleasant surprise."

"If you hurt her, Phoenix, I'll bury you."

Jonas sighed. "I didn't kidnap her, Harrison. She wanted to come. She's a big girl."

"Put her on the phone."

"Nice talking to you, too, buddy." Jonas handed the phone to Deanna.

Deanna snatched it out of his hand. "Before you open your big, stupid mouth, you better remember that I don't answer to you. Nor do I answer to Wade. I came on this trip because I wanted to spend time with Jonas, so back off!"

What did it say about a guy who got a hard-on over his woman's anger? Jonas's dick was so hard he felt like he could drive nails through a two-by-four. She went quiet, and Jonas was curious what Dean was saying. When Deanna's eyes began to water, a red haze of rage clouded Jonas's vision.

"Yes, we'll talk when I get home." She paused, her gaze on his when she ended the call by saying, "I love you too."

In Jonas's mind, he heard her saying those words to him someday. It was a nice thought. He wasn't sure he deserved a woman like Deanna, but a guy could dream. After she closed the phone, she handed it back to him. He tossed it onto the table and wrapped his arms around her, pulling her in for a tight hug. "What'd he say, kitten?"

"You won't like it."

He shrugged. "I don't like you upset, either."

"First he complained about my phone not being on. I didn't get a chance to tell him I'd merely forgotten to charge it today."

"And then?" He nudged her, knowing there was a hell of a lot more.

She smoothed one hand up and down his bicep and softly answered, "He told me you're just using me. That you just wanted to get me into bed and you knew this was your best chance at achieving that goal."

The son of a bitch. If he weren't Deanna's brother, Jonas would beat the shit out of him. But he was family, which meant hands off. Christ!

Jonas took hold of Deanna's shoulders and pulled her off his chest so he could look her in the eye. "Did you believe him?"

"No."

She answered with such vehemence that Jonas knew she told him the truth. Thrilled she hadn't let Dean get to her, Jonas kissed her, keeping it quick. "Good, because it's not true. I understand he's concerned for you, but he doesn't know what he's talking about. Not about this. Not about us. The only thing that could screw that up is you and me. That's it."

She cupped his cheeks in her hands and leaned close. "I misjudged you and for that I'm sorry."

He quirked a brow at her. "You mean the oversexed playboy thing?"

"Well, you do have quite the overactive sex drive." She kissed his nose, which Jonas found completely adorable. "But I was way off about the playboy remark."

"I like to think of it as an over*achieving* sex drive, and only with you, kitten."

She laughed. "I enjoyed it when you tied me up," she whispered. "I got all hot and bothered when you spanked me. The ice, though cold as heck, was even exciting. It occurs to me that maybe we're both overachievers."

"And don't forget you sucked my dick and swallowed my cum, because I sure as hell won't be forgetting it anytime soon."

Deanna drew in a breath. "It was certainly memorable."

"Damn straight." He wrapped his arms beneath her ass and stood with her in his arms. Ready to take her to bed where he could hold her in his arms the rest of the night. "So, maybe you could give us a chance?"

"Yes, I'd like that."

The quiet answer sent a jolt of electricity straight to his heart. "You won't regret it, kitten."

She smiled. "I know."

"Time for bed. Tomorrow's our last day, and I want to hold you in my arms for a while."

Deanna rested her cheek against his chest and let him carry her out of the kitchen. "I'd like that, too, Jonas, very much."

16

It was early Monday morning, and Deanna had been awake for hours. She'd wanted to make a few adjustments to the computerized design she was going to present to Valdez when they met on Wednesday. *If* they met. She still needed to talk to Jonas about his suspicions that Valdez was a criminal. She had the design nearly finished and it was gorgeous. Deanna only hoped it wasn't going to be all for nothing. If Jonas was right and the gentle, older man truly was a drug dealer, then she'd just have to eat the time and trouble she'd put into the job, because she wasn't going anywhere near the guy.

When she heard the doorbell, her heart began to race like a little puppy doing laps around a living room. It was pathetic how much she missed Jonas. It'd been less than twelve hours since he'd dropped her on her doorstep with a promise to call on his lunch hour.

She glanced down at the time on her computer monitor and frowned. Who on earth would be at her front door at eight in the morning? Even though she knew it couldn't possibly be

Jonas, she still crossed her fingers, hoping he'd decided to bring her breakfast again.

The doorbell chimed once more, forcing Deanna to shout, "I'm coming! I'm coming!"

As she ran down the steps and approached the front door, she realized she'd forgotten to grab her robe. She was still wearing her black pajama shorts and tank. Deanna peeked through the peephole and frowned. She twisted the lock and flung the door open. "Dean? What is it? Is something wrong?" It wasn't like him to visit so early. He should've been at some construction site the way he always was this time of day.

"Can't a guy visit his sister without there being an emergency?"

"Yes, but not this early in the morning."

He looked her over and scowled. "Were you in bed?"

"No, I was up working on a design for a client."

"Then can I come in?"

She stepped aside to let him enter. "Of course. Sorry."

He shrugged and walked through the door. "Don't suppose you have coffee? It's cold as shit outside." He unzipped his heavy cotton work coat and tossed it onto the couch, then started to rub his hands together to chase away the chill.

Deanna laughed as she started toward the kitchen. "Cold? With that thick thing?"

As she went about making a fresh pot, Deanna heard Dean let out a weary sigh. "I do love that coat, but I swear Ohio winters get colder and colder every freaking year."

"You'll get no arguments from me." Since Deanna had just come from warm, sunny Florida, she wasn't all that in love with the cold Ohio winters either. "So, to what do I owe the honor of your presence?" she asked, even though she suspected it had something to do with Jonas.

He went to her cupboard, took down two mugs, and brought them to the table. "I think we both know why I'm here, Dee."

Deanna's hopes fell flat. "Jonas."

"Yeah, him," he muttered.

As he sat down in one of the chairs, it creaked a little, causing Deanna to ask, "You've put on a few more pounds of muscle, haven't you?"

He nodded. "Been working out."

"Me too. I might even be able to take you in a match." She flexed her bicep, as small as it was, and grinned. "Care to place a bet?"

He laughed. "Best save your money now that you're a freelance interior designer. It's not an easy gig."

Deanna sat across from him and waited for the coffee to finish brewing. "You're just afraid I might show you up." When Dean didn't say anything but simply stared at her, Deanna slumped in her seat. "Might as well start the interrogation."

"It's not like that. I'm just worried about you. Why didn't you tell me you were seeing Jonas?"

"Because until this past weekend, I wasn't."

He leaned forward in his chair. "You went out of town with the guy and he hasn't even taken you on a date?"

"He tried to take me on a date." Deanna pulled her feet up under her to warm them. She loved her hardwood floors, but they were cold in the winter and she hadn't bothered with slippers. "He tried to take me on several dates, but I kept turning him down."

"That was smart. Going to Miami with him, not so much. What were you thinking?"

"I like him, Dean," she explained. "And he likes me. What's so bad about that?"

"This is Jonas we're talking about, sweetheart. The guy would make a porn star blush."

She snorted. "Don't you think you're exaggerating just a tad?"

"If it's all so wonderful, then why didn't you tell me you were going away with him? Why did I have to find out from Mom?"

"Because you would've tried to stop me," she shot right back. "You wouldn't have approved, just like you never approve of the guys I date."

"I've never tried to interfere in your personal life."

She didn't speak, merely quirking a brow at his blatant lie. When the alarm on the coffeepot beeped, signaling it'd finished brewing, Deanna stood to retrieve it. After she poured them each a cup, she placed the pot back on the warmer and sat back down. She watched as Dean attempted to gather his thoughts. She could practically see him formulating a plan of attack. He was terrible at hiding his feelings from her. What he didn't know, what she hadn't even realized until she'd woken up without Jonas beside her, was that she loved Jonas. And no one, not even her well-meaning twin, was going to keep her from having a chance to explore that wonderful new feeling.

"Okay, so I worry." He crossed his arms over his chest. "I don't want to see you hurt."

"You mean the way you were hurt by Linda?"

Dean stiffened. "She has nothing to do with this. This is about you and Jonas."

Deanna hated the pain she heard in her brother's voice. It tore her up to know how much Linda's betrayal had changed him. "That's not entirely true," she said in a soft voice. "You're worried Jonas will hurt me because you were hurt. But I don't want to shut myself off from love, Dean. I care about Jonas. I need to see where this could go."

"And if he hurts you?"

Yeah, that's the part she was concerned about too. "Then I'll deal with it," she answered, hoping he didn't hear the catch in her voice. "It wouldn't be the first time a guy hurt me, Dean."

His frown darkened. "What's that supposed to mean?"

"Uh, newsflash, bro, I'm not a virgin. I have been in relationships, believe it or not."

"Yeah, I'm aware, smart-ass. What I'm asking is which of those asswipes hurt you."

Deanna picked up her cup and took a sip. Good. A little strong, she thought, but good. "That's not the point. The thing is, I was hurt, but I got over it. I moved on."

Dean shook his head and picked up his own mug. "Puppy love isn't the same thing, Dee."

"No, you're right," she conceded. "It would hurt more if Jonas betrayed me."

"Wait, are you saying he's the one? That you're in love with the guy?"

"I—" A loud pounding on the front door interrupted her morning confession. She stood to go see who it was. "This place is turning into Grand Central Station."

"Deanna," Dean growled as he shot to his feet. "You aren't even dressed. Go put something on while I see to your visitor."

Her face heated as she imagined opening the door to the UPS guy. "Uh, not a bad idea. I just want to see who it is first," she said, still hoping Jonas would stop by.

As Deanna approached the door, she looked through the security hole. Her heart rate picked up when she spied Jonas standing on her porch. He was wearing a brown leather jacket and jeans. Ooh, yummy. Deanna quickly turned the knob. Between one breath and the next, Jonas crushed her against his muscular chest, his arms wrapped around her waist so tight she thought she might break a rib.

"Damn, I missed you," he groaned as he nuzzled her.

"Jonas." Her arms snaked around his neck, and she inhaled

his warm, masculine scent. "I thought you were going to call at lunchtime."

"Yeah, that was the plan," he murmured as he loosened his hold and leaned back to look at her from head to toe. "Christ, you look good enough to eat, kitten. In fact . . ." His sentence drifted off as he slammed the door with his foot and took her mouth in a hard, claiming kiss. His tongue demanded entrance, and Deanna was helpless to the passionate assault. She sighed and parted her lips. Jonas delved in, tasting and playing. Deanna melted against him, and she heard a low growl deep in his chest. When he dipped his tongue out and licked over her bottom lip, Deanna felt as if she were drowning in bliss.

Oh, my, the man could kiss. Before she had time to think clearly, his hands slid down her back to cup her bottom. When he started tugging her shirt upward, Deanna forgot everything else and surrendered. Having Jonas so hungry for her had a way of doing that. Her body tingled everywhere his hands touched. Excitement skittered down her spine when she felt his rock-hard arousal against her belly.

Then someone cleared his throat.

Too late, Deanna remembered they weren't alone. She broke away just as Jonas glanced over the top of her head. He scowled as he straightened. Deanna noticed he didn't bother to release her. "Dean," Jonas muttered, clearly unhappy at the interruption, "what a pleasant surprise."

"I take it you didn't see the big red pickup parked on the street in front of Dee's house?"

Jonas grinned down at her. "I was a little distracted."

"I noticed," Dean said as he glared at her. "Maybe some clothes would be good?"

Deanna rolled her eyes. "Fine." She looked up at Jonas and smiled. "I'll be right down. There's fresh coffee. Help yourself."

Jonas placed a gentle kiss to her forehead before releasing her. "Take your time." He winked and patted her on the bottom. "Dean and I can entertain ourselves."

"Yeah, by engaging in a few rounds of boxing, no doubt." Deanna had the forethought to send up a silent prayer for her furniture. "Anything gets broken and you'll both pay dearly." With that deadly warning, Deanna turned and left the room.

Jonas wasn't a happy camper. He'd been hoping to find Deanna alone, maybe even a little rumpled from dragging her out of bed, which he would've dragged her back into. Instead, he had to deal with her overprotective twin. Oh, joy.

"So, what brings you to Deanna's this early?" Jonas asked as he unzipped his coat and laid it over a chair. "Shouldn't you be on a job somewhere?"

Dean scowled. "Do you always leave Wade to do all the work, or is this just a special occasion?"

"Wade knows I'm here." Jonas shrugged. "He's fine with it."

"I'm not Wade."

Jonas snorted as he headed for the kitchen. "Thanks for the heads-up on that one."

Dean stepped in front of him before he could get to the coffeepot. "Look, Phoenix, for whatever reason, my sister cares about you. I think she has poor taste in men, but that's beside the point. I can't stop her from seeing you. Just know that if you hurt her, you will pay."

Jonas's morning was seriously turning to shit. He dragged his fingers through his hair and muttered, "I told you before, I have no intention of hurting Deanna. What's your problem with me, anyway?"

Dean's eyebrows shot up. "Christ, are you serious? I know some of the things you've done. The women, the dangerous ops you eagerly participated in. Life is a game to guys like you.

Do you honestly think I want my sister with someone like that?"

Jonas clenched his fists at his sides in an effort to keep from strangling Deanna's brother. Something like that would surely put a crimp in their new relationship. "You're on dangerous ground, Harrison," he warned. "Watch it."

Dean stepped closer so that only a few inches of air separated them. "What's wrong, Jonas, can't handle the truth?"

"Deanna isn't a game to me," he gritted out, vying with his anger for control. "And while I'm willing to be your punching bag for her sake, don't ever put her in that category again."

Dean frowned. After several tense seconds of silence, he asked, "You're serious?"

"About Deanna, yes. That's what I've been trying to tell you."

Dean studied him another few seconds, then nodded and moved out of the way. Hallelujah. "Now that we've settled that, I'm hungry."

Jonas headed to the fridge but stopped when he heard Deanna's husky voice behind him. He turned around to find her dressed in a pair of black jogging pants and a yellow V-neck T-shirt. The sweats were baggy, but the T wasn't. He couldn't really see the outline of her areolas, and yet his mouth watered for a taste or a lick, anyway.

"What'd you say?"

"I said I'll cook breakfast for you two, if you promise to play nice."

"Omelets?" Dean asked as he pulled out a chair and sat. "You make the best omelets, Dee."

Jonas wanted Dean gone. He wanted to feast on Deanna. He wanted to start the day all over again, only this time he never would've left Deanna to sleep alone. He would've stayed so he could wake her up with kisses. They could've made love, real slow and sweet. He sighed, knowing it would be hours before he could have her all to himself again. Shit, shit, shit.

"Jonas?"

"Uh, yeah, omelets sound great." Their gazes connected and Jonas saw the same longing reflected back at him. Knowing she wanted him as badly as he wanted her was going to make playing nice with Dean pure torture.

After Deanna had made them omelets, Dean left, finally leaving Jonas alone with Deanna. All he could think about was stripping her naked and was about to say as much when his cell phone started playing the tune "Renegade," interrupting his mental fantasy.

"That's Wade," Jonas cursed. "I need to get that." He pulled his cell phone off his belt and flipped it open. "What's up?"

"I need your computer skills," Wade said.

"My brother has his own ring tone?" Deanna asked in a hushed voice.

Jonas nodded, completely tuning Wade out.

"Jonas? You still there?"

"Do I have a ring tone?" Deanna asked.

Jonas grinned. "Hang on a second, Wade." He wagged his eyebrows at Deanna and murmured, "I added one for you after you agreed to go to Miami with me."

Her eyes lit up. "You did? What is it?"

" 'Feel Like Makin' Love,' the Bad Company version," he answered her as he patted her bottom and stepped away.

"So every time I call you, it plays that tune." She laughed. "Figures." Deanna went back to cleaning up their breakfast dishes, and Jonas put the phone back to his ear.

"Sorry about that," he said. "Now, what's this about my computer skills?"

"Gracie got a phone call this morning from a woman claiming to be her long-lost sister."

"How is that possible? I thought her mother was history. Unless it's a sibling on her father's side?"

"No, she claims they have the same mother. Gracie's a mess. I need you to run a check on this woman. She's not coming anywhere near Gracie until I know she's telling the truth."

Jonas watched Deanna bend to pick up a fork she'd dropped. Her ass stuck up in the air, and he had to tamp down the need to reach out and grab a handful. "Okay, I'll be right there."

"Thanks, man."

"No problem." Hell, he was supposed to be at the office anyway, not playing around with Deanna.

Jonas flipped the phone shut. "I need to go."

Deanna swiveled around, a frown marring her pretty face. "Already?"

"It's important. Someone called Gracie, claiming to be her sister. Wade wants me to check into it."

She sucked in a breath. "Oh, wow. Gracie must be going crazy."

Jonas nodded. "Especially considering this could potentially be the only living relative Gracie has left. Unless you count her worthless drunk of a father, which I don't."

Deanna looked down at the floor. "I'm happy for Gracie, really I am, but I was hoping to show you the design I've been working on for that client I told you about. I'm really excited about it."

"Are you talking about Valdez?" Jonas couldn't believe his ears. "I thought we agreed, Deanna. Valdez is bad news."

Her head snapped up. "We didn't agree I'd dump the guy based solely on your word," she said as she moved around the kitchen, cleaning up and putting things away. "If I remember correctly, you all but ordered me to tell him to find a new designer."

He forced himself to calm down. If he came at her with ultimatums and went all dictator on her, she would only dig her heels in further.

Moving up behind her, Jonas grasped her shoulders, urging her to look at him. She refused to turn around. "Okay," he said, relenting. "Then at least let me run a background check—before you meet with him. There's no harm in being cautious, right?"

She turned around and planted her hands on her hips. "I'm not an idiot, Jonas. Of course I'd rather be safe than sorry."

Jonas took her into his arms. She was stiff at first but slowly relaxed. "I'm only concerned for you, kitten. I'm not trying to tell you how to run your business."

Her gaze sought his, and again Deanna's sweet nature kicked Jonas square in the chest. She saw the good in people, while Jonas knew not everyone had a good side. Like Valdez, for instance. The guy specialized in using kids to run his drugs for him. In Jonas's mind, the guy was the lowest form of scum.

"It sure sounds like that from this end, Jonas. And I don't want another person in my life treating me like a child."

"Trust me, you're all woman in my eyes," Jonas growled.

"I'm serious."

"I am too. Your safety is the only thing that matters to me, Deanna. I'm not trying to take over." Jonas did a mental survey of her home and wondered why she didn't have a security system. "Speaking of safety, I'm surprised Wade hasn't installed an alarm for you."

"He and I have talked about it, and I intended to get one, but I've been busy trying to get my design business off the ground."

"I could install one for you if you want. It's no big deal."

Deanna sighed. "We spent one weekend together and you're already screening my clients and talking about installing an alarm?"

When she put it like that, he felt like a complete ass. "First off, it wasn't just a weekend. We mean more to each other than that. Don't reduce it to a meaningless fling."

She winced. "That's not what I meant. It's just that we've barely had time to explore this relationship and you're already bulldozing your way through my life!"

"I'm a PI and an ex-soldier. Safety is more than just my job—it's who I am. You're mine and I won't apologize for taking care of what's mine."

Deanna looked at the clock on the wall and stepped away from him. "You need to go. Wade's waiting."

Damn it, he didn't want to leave it like this. "I'm sorry, kitten. I didn't mean to start issuing orders. I am only thinking of you. I don't want anything to happen to you." He grabbed her upper arms and pulled her into a tight embrace meant to soothe. "Let me check out this Valdez character, okay?"

She nodded and pushed out of his arms. "I'll get my purse. I have his business card in there." She walked out of the room and came back a few minutes later with a white card in her hand. "Here. It has his address and phone numbers. Will that be enough?"

Jonas had a bad feeling in the pit of his stomach. Like he'd broken something between them and he had no idea how to fix it. "Yeah, this is fine."

He tried to take her back into his arms, but she moved out of his reach. "Deanna?"

"You need to stop and consider the fact that I've been getting along just fine without you. Believe it or not, I do have a brain in my head, and I'd already decided to wait for you to check Terrance out, but you couldn't know that because you jumped to conclusions before I had the chance to say anything." He started to speak, but she simply leaped right over him. "I know you care, that you worry, but I don't want another keeper, Jonas. I can't live my life with someone like that."

"I know. I'm sorry," he said in a voice rough with emotion.

Deanna closed the distance between them, then went up on her tiptoes and kissed him. A too-quick peck, but Jonas would take whatever he could get. "Go. Gracie needs your help."

"Can I come by later?"

She bit her lower lip and looked away. "I think I need some time alone. I need to think."

Christ, he'd royally screwed up. "Will you call me?"

"Yes. I'll call." She looked back up, and he saw tears in her eyes. Tears he'd put there. "Be careful."

"Always, kitten."

Leaving Deanna standing in the kitchen alone and upset was the hardest thing Jonas had ever had to do.

17

Deanna didn't let the tears fall until she heard the front door close. That's when the dam broke, and once the waterworks started, she couldn't seem to turn them off. She wanted to believe Jonas only had her safety in mind, but she knew that at least part of the reason behind Jonas's attitude about Valdez was because he wanted to put her on a shelf, as if she were made of fine china. Being a woman meant she had to have a man make the decisions for her, right? God, she was so sick of that attitude from the men in her life. That's not what she wanted with Jonas. She wanted him to see her as an equal. A partner.

Deanna swiped away the tears and went up the stairs to her bedroom. She needed to get out of the house, to get her mind off Jonas for five freaking minutes. She slipped into her tennis shoes and coat, then picked up her purse and located her keys inside one of the pockets. She jogged downstairs and grabbed her cell phone from the cradle near the stove, and dialed her mom.

"Hello?" her mom answered.

She sounded sleepy, and Deanna wondered if she'd woken her from a midday nap. "Hey, Mom. Were you sleeping?"

"Nope, just reading. You know how that always makes me drowsy."

"I was thinking of coming over. Do you want company?"

She heard a rustling sound in the background. "How about we meet in town for coffee. I need to go to the store anyway."

Deanna thought of their favorite little coffee shop in town. "Java Rush sound good?"

"Yeah, it's next to the store. Two birds with one stone." She was quiet a moment. "Is everything okay, dear?"

Deanna's throat closed with emotion. Her mother could always tell, even through the phone line, whenever Deanna was upset about something. It boggled her mind how she did that. "Not really."

"Is it Jonas?" she gently prodded.

Nothing like a mom's soft voice to make you feel better almost instantly. "Yeah. I'll tell you about it when I see you."

"Okay, but be careful driving," she cautioned.

"I will," Deanna promised as she strode toward the door. "You too."

"Love you, sweetie."

"I love you. See you in a bit."

Deanna ended the call and went out the door, locking it behind her. As she got in her car and started the engine, she took a moment to pull herself together. The only thing going through Deanna's mind was the tone of Jonas's voice. He'd been so quick to decide Valdez was a bad person and therefore she should drop him as a client. After everything they'd shared and all the little pieces of herself she'd freely given him, he thought to come into her life and start giving her orders?

Somehow, someway he needed to get it through his thick skull that she wouldn't allow him to tell her what to do. A man leading her around? Uh-uh, not in this lifetime.

Deanna thought about how attentive and loving Jonas had been in Miami. So intent on making the weekend perfect for them. She wanted to go back there. To forget the last few hours had ever occurred. *If only time would stand still,* she thought wistfully.

Pulling into a parking spot near the front of Java Rush, Deanna killed the engine. She grabbed her keys and purse and headed toward the entrance to the little café. She and her mom had spent hundreds of hours mulling over life's many problems inside the small, cozy restaurant. Now, like so many times before, her mother was the one person she could count on for sound advice.

Deanna spotted her mom, sitting with her hands wrapped around a mug at a booth near the back. When Deanna started in her direction, Billy, one of the waiters, caught her attention.

"Hey, Deanna. How's it going?"

"Good," she lied. "How's school? Did you ace that test you were so worried about the last time I was here?" Billy was gorgeous, had beautiful dark hair that women drooled over, was flirtatious as all heck, and way too young for her, considering he was only in his sophomore year of college.

"Calculus, and no." He blushed, which Deanna thought was adorable. "I suck."

She tsked. "You don't suck, but did you at least pass?"

"Yeah, it's cool. They're not kicking me out yet."

She laughed. "It'll be over before you know it; then you'll have that fancy degree to brag about." She winked. "Hang in there."

"I will. By the way, have you thought any more about going out with me?" He grinned from ear to ear.

Deanna shook her head. "I'm not the woman for you, Billy. Besides, I'm too old for you." She wasn't exactly sure how old he was, but he was at least seven or eight years her junior. Not to mention the fact that Deanna had already handed her heart to Jonas—the idiot just didn't know it yet.

"You're not that old. Smokin' hot? Yes. Old? No way."

"How about a latte instead?"

"Fine, but I'm not giving up on you."

She laughed. "Thanks, Billy."

Just then, her mom glanced up from the table and waved her over. Deanna closed the distance, then leaned down for a quick hug. "Black coffee again, huh?" Deanna shook her head. "You know, they have a great variety of drinks here. You should mix it up a little every once in a while, Mom."

"And I'll bet Billy's getting you a latte even as we speak, right?"

Deanna grinned as she shimmied out of her coat and tossed it onto the seat before sitting down. "Like mother like daughter, I guess."

"Okay, what happened? Was the weekend horrible?"

That was Audrey Harrison, always direct. She didn't dance around a problem. "It was wonderful," Deanna answered, wishing she were back there all over again. "We went to the beach, and he took me shopping. We ate really terrific Mexican food." She felt her cheeks heat when she leaned close and whispered, "And spent the rest of the time inside the house."

She smiled and patted her hand. "Sounds like a fun time. So, when did the happy bubble burst?"

"Today." Deanna was about to tell her what had happened when Billy showed up with her latte. He put her drink on a napkin in front of her, threw her a wink, then sauntered off. Deanna picked up the mug, took a sip, and proceeded to moan. Sheer perfection. Billy had outdone himself this time. She made a mental note to give him a big tip.

"Everything was going really well," Deanna continued. "He and Dean even had a civil conversation this morning. Dean seems to be accepting the fact that Jonas and I are dating, which is nothing short of a miracle, considering how protective Dean can be about the guys I date."

"Yeah, he can be a real bear. He blasted me for letting you go to Miami." Her mother scowled and shook her head. "As if you were a teenager or something. That boy can sure try my patience sometimes."

"Mine too. Anyway, I fixed omelets and all was wonderful in the world. Then I brought up my newest client."

"The one you're doing the Asian design for?"

"Yeah, that's the one. Jonas thinks he's a drug dealer. He wants me to drop him as a client. Actually, he all but demanded it." Thinking about it had Deanna getting angry all over again.

Her mother's eyes widened. "Oh, my, a drug dealer? Is he positive?"

Deanna threw her hands up in the air. "That's just it—no, he's not sure. It's all conjecture. I told him that if he had proof that Valdez is the guy Jonas says he is, then I'd tell the man to find a new designer. I'm not going to work for criminals."

"That seems like a reasonable compromise. So, what's the problem?"

"It's annoying that he'd even think to tell me how to run my business. I don't want, nor do I need, another father figure in my life. Dean and Wade are enough."

"Maybe he was simply concerned?" she ventured before taking a sip of her coffee. "It sounds to me like he wants you safe. I don't think he meant to undermine your opinion, dear."

Deanna slumped in her seat, no longer interested in her latte. "I understand his worry. If the situation were reversed, I'd be worried too. But I don't want to be with a guy who tells me what to do all the time. I want someone who will work through a problem with me. Someone who will see me as a levelheaded, intelligent adult." She pointed to her mom. "I want a relationship like you and Dad had."

Her mom's eyebrows shot up. "Like your father and I?"

"Yes. You and Dad always talked things out. He didn't just point his finger and expect you to sit quietly and listen."

Her mom laughed. "Are you kidding me, Deanna?"

Deanna frowned. "What's so funny?"

"Listen, I loved your father with all my heart and he loved me. But it wasn't all roses. We had our share of problems. One of them was pretty much exactly what you're dealing with right now."

"How so?"

She sighed. "Back when your father and I first got married, he was very . . . autocratic. It was his way or the highway. Well, as you can imagine, that didn't sit well with me."

Deanna snorted. "Uh, no."

"We had our arguments. No, that's not true. They were fights. Downright ugly sometimes too."

"Really?" Deanna couldn't believe what she was hearing. She'd always thought her parents had had the perfect marriage. That nothing could pull them apart. It was oddly comforting to know they had had problems.

Her mother took the last sip of her coffee and smiled when Billy arrived out of nowhere to refill her cup. After he left, she asked, "What were we talking about?"

"You and Dad," Deanna reminded her.

"Of course. As I was saying, we had our fair share of issues, but we were good at hiding it from you kids. One of those issues centered around me working as a nurse."

She couldn't have heard her mom correctly. "Wait, Dad didn't want you to be a nurse?"

Her mom shook her head. "Nope. He thought my place should be at home raising you kids."

"Well, you won that argument, obviously." *Score one for Mom,* Deanna thought with no small amount of pride.

"Yes, I did. But one of the reasons he hated it was the hours. I had some crappy shifts back when I first started. He worried about me. Bad things happen every day. Muggings, rapes, murders. And back in those days, I got off really late at night."

"I remember when we were little you'd come into the bedroom in the middle of the night and kiss us."

Her mom smiled. "I hated those late shifts. I wanted to be the one to tuck my babies in at night. Instead you three had a babysitter doing it."

Deanna reached out and patted her mom on the arm. "It worked out okay, though. You didn't work those hours forever."

"You're right." She took a deep breath, then exhaled. "The thing is, your dad used to worry something fierce. And since I wasn't about to quit my job, he figured the next best thing was to take me back and forth to work every day. I fought him on it at first; then it dawned on me why he was doing it."

"Why?"

"Because he didn't want to lose me. I was his world. You kids and I were everything to him. He wasn't trying to tell me how to live my life; he just didn't want to lose me." She shrugged. "Knowing that changed the way I looked at some of his actions."

"And you think that's the reason behind Jonas's attitude?"

"Think about it, dear. Jonas is a loner. His own parents don't seem to care if he lives or dies. Now he has you. Don't you think he'd want to hang on to that with all he's worth?"

Deanna could see her mother's point. "So I'm supposed to shut up and deal?"

Her mother stiffened. "I didn't say that. Hold your ground. Go head-to-head with him if you have to. Just don't give up before you even have a chance to find out how good things could be between you. Some of my best years with your father were toward the end. Each day becomes important when you get older. Don't give up the chance to know what that feels like because your pride is taking a beating."

And this was why women went to their mothers for advice. "Mom?"

"Yes, dear?"

"I love you."

"I love you, too, sweetheart," she said, her voice growing a little unsteady. "You and the boys are the best thing to ever happen to your father and me."

Deanna smiled. The rest of their conversation revolved around current events and the latest trends in fashion. By the time they left Java Rush, Deanna felt like she could take on the world. Or at least one stubborn ex-soldier.

18

When Jonas walked through the door of Phoenix-Wade Investigations, his mind was on his conversation with Deanna. He hadn't meant to hurt her, and that's exactly what he'd done. Damned if he could figure out a way to make it right, though. It was as if he was destined to mess up every time he opened his fool mouth around the woman. Their weekend had gone so well too. Damn it. A curse from across the room tore Jonas out of his miserable thoughts.

"Piece of crap," Wade muttered as he pounded on the keys of his laptop.

Jonas chuckled. "It's not the computer—it's the user."

Wade's head shot up. "It's about time you got here. It's been a hell of a day so far."

Jonas snorted. "I hear ya." When he reached the side of Wade's desk, he shoved at his shoulder and ordered, "Get up so I can see what damage you've done."

Wade stood and raked a hand through his hair. "I'm like jinxed with this stupid thing. Whenever I touch it, something new screws up."

As Jonas went to work fixing Wade's computer—again—he asked, "So, tell me about this woman claiming to be Gracie's sister."

"Her name is Catherine Michaels. She called Gracie this morning and told her that she tracked her down through some letters she found."

Jonas hit a few more keys, then turned the computer off. "Letters?" he asked as he waited for it to finish shutting down.

"Yeah. She says she never knew about them until recently. Apparently, Catherine's adoptive mother had them stored away. Catherine found them when she began to deal with her parents' estate. Catherine's biological mother wrote the letters and sent them to Catherine's adoptive parents."

Jonas frowned. "And Catherine is claiming that the woman in the letters is not only her mother, but Gracie's as well?"

"Yep."

"Well, you have a name, at least. That's a place to start. Anything else?"

"She gave us her address and phone number. She seemed to understand our need to look into her story."

"What did Gracie say? And why didn't her father know about this woman?"

Wade threw his hands up. "Gracie's all ecstatic. Wants to meet her." His voice turned hard. "And Gracie's family tree is so crooked, who knows if Gracie's dad even knows about Catherine."

Jonas scowled. "Damn, Wade, if this woman turns out to be some nutjob, Gracie's going to be crushed. Why didn't you stop her?"

"Christ, I didn't know about the woman's phone call until after the fact! When I told Gracie we'd need to run a background check on Catherine, she went ballistic." Wade slumped into the chair across from the desk. "I might be sleeping on the couch tonight."

Jonas hit the power button and watched as Wade's computer came back on without any trouble. "Bummer, man. Good news, though, your computer is working."

Jonas stood and went to his own computer and booted it up. He took the business card out of his shirt pocket that had Valdez's information on it and stared at it. It looked so innocent. Jonas could understand why Deanna would think the man was an upstanding guy. A regular businessman. Jonas knew better. He'd seen Valdez's type too many times to count, and if there's one thing he'd learned, it's that dirtbags rarely actually looked like dirtbags.

"Thanks," Wade said as he took his seat back. "So, how'd the weekend with Deanna go?"

Jonas chuckled. "Took you long enough to ask. Afraid I corrupted her, are you?"

Wade glared at him from across their desks. "Don't be a prick. That's my sister you're talking about."

Jonas winced. "That was a dumbass thing to say. Sorry."

Wade waved the apology away. "Yeah, yeah. So . . . ?"

"The weekend was great. Hell, better than great. She was great. We were great together. But I'm pretty much in the doghouse with her right now, which isn't so great."

Wade sat back in his chair and folded his hands behind his head. "Did you do something I'm going to have to punch you for?"

Jonas rolled his eyes. "Nothing like that. I pretty much told her to drop her latest client because I think he might be bad news. As you can imagine, she didn't really care for that highhanded idea."

Wade shook his head. "Deanna doesn't like to be told what to do. Dad used to have a hell of a time getting her to mind him. Stubborn as hell from the time she could walk, he used to say."

"Stubborn and smart and sexy and funny and sarcastic." Jonas let out a breath. "She's the whole package."

Wade quirked a brow. "Sounds like you're serious about her."

"I'm pretty sure I'm in love with her, which is why it sucks that she's so pissed at me right now."

"Deanna doesn't hold a grudge. You two will figure it out." He frowned. "But this client. What makes you think he's bad news?"

Jonas glared. "His name." He got out of the chair and handed the business card over to Wade.

Wade took it. A few seconds later, he cursed. "You're joking. Tell me my sister isn't anywhere near that motherfucker."

Jonas shook his head and sat back down, then started to run a search on Catherine Michaels. "She's waiting for me to check him out first. But she's excited by the design she did for him. I feel like it's partly my fault that she's going to have to scrap the whole thing."

"It's not your fault that Valdez is the scum of the earth. If she's promised to stay away from him until you can get her some answers, then get her some answers."

Jonas continued searching. "I intend to," he vowed. "The only thing that matters is Deanna's safety."

"Agreed." The front door chimed, signaling someone's arrival, and Wade frowned. "Were you expecting anyone?"

"No." Jonas stopped what he was doing and stood. "We need a receptionist." He frowned at Wade. "Why don't we have a receptionist?"

Wade shrugged. "Hell if I know. Maybe we should put out an ad."

"Good idea." Jonas headed for the front room. "In the meantime, I'll go see who that is."

"And I'm going to check a few of my sources and see what I can find out about Valdez."

Jonas nodded. "The sooner we have proof, the better."

* * *

"I'm sorry to just burst in here like this without an appointment. I didn't know where else to turn."

"It's not a problem." Jonas watched as Ray Moseley paced back and forth. He'd known the guy for years. They'd met at a Cleveland Browns football game and had been friends ever since. Still, Jonas had never seen him so frantic. He looked as if he hadn't slept in weeks.

"Just start at the beginning, Ray," Jonas offered.

"It's that damn Valdez," Ray said, waving a hand in the air. "That bastard has Cade hooked on cocaine."

Jonas tensed when he heard the drug dealer's name in combination with Ray's seventeen-year-old son. "Terrance Valdez?"

"The one and only."

Jonas was getting a headache, and he was beginning to really hate that goddamn name. "How did you find out that Cade is mixed up with that guy?"

"I installed a chat-nanny program on Cade's computer without him knowing it."

The computer geek in Jonas was impressed. "Some would say that's an invasion of privacy. Not me, of course. I'm all about invading one's privacy."

"Some don't have a son bent on destroying his future."

"I don't imagine raising a teenager is a picnic."

"That's just it; Cade has always been a good kid. Always on the honor roll. He plays the trumpet in his school band too. He's really good. Cade isn't the type to skip school and go to parties. I've never had to deal with any of that like most parents do." Ray shook his head. "Lately that's all he seems to be doing, and I'm not sure what to do."

"Let's take one problem at a time. So, you decided to find out what he's up to. That's a good start. What'd you find out?"

"Nothing at first. A lot of talk about girls, favorite bands, lame movies. All the normal stuff. Then the other day he was instant-messaging with someone with the user name 'addicted241.' " He pulled out a piece of paper and handed it to him. "It's all there. See for yourself."

Jonas scanned the chat transcript and whistled low when he reached the bottom. " 'Gonna take you up on that offer,' " Jonas read aloud. " 'Valdez is loaded. Might as well have a piece of that since he's willing to share.' "

"He's supposed to meet with him on Friday, Jonas," Ray said as he started pacing again. When their gazes met, Jonas could see his friend's anguish. He looked as if he'd aged ten years since Jonas had last seen him, which had only been a few months ago.

Jonas folded the paper and said, "I'll take care of it, Ray. In the meantime, hang tight. Cade's a good kid. He's mixed up with some nasty people, but he'll come around."

"Everything changed after Karen died last year." He looked down at the floor and shook his head. "She was a terrific wife and the best mom a kid could ask for. Unfortunately, I haven't been the best father."

After Ray's wife had died from breast cancer, Ray had fallen apart for a while. But he'd picked himself up, for Cade's sake. "Don't beat yourself up. Let me see what I can find out about Valdez. The sooner he's put away, the better off this whole county will be."

"How will you get enough evidence? He seems to be un-touchable."

"That's because he has kids like Cade do all his dirty work for him. But we'll get him. Don't worry. In the meantime, get Cade into rehab. The sooner you two confront this issue, the better."

"He's not going to want to go, not without a fight."

"Then you fight," Jonas insisted. "When it's family, when it's someone you love, you do what you have to." Jonas thought of Deanna. He loved her and he would do whatever he had to in order to keep her safe.

Ray nodded. "Thanks, Jonas. I owe you."

Jonas waved a hand in the air. "You're a friend, Ray. Do what you can for Cade and let me handle the rest. I'll call you as soon as I know something."

After Ray left, Jonas headed back into his office and started continuing the search for information on Michaels. He wanted to get it out of the way so he could concentrate all his efforts on taking down Valdez. After about an hour, Jonas found what he was looking for.

"Okay, I had to do a bit of hacking, but I got it," Jonas said as he looked at Wade across the room.

Wade glanced up from his computer. "What do you have?"

"Catherine Michaels, twenty-five years old. Adopted by Russ and Jean Michaels. She's an only child."

Wade rolled his eyes. "Show-off."

Jonas chuckled. "She's not married. Her parents . . ." Jonas grimaced. "Damn."

"What about her parents?"

"They died in a car accident. A semi lost control. They were killed instantly."

"That's rough."

"Catherine grew up in Atlanta, Georgia. No criminal record, unless you count a few parking tickets. I don't know, Wade. I think this woman is legit." Jonas clicked a link to an article, and a picture popped up. It was a write-up in the Sunday edition of what appeared to be a small, local newspaper about Catherine Michaels's prize-winning roses. "Uh, she's definitely Gracie's sister."

"How do you know?"

Jonas pointed to the monitor. "I'm looking at her picture. She could be Gracie's twin, Wade."

Wade shot out of his chair. In two strides, he was next to Jonas's desk and staring at the computer screen. "Wow. Right down to the red hair and green eyes. It's uncanny."

Jonas leaned back. "I say invite her here and have her bring the letters."

Wade straightened. "I'm going to have to eat crow, aren't I?"

"Yes. But the upside is that Gracie has a sister, and you won't have to sleep on the couch." He grinned as he hit the PRINT button.

"That's a damn good upside," Wade said as he went to the printer and took the picture out of the cradle. "Oh, man, Gracie's going to cry when she sees this."

"After living with a drunk for a father her whole life, I'd say she's due for some good family news."

"What good family news?"

At the feminine voice, Jonas swiveled around in his chair and saw Gracie standing in the connecting doorway to the converted warehouse that she and Wade called home.

"Hi, angel," Wade said as he went to her and pulled her into his arms.

As Wade kissed her, Jonas felt a pang of jealousy for his friend. What he wouldn't give to have Deanna to come home to every night.

"You're home early."

"Yeah, it was a slow day, so Marie let me go early," she explained as she stepped out of Wade's arms. Gracie looked at Jonas and asked, "What's this about good family news? Is it about Catherine?" Gracie crossed her arms over her chest. "You two look like you're up to something. Out with it."

Jonas looked at Wade for help. Wade handed Gracie the picture and said, "She's definitely your sister, Gracie."

Gracie stared down at the image for so long Jonas started to get a little worried. When her head lifted, she looked at Wade first, then at him. Jonas could see tears in her eyes.

She lifted onto her tiptoes and kissed Wade, then murmured, "Thank you."

Jonas came out of his chair and strode up to her. "Hey, I did all the searching. Where's my kiss?"

Gracie laughed, which had been his intention, and placed a gentle peck on his cheek. "I don't know how you managed it, Jonas, and I'm not sure I want to know, but thank you for this." She held the picture against her chest. "It means more than you know."

Wade took her into his arms and held her tight. "How about we give her a call? We could invite her up for a visit so you two can get to know each other."

Gracie nodded and smiled. "That's a wonderful idea."

"Want me to come with you? Keep you company?"

She shook her head and started for the door. "No, I'm fine, Wade, but thank you. I need to talk to her alone."

Wade winked. "I'll be here if you need me, angel."

She nodded and left.

Jonas took a deep breath. "I thought she was going to start crying there for a minute."

"Me too." Wade pushed a hand through his hair. "It breaks my heart when she cries."

Jonas mock shuddered. "Women in tears are my kryptonite."

Wade laughed. "I hear that. Now, back to Valdez." He cocked his head to the side and asked, "What's your plan?"

"You heard Ray?"

"Yeah. Poor guy's an emotional wreck."

Jonas swiped a hand over his face. "He doesn't deserve this shit. Valdez's days are numbered. He just doesn't know it yet."

Wade sighed. "Are you going to do anything illegal?"

He bobbed his eyebrows. "Nothing that'll get me the chair."

"Well, I managed to find out a few tidbits that might come in handy."

"Yeah?"

"My source tells me that Valdez has a few quirks. Seems our friendly neighborhood lowlife doesn't allow anyone in his house if he's not there. Which means that even though he's loaded, Valdez has used the same woman to clean up after him for the last eleven years. And she's never there past six at night."

"No bodyguards or personal assistants?"

He shook his head. "Nada. He doesn't trust anyone to get that close."

That was damn good intel, considering what Jonas had planned. "Who's the source?"

"A kid I helped out once. It was before you and I set up shop. Long story short, he needed a fix so he tried to rob me. Now he's a counselor at the youth center."

"No shit? How come you never told me about this?"

Wade quirked a brow at him. "What, are we married?"

Jonas gave him the finger. "You're not my type," he said as he went back to his computer and got to work.

Jonas searched every database he knew in an attempt to gather information on one Terrance Valdez of Rolling Hills Avenue. Nothing incriminating came back. "The only thing I can find on the prick is a few newspaper articles talking about his fan-fucking-tastic business deals and his driver's license picture." Jonas clicked the PRINT button. "He has no criminal record and no other pictures that I can find."

"Is the driver's license photo clear enough?"

Jonas nodded as he stared at the computer screen. "I saw him once. I was in court testifying for Williamson." Jonas glanced up at Wade. "Remember him?"

"Williamson," Wade repeated, as if attempting to recall the case. "Wasn't he the guy getting ripped off? His friend was stealing money from his business or something like that, right?"

"He was taking computer parts and selling them on the side.

Hundreds of thousands of dollars' worth of equipment," Jonas said as he stood and went to the printer to retrieve the driver's license image. "I had to be up at the courthouse when the case went to trial. Valdez was coming out of the bathroom when I was going in. He looked familiar to me at the time, but I didn't really know anything about the guy then. There were a couple of cops in the bathroom, though, and they were going on and on about what a loser Valdez was." Jonas folded the paper and stuck it in his pocket.

"The driver's license will be enough to convince Deanna to find another client, but how can we get any decent proof for Ray? Shit just rolls off Valdez."

"I'll find a way."

"You need me to do anything?"

"Not yet. I'll let you know."

Wade nodded and grabbed his keys off his desk, then waved them in the air. "I'm going to see how the phone call went between Gracie and her sister. I'll probably take her to dinner or something." He paused, then asked, "You've got Deanna covered, right?"

"If I have to hog-tie her, she's not going anywhere near Valdez," he assured him.

Wade chuckled. "Most men wouldn't even attempt something like that with Deanna, but I think if anybody could manage it, you could." He frowned. "Which is both reassuring and unsettling at the same time." Wade headed for the connecting door to his home. "Don't wait up, dear," he said.

"Hugs and kisses, princess," Jonas shot right back.

19

Once Jonas was alone, he was free to think of the dark-haired, brown-eyed siren. He recalled how she had looked when he'd left, standing in the kitchen, tears filling her eyes. That image was killing him. He needed to hear her voice. He needed to see her looking all flushed from arousal, with a sleepy smile on her face and her hair all mussed from his hands.

Hell, he just needed *her*.

He picked up the phone and dialed her cell phone. She answered after two rings. "Hello?"

"Hi, kitten, you busy?"

"Just finished a late lunch." There was a pause, and then, "A really late lunch now that I look at the clock. I have a few minutes, but then I need to go. I'm meeting with a potential new client."

Jonas heard the excitement in her voice and he smiled. "You're going to be rich if this keeps up."

Deanna laughed. "Hardly, but it's nice to have work. This woman was referred by another of my clients."

"Oh, yeah? What does she want done?"

"It's a bathroom redesign. I'm going to be using Dean's construction business for this one, I think. She wants a wall knocked out and a bigger tub installed."

He whistled low. "That sounds like a big project."

"In some ways it will be. But I love doing bathrooms, so it should be fun." There was a beat of silence, and then, "So, uh, did you find out anything about Terrance?"

"I've got a driver's license picture. I'll bring it over tomorrow so you can see if he's the same guy."

"Oh, that sounds good."

Jonas didn't want to talk about drug dealers. Instead, he admitted, "I miss you, kitten. I needed to hear your voice."

Her soft, husky laugh filtered through the phone line and vibrated clear through to his bones. "I just saw you this morning, Jonas. Speaking of that, did you find out whether that woman claiming to be Gracie's sister is for real?"

"She's definitely her sister. Actually, she could be Gracie's twin." He paused, then added, "And it doesn't seem to matter if it's a few hours or an entire week, I still miss you."

She was quiet a moment, and then said, "I miss you too."

Jonas perked up at her small confession. "Does that mean you're not still mad at me?"

"I'm not mad. Frustrated, but not mad."

"Can I come over tonight?"

"No, and don't push," she chastised. "I just need a little breathing room. Okay?"

"Okay. One more question and I'll let you go so you can get to your appointment."

"Sure, what is it?"

"Do you have a webcam and Skype?"

"Uh, yeah, why?"

"You'll see tonight," he growled. "What's your user name?"

"Deanna dot Harrison twenty-nine."

"Got it. I'm going to add you to my contacts," he growled. "Talk to you tonight. Take care, kitten."

"You, too, Jonas," she said, her voice a little unsteady.

After they hung up, Jonas went into the storeroom and grabbed the small wireless camera, complete with audio, off a shelf, and a few other supplies, then headed for the door. With any luck, Jonas would be able to catch Valdez doing something illegal. It wouldn't be admissible in court since he'd be obtaining the information by illegal means, but it would be a place to start. Anything was better than the nothing he had now.

Ray's son, Cade, was a little trickier. Jonas had a feeling that the only way the kid was going to keep away from the allure of Valdez's money was to have his life or freedom threatened. Jonas would have to tread carefully there. He couldn't let Cade meet with Valdez on Friday. One way or the other, Jonas had to teach the kid a hard lesson.

He had an idea about Cade, but for now, Jonas had a house to break into.

Jonas's back was cramping up and he had pine needles sticking into his ass. "Damn it," he mumbled as he checked his watch. "I freaking hate surveillance work."

He wanted to get the job done so he could go home and wait for Deanna's phone call. Hiding behind Valdez's evergreen bushes wasn't his idea of a good time. He had plans for Deanna. Hot, erotic plans. He might not be able to see the woman in person, but Jonas was nothing if not creative. Hell, with today's technology, there was more than one way to go on a date.

After Jonas had left the office, he'd gone home to change and grabbed his knife; then he'd driven to the address he'd gotten from the DMV database. But he'd been sitting in pine needles for the last two hours watching the man's house, hoping for an opportunity to slip inside and plant the camera.

Jonas was just about to give up and head home for the night when a balding man with a potbelly walked out of the front door, a woman on each arm—both of whom looked half the guy's age—and got into a black BMW. Valdez. Once the car pulled out of the driveway, Jonas stepped into action.

Jonas found the house perfect—secluded on a two-acre lot; no snooping neighbors around to see him and call the police. The place Valdez called home sweet home happened to be a massive three-story estate large enough to house three families. A beautiful structure, no doubt about it, but to Jonas's way of thinking, built on the backs of the innocent kids he'd addicted to his damn drugs.

It was dark as Jonas moved across the neatly trimmed lawn and slipped onto the back porch. All the money the guy had and no cameras or spotlights in sight? Jonas shook his head in disgust. What a dumbass. The man was so confident he couldn't be touched that he'd left himself completely vulnerable. That's what having an inflated ego did for you, Jonas thought, made you feel invincible.

It took only a few minutes to bypass the alarm system. Within seconds, Jonas slipped into the living room. He looked around until he found what he needed along the south wall near the ceiling—an air-return vent, the perfect place for a hidden camera. Jonas took out a small pack of tools and the pinhole camera he'd brought along and went to work.

After Jonas had Valdez wired for video, he looked at his watch—eight minutes and twenty-two seconds. Not bad. Not his best time ever, but nothing to laugh at either. Jonas went out the way he came in, through the back entrance, then sprinted back across the yard to his car. He'd parked half a mile down the road to keep Valdez from noticing anything suspicious. By the time he reached the sleek, black machine and got in behind the wheel, Jonas's adrenaline was pumping hard. Nothing new there, but Jonas didn't think it had anything to do with the job. This time his blood was pumping hot in anticipation of Deanna's phone call.

Picking up the monitor that came with the camera, Jonas took a moment to test the feed. When Valdez's living room came into view, Jonas was satisfied he'd done all he could for one night. Unfortunately, having the camera in place was only the first step in the plan. He still needed to stay close in order to capture the feed, which meant more surveillance work, and more time away from Deanna. As his cell phone started to ring to the tune "Feel Like Makin' Love," thoughts of drug dealers quickly disappeared.

He picked it up off the dash where he'd left it, flipped it open, and said, "Hi, kitten."

"Hi," she said in that throaty, bedroom voice that Jonas loved so much. "Sorry I'm late calling. I got busy talking with that client and lost track of time."

"No problem. I was doing some surveillance work anyway." He took his keys out of his pocket and revved the engine. "Where are you?"

"In bed working on the computer."

Jonas thought of Deanna in bed and asked, "Are you wearing those little black pajama shorts you had on this morning? The ones with the tiny red hearts all over them?"

"Yeah, why?"

He had to suppress a groan as an image of Deanna in the barely there pj's sprang to mind. "You're killing me, woman."

She was quiet a moment, and Jonas was afraid the call had dropped. "Do you like my pajamas, Jonas?" she asked finally.

"Yes, a little too much," Jonas growled as he took off down the street.

"Hmm, good to know."

"Little tease," he murmured as his cock stood at attention. "Are you tired?"

"Not really. I'm sort of wired from my meeting. It's always exciting to start a new project."

"Do you have to give her a bid, or did she hire you right out?"

"She hired me because she liked what I'd done with her friend's living room. She kept going on and on about it."

A shot of pride burned through Jonas. "You're going to get a reputation soon. It won't be long and you'll be turning down clients because your schedule is so full."

Deanna laughed. "I don't know about that, but it's a nice dream."

"So, are you still frustrated with me, kitten?"

"That depends."

"On?" he gently prodded.

"Do you intend to tell me which clients I can take and which ones I can't?"

Jonas's hand tightened on the steering wheel. "That seems like one of those questions that could get me into trouble."

Deanna sighed. "It's a simple yes-or-no question, Jonas."

"Then, no, I don't intend to pick your clients for you."

"But?" she asked. "Do I hear a but?"

"But," he confirmed, "I do think I have a right to know who they are. And I do think I have a right to protect you from danger. I don't think that's too much to ask, Deanna."

"No, it's not. I just don't want to be ordered about."

He relaxed at once, glad that she appeared to be softening toward him. "By the way," he said, remembering the printout he still had tucked in his pocket, "I have a picture of Valdez. I'll bring it by tomorrow."

"That's what you said earlier. By the way, I have an apology to make about that."

That shocked him so much he nearly ran a red light. He slammed on his brakes and barely kept from ending up in the middle of the intersection. "You do?" he asked.

184 / *Anne Rainey*

"Yes. Don't let this go to your head, but you were right when you said it's highly unlikely that there are two Terrance Valdezes living in Zanesville. I did a quick search and only one popped up."

Jonas couldn't have been more surprised if someone had yelled *fire*. "You ran a search on him?"

"Nothing fancy like you. Just an online search engine. And don't laugh, Mister Computer Genius."

"I'm not laughing," he murmured. The light turned green and he hit the gas. "That's the first thing I do. Amazing what you can find out about people when you Google them, huh?"

"Yeah. I think I might be doing that more often too. Still, I do want to see the picture, just in case."

"No problem." He turned down his street and wished like hell he was heading to her house instead of his cold, lonely bed.

"Jonas?"

"Yeah, kitten?"

"Earlier, you asked if I had Skype. I got your friend request and accepted."

"Thanks," Jonas said as he pulled into the parking lot to his apartment. "Can I call you back in about fifteen minutes?"

There was a beat of silence, and then, "I'll be waiting."

Damn, he liked the thought of that. Jonas kept his voice gentle when he ordered, "Have your Skype up, kitten. I'm going to call you on that."

"Okay."

Jonas sucked in a breath at her one-word reply. Already he could picture her all tucked under the covers and looking sexy as hell. His dick urged him to move his ass along already. "Do you know how turned on I am right now?"

"I think I can imagine it, yes."

He turned off his car and yanked out the key. "It?"

"You," she answered in a soft voice.

"Good," he gritted out, "hold that thought. Fifteen minutes, kitten."

Jonas heard a small laugh. "I'll be here, Jonas."

The idea of Deanna waiting in bed for him sent a bolt of lightning through his bloodstream. Christ, how he wished he could go there now, strip her naked, and make slow, sweet love to her the rest of the night. Instead, he was going to have to rely on a webcam, a poor fucking substitute for Deanna's warm, curvy body.

20

He was the most voracious man Deanna had ever known. Even from a distance, Jonas managed to have her panting and ready. It was humbling how effortlessly the man could get to her. As Deanna waited for him to call, she opened her Skype account and stared at Jonas's status, willing it to change from offline to online. When it turned green, her heartbeat sped up. She looked at the clock on the right corner of her monitor. Fifteen minutes exactly. Well, of course he was on time; this was Jonas she was talking about. The man was perfect, and she was in love with him. She wasn't sure how to feel about that morsel of data. What if he never felt the same way about her? A part of her was afraid he'd get bored with her and move on. For Deanna there wouldn't be any moving on. What she felt for Jonas was the real deal. She ought to know, because she'd never felt it before.

The ringing over the computer speaker jarred her out of her love-struck musings. She hit the little answer button, and instantly she could see Jonas. He was shirtless and wore only a pair of black boxer-briefs. Holy mother, he was hot. His tanned, muscular chest and shaggy, unkempt hair stared her in the face. A lick, was it so much to ask?

"H-hi," she said. Crap, she'd stuttered. Real sophisticated.

"Hi, kitten," he murmured as he looked her over. "Don't get pissed, but did you lock up?"

She laughed. "Yes, I locked up. And I'm only going to get pissed if you make decisions for me or treat me like I'm a two-year-old. Being concerned is sweet, Jonas."

"Sweet?" he snorted. "That's new. I've never been accused of that before."

"You can also be annoying," she said as she shifted her pillow to get more comfortable.

He chuckled and leaned back against what appeared to be a headboard. She couldn't see much more than his face and chest. "Now, that I've heard."

Curious about his surroundings, she asked, "Where are you right now? Your bedroom?"

He nodded. "Yeah, want to see?"

She wasn't about to pass up that opportunity. "Yes."

The camera moved as he started to stand. Deanna saw a black comforter; then he pointed the computer away from him so she could see the rest of the room. He moved it in a slow arc. Plain white walls, black-and-white striped curtains on the window, and a large wooden desk against one wall. When it stopped on what appeared to be a couple of computer monitors and a black metal tower of some sort, Deanna asked, "What is all that?"

Jonas brought the laptop back around and she was once again staring into his face, only this time he was closer and she could see his dreamy blue eyes up close. God, why had she told him he couldn't come over? Was she a masochist?

"The big thing is a server," he said. "The multiple monitors are for work."

Deanna frowned. "Why on earth would you need all that?"

"Hacking into databases isn't easy," he explained. "It's time-consuming work. The multiple workstations allow me to let a program run on one while I work on the other. Saves me hours of waiting around."

Hacking? That surprised her. She'd known he was a computer geek, but she hadn't known he was capable of that. "You break into people's computers?"

"Hang on," he said; then the camera moved off him and bounced up and down a few times before finally settling on him once more. "Sorry, I needed to get back into bed. And to answer your question, yes, sometimes it's necessary. I don't do it to get my jollies and it's not because I get off on invading a person's privacy." He rubbed his chin, then said, "Although your brother seems to think I get way too much enjoyment out of it."

Deanna laughed. "And do you?"

He wagged his eyebrows. "I can find my pleasures elsewhere. Take *you* for instance."

"Take me?" she asked, hoping her voice didn't sound quite as breathless as she suspected. "Where would you take me, Jonas?"

"To heaven, kitten," he answered in that deep, gravelly tone that told Deanna he was more than a little aroused.

She made a valiant attempt to tamp down her mounting desire, but it didn't work. Jonas was simply too potent.

"You took me to heaven in Miami," she admitted.

Jonas put his arm behind his head and murmured, "How about I take you there again? Right now? Would you like that, Deanna?"

Deanna bit her lip, unsure. "Could anyone see this? Like a hacker?"

Jonas shook his head. "No one will see, I promise. It's just us, kitten."

"Because my computer's been acting a little flaky lately, and I haven't called to have it fixed."

"I'll fix it," he said, his voice suddenly hard and unyielding.

"You?"

"I don't want some stranger's hands on your computer."

Deanna's heart raced. "That's somehow a turn-on. I'm not sure why, but it is."

"You're mine. No one touches what's mine, kitten."

"Jonas." His name came out on a sigh.

"Show me what you're wearing," he growled. "Pretty please?"

"God, I feel so awkward."

"Don't," he whispered. "It's just me. Pretend I'm there. Remember in Miami when you sat across the table naked and ate that sandwich?"

Her face heated. "I'll never forget. I can't believe I did that."

"I fucking loved it." He paused, then softly ordered, "Put the laptop on the bed and sit in front of it so I can see you."

Deanna obeyed Jonas's command, knowing full well that whatever he had planned was going to send her head-on into an orgasm. Knowing that sure helped tamp down her nervousness. "There," she said when she had the computer on the bed. "Can you see me okay?"

"Hell, yeah. Move those yellow blankets off you. Show me that pretty body, Deanna."

Deanna gripped the blankets as if they were a lifeline. "I feel like I'm being naughty. Like I'm going to be caught by my mother at any moment. Silly, huh?"

He chuckled. "I could just come over there and move the blankets myself if you'd rather."

The idea had her pussy dripping with need. But she knew if he came over, she wouldn't want him to leave. Ever. And she still needed time to think about things. Like the fact that she loved him and he might never return those feelings.

"I can see those thoughts running through your head, Deanna. I won't push if it's making you uncomfortable."

"I do want you, Jonas."

"Then show me," he urged as he pointed at the camera. "If I can't touch you, taste you, at least give me this, kitten."

Deanna released her tight grip on the blanket and pushed it down, revealing her body to him a little at a time.

Jonas cursed and she could see him shifting around on the bed. "You said you were wearing those pj's," he growled. "Those cute, pink, satin panties don't look a thing like your pj shorts."

"I did have them on, but I took them off. I don't like to sleep in them very much."

"I should spank you for misleading me, don't you think?"

Deanna squeezed her eyes shut. "Oh, God, Jonas."

"Damn. You look so good on my screen. So pretty. I want this as my desktop background."

Deanna's eyes shot open and she sat straight up. "Don't you dare!"

His laugh came through the speakers loud and clear, the sound of it vibrating all over her too-sensitive skin. "No screen capture," he assured her, "got it."

She relaxed back onto the bed. "I mean it, Jonas."

He reached down and adjusted himself, and Deanna's gaze followed the path of his hand. He was fully aroused and her mouth watered. "Someday you're going to let me take pictures. I want lots of them of you, kitten."

Deanna smiled, a little too pleased that he was already think-ing of a future with them together. "Jonas?"

"Yeah?"

"Take off your boxers."

He didn't even blink. Within seconds Jonas sprawled out on the black comforter completely nude. His hard cock jutted out from his body, all but begging to be sucked. "I have a confes-sion to make."

"Uh, okay. I'm all ears."

"I love your cock," she said, as if admitting some deep, dark secret. "I want to taste it so badly right now."

"Fuck, Deanna," he growled as he wrapped a hand around the heavy length. "You need to be here, damn it."

"But I'm not. You'll just have to stroke it for me, won't you?"

"I will if you will," he challenged.

The promise of seeing Jonas masturbating was more than enough incentive. Deanna took hold of the hem on her tank top and tugged it upward. She tossed it onto the bed next to her, then removed her panties next. Once she was completely naked, she lay back against the pillows and wrapped both hands around her breasts and squeezed.

"Mmm, that's my girl. Now, open your legs for me. Show me that hot, little pussy."

Deanna slowly spread her legs wide until they were on either side of the laptop. "Better?"

"Much. I'm so damn hard for you right now."

"I can see that, and it makes me very thirsty."

Jonas squinted. "Be very careful what you say, kitten," he cautioned in a rough voice. "I'm staying away from you only because it's what you want. If I had my way, I'd be there on that bed, right between those silky thighs, lapping you up."

Deanna wanted to laugh, to lighten the mood, but she was too aroused, too ready to sail over the cliff into oblivion with Jonas. When his hand moved up and down his cock, she nearly whimpered. "You have a very talented mouth, Jonas. And an absolutely gorgeous cock."

"Since I can't use either of them on you properly, then I think the only thing to do is let you play. Will you touch your pussy for me?"

Deanna skated one hand down over her belly until she reached her mound. She stopped and cupped herself. She heard

Jonas curse. "Well, since we're both in bed and naked, I think it would be a pity to waste the opportunity."

"Exactly," he murmured as he continued to pump his cock.

Deanna massaged her hand up and down her pussy. "Like this?"

"Use your fingers and open your pussy lips. I want to see you, kitten."

Deanna's breathing increased as she used both hands to open her slick, swollen folds.

"Yeah, that's it. Fucking sweet as honey. Damn, I want that," he gritted out. "I need to bury my dick in there, sweetness."

Deanna bit her lower lip and closed her eyes as she stroked and teased. "What's your favorite position?"

"With you, any position is my favorite. But if I had to choose, then I'd want you on top, riding me. I want to watch your tits bounce with each thrust, your head thrown back. All wild like you were when you took me against the door at the beach house."

The images flitted through her mind like an erotic film, tossing her into a firestorm of need. She started to slide her finger inside her pussy, when Jonas said, "No, not yet."

She opened her eyes and stared at him on the screen. "What? Why?"

"No finger-fucking yet, kitten."

"Please, Jonas," Deanna begged, beyond caring about pesky things like modesty or feminine pride.

"Soon," he promised. "First, I want you to play with that little clit. Pinch it, Deanna."

"You're making me crazy, Jonas."

"So make me even crazier. Tease me into a drooling, begging stupor."

"Just remember, you asked for it," she warned; then she took her clit between her fingers and squeezed.

21

Jonas was a breath away from exploding. Christ Almighty, the woman was as hot as TNT. With her body all spread open and on display for him, it was all he could do to keep from tearing out after her. She had him so turned on he'd probably kill himself trying to get to her.

He watched as she toyed with her little button, her eyes closed and her bottom lip clamped between her teeth. A single capture and he'd be able to immortalize her, but he'd promised no pictures. Shit.

"Open your eyes for me, kitten."

Deanna's eyes drifted open, and she looked down her body at the monitor.

"That's it, there're those sexy brown eyes. Keep them on me, Deanna. No closing them."

She didn't speak, only shook her head. She was as close to coming as he, but Jonas wasn't through with her, not by a long shot.

"I want you to slip your finger into your mouth. Get it good and wet."

"Why?"

"No questions. Just feel."

Deanna hesitated. She had a thing about control, he'd discovered. It wasn't easy for her to surrender, which made it all the sweeter when she did. When her index finger disappeared between her lips, Jonas groaned, wishing like hell it was his cock she sucked instead. She pulled it out, and Jonas issued another demand. "Now, slide it down your slit, and don't stop until you reach that tight, pink pucker."

"You want . . . But, Jonas, I'm not sure about that."

"You can close your eyes, pretend it's my finger if you want. Remember how good that felt?"

"Yes," she cried out as she placed her finger between her puffy pussy lips. She moved it up and down, wetting it with her juices; then she glided it down farther. When she pressed it against her anus, Jonas pumped his cock faster.

"Push it in, kitten." Her moans turned to cries of passion as her finger entered her ass a bare inch. "Son of a bitch, you're beautiful. Fill it, Deanna."

She wiggled and her finger went in a little deeper, and she threw her head back and cried out.

"Pump it," he said. She started out slow, in and out, fucking her own asshole with her slim, delicate finger. Then her movements turned more frantic, her cries louder. Jonas tightened his fist around his cock and pumped it up and down. Suddenly Deanna's gaze came back to the monitor, and he could see the intensity of her desire. She was so damn close. Her words only confirmed it.

"I need to come, Jonas. Please," she pleaded.

"Now, Deanna," he ordered. "Fuck that pussy while I watch." When her finger slipped out of her ass, Jonas reached down and cupped his balls. "Do you know what I want to do with you, Deanna?"

"What?" she asked in a low, husky voice, turning Jonas on further.

"I want my dick where your fingers are right now," he admitted as he watched her push her ring and middle fingers inside her tight cunt. "Quick and hard and deep." Shit, he was too close. He pulled his hand off his cock and watched as Deanna's eyes opened and locked onto his through the screen. "I want you, kitten. Only you. I want to pound my dick into you over and over again."

"God, yes. I want that so badly," she moaned. "You're driving me crazy."

Jonas watched and waited, giving her a minute to catch up. "Do you like when I talk to you, Deanna? Do you like hearing my voice as you touch yourself?"

She didn't speak, making only soft whimpers of sound as she continued to tease and play with her pussy.

"You'll have to tell me, kitten. Tell me what you want."

"Yes, I like it."

"You like it, huh?" Jonas wrapped a fist around his cock again and stroked. Deanna obviously didn't want him to stop, but he wanted more from her. Jonas wanted her to let down her guard and give him everything. "If I were there, would you want me to make love to you? So that it lasted all night? Would you like that, sweetness?"

"Oh, yes," she breathed out. "I want you deep, Jonas. So deep that you fill me up."

Jonas pumped harder. "Look at my cock, Deanna." Once her chocolate gaze was on him, he asked, "Do you like what you see?" He ran his thumb back and forth over the tip.

"I love your cock. I want my tongue there, licking and teasing that little slit in the tip."

"Hell yeah," he said as the image she described filled his mind. "Keep playing with that lovely clit, Deanna," he demanded. "Don't stop."

"I'm so close. Oh, Jonas," she moaned.

Goddamn, he wanted her so badly it hurt. "Use your other hand and massage your tits." When her hand lifted and covered one creamy swell, Jonas growled, "Mmm, such pretty titties. I want that nipple in my mouth."

He stroked faster as he imagined the tight fist of her pussy sucking his cock deep. Her creamy heat would surround him and take him straight to paradise. As Jonas watched, Deanna used her delicate fingers to knead and stroke. Her dark mauve nipples puckered and stiffened to hard points that he wanted to nibble on for hours.

"Can you feel my mouth on your nipples? I can almost taste you, Deanna." He saw her chest rise and fall, growing more rapid as her passion mounted. Jonas continued the erotic words, making love to her the only way he could in that moment. "If I were there, I'd suck your nipples first, and then bite them. Gentle love bites, enough to make you grab at my hair the way you do when you get all wild."

"Jonas."

His voice turned hoarse with his own need. "Cum for me, kitten. Cum all over your fingers while I watch."

"No," she said, surprising him. "Not without you."

"Look at me, kitten." When her gaze locked onto his, he murmured, "That's it." Jonas pumped himself harder, until suddenly he felt his release coming on. "Now," he growled.

Deanna cried out his name and arched her back. The image of her on his screen sent him careening over the edge. He came on a shout, shooting his cum all over his hand.

Jonas collapsed against the headboard and closed his eyes. "Fuck."

"Yeah," she said. Even through the computer speakers, Jonas could hear her out-of-control breathing.

He reached over to the bedside table and grabbed several tissues. After he cleaned himself off, he said, "I'll be right back."

"'Kay," she mumbled.

Jonas got up and stretched his legs, then went to the bathroom to get rid of the tissues. He quickly washed up, then went back out to the bed. As he sat, his gaze went straight to the laptop screen. He smiled as he saw Deanna, limp on the bed, her legs spread open and her fingers still imbedded inside her pussy. Her eyes were closed, and he wondered if maybe she'd drifted off that way. "Deanna?"

"Shhh," she muttered. "I'm busy enjoying the afterglow."

He chuckled. "And here I thought you'd fallen asleep."

She lifted her eyelids and looked at the camera. "I can honestly say that I've never had an orgasm via video chat before."

His gaze was riveted as she slid her fingers out of her pussy and closed her thighs. "Does that mean I popped your video cherry?"

She grinned. "Something like that." He saw her reach for something; then she came back with a tissue.

As she went about cleaning off her fingers, Jonas was compelled to say, "There wouldn't be anything to wipe off if I were there."

"Ditto."

He shook his head and picked up his laptop, then lay back against his pillow. "What are your plans for tomorrow?"

"I'm going to be working up an estimate for that new client. You?"

"I have a few things I need to take care of too. Want to go out to dinner afterward?"

Deanna looked down at the bed for a second before answering. "Yes," she said as her gaze came back to his. "I'd like that."

Jonas raked a hand through his hair and yawned. "I haven't taken you on a proper date yet. I think it's about time, don't you?"

She laughed. "We went out on a date in Miami, Jonas."

"Kitten?"

198 / *Anne Rainey*

"Hmm?"

"I want to hold you in my arms right now," he murmured. "My bed is going to be damn cold tonight."

"Mine too. Maybe tomorrow night we can make up for that."

He stilled. "Are you inviting me to spend the night?"

She smiled. "Yes, I think I am."

He let out a breath and groaned, "Thought you'd never ask."

She was quiet a moment. He wondered what she was thinking because her gaze turned serious. She seemed almost sad. Jonas didn't like it, not after what they'd just shared. "What are you thinking, kitten?"

"I was thinking that I'm starting to fall for you."

Jonas had to be hallucinating. It wasn't possible that Deanna had just confessed her love, right? And yet, she seemed totally unaware of the precious gift she'd just given him. "You aren't the only one falling, sweetness," he murmured.

Deanna's gaze darted to his. "I'm not?"

Jonas smiled at her surprise. Did she still think he was just in it for the sex? "No."

"But what—"

"Wait," he said, stopping her before she said too much. "Not over a video chat. I'd rather do this in person, wouldn't you?"

"You're right."

"Rest for now. Tomorrow I'll pick you up and we'll go to dinner."

"Sweet dreams, Jonas."

He pressed a kiss to his palm and blew it at her. "Sweet dreams, kitten."

As he shut down the video chat screen and logged off Skype, Jonas's mind went haywire. Had she been aware of what she'd said, or had she just been feeling emotional because of what they'd shared? He didn't know and he suspected the not knowing was going to keep him up most of the night.

Jonas tried to remember a time when someone had said those three little words to him. *I love you.* No memories sprang to the surface. His stomach knotted when he thought how fucking pathetic that seemed. Hell, people said the words all the time. Mothers, fathers, husbands, and wives. Sometimes they said them without thinking, but to Jonas those three words were sacred. Maybe because he'd never had them directed at him—not even by his parents. Sure, they cared—in their own screwed-up way. But love? That wasn't something they were familiar with.

Jonas knew beyond anything else that with Deanna he didn't just want to say the words; he wanted to shout them from the rooftop. He wanted the world to know she belonged to him. Being with her, even for five minutes, was precious time spent to him. He tried to remember exactly when it had happened, when his feelings for her had shifted from desire to this all-consuming need to be with her, but he couldn't recall.

Jesus, he'd never had a yearning to wake up next to the same woman day in and day out. To share coffee and breakfast with her. Yet, he ached to have that very thing with Deanna. Going to bed with her tucked up real close, watching movies on a lazy afternoon, even listening to her share her day, Jonas wanted it all.

Tomorrow, when they went out on their date, he would tell her, lay it on the line, and pray like a man possessed that she didn't toss his heart into the trash.

22

The next morning, after Jonas handed the monitor over to Wade so he could stake out Valdez, Jonas headed to a meeting with a friend. He'd decided the only way to get Cade back on the straight and narrow was to put the fear of God into him. Barring that, the fear of Granger Manet.

He and Granger had gone through basic training together, but when Jonas had moved on to the Special Forces, Granger had finished his four-year enlistment, then later went into police work. Now he was one of the most respected narcotics officers on the force, and one of the toughest.

As Jonas pulled into the parking lot of Raven's Diner, he saw Granger's hunter-green SUV parked near the front. Jonas shook his head. The man always showed up at least fifteen minutes early to a meeting.

Entering the restaurant, Jonas went straight to the counter where a broad-shouldered African American sat devouring a stack of pancakes.

"Eating enough to feed a small country as usual," Jonas said as he took the empty seat on Granger's right.

"A man needs to keep up his strength, doesn't he?"

Jonas rolled his eyes. "Keep eating like that and you'll be in the hospital."

Granger snorted. "Like you're the first asshole to tell me that line of crap."

Jonas waved the waitress over and asked for a cup of coffee. After she left, he turned his attention to Granger. "Thanks for meeting me."

"I knew if you were asking for a favor it must be serious," he said around a mouthful of food. "So, spill."

"A friend of mine, Ray Moseley, his son's gotten himself into some trouble," Jonas replied, getting right to the point.

"What kind of trouble?"

"Cade's been messing around with drugs. If that isn't bad enough, the kid's decided he wants to go work for Valdez."

Granger dropped his fork on the counter and glared at him. "You couldn't have waited until I finished eating to bring up that asshole's name?"

Jonas chuckled. "Sorry."

"Yeah, you sound it," he grumbled as he pushed his plate away. "Might as well tell me the rest."

"Ray's wife died last year. Since then, Cade is all Ray has left. He's done his best, but Cade seems hell-bent on screwing up his life. It's killing Ray."

"Teenagers." He shook his head in disgust. "Damn, I hope I never have kids."

"Uh, you'd have to have a woman first, bud."

"Screw you, I date," he muttered.

"You're married to the job and we both know it," Jonas said as he finished off his coffee. The waitress came over and gave him a refill, and Jonas noticed the way the tall brunette shyly peeked over at Granger.

Granger shrugged and took a sip of his coffee. "The job is easier to figure out than women."

202 / Anne Rainey

"Not nearly as much fun, though." He gestured to the waitress and bobbed his eyebrows.

Granger's frown turned fierce. "I come here for the food, not the company. Speaking of which, get on with it, will you? I'd like to get to work sometime today."

Jonas chuckled. "You're all roses and sunshine, aren't you?"

Granger slammed his hand down on the counter. "Do you want my help or not?"

Because Jonas knew that Granger was more bark than bite, he tweaked him a little more. "Now, now, you're scaring the nice customers."

"You're running out of time, Phoenix," he warned.

"Look, all I need is for you to meet the kid. Show him that drugs are bad for his health."

Granger rubbed a hand over his smoothly shaved head. "An intervention, Granger style?"

Jonas nodded. "Keep him from being Valdez's bitch and I'll owe you big-time."

Granger picked up his fork and tapped it against the counter. Jonas noticed his friend performed the ritual whenever he needed to think through a problem. Jonas found it irritating as hell.

After a few seconds, Granger said, "I sort of like the idea of you owing me."

"Figured you would." Jonas thought of the skinny Cade meeting the big badass Granger Manet. "Uh, we are on the same page here, right? You're just going to scare him a little."

"Let me worry about that," he said as he glared at the waitress. "You just arrange the meeting."

What had he just gotten the kid into? Jonas recalled the look of defeat on Ray's face when he'd come into his office. As if reading his thoughts, Granger said, "I'm not going to hurt him. Relax."

"Never doubted you for a second, buddy," Jonas lied.

"Whatever." Granger glared harder at the waitress. As if sensing him, the woman turned and started in their direction. Jonas noticed the softening in Granger's eyes. To anyone else it would've been imperceptible. But Jonas had been friends with the guy too long. "You come here for the food, huh?" Jonas said, grinning.

"Jonas?"

"Yeah?"

"Scram," he growled.

Jonas barely suppressed a laugh as he stood and took out his wallet. He tossed a few bills onto the counter. "Breakfast is on me," Jonas said; then he left Granger to his bizarre courtship. His next stop was Ray's house. It was time they had a little chat.

When he pulled into the drive, he saw Ray's pickup truck, covered in what appeared to be months of dirt and grime. He got out of his car and grabbed his computer case and the hardware he'd brought along, then headed to the door. He knocked and waited. Sometime in the middle of the night, while Jonas lay awake thinking of Deanna's confession, he'd managed to come up with a way to keep Cade from going to the meeting on Friday and possibly get him back on the right track at the same time, but he needed to get into Ray's home network for his plan to work.

He rang the bell and waited. After a minute, Ray appeared, looking as if someone had shoved him in the dryer and hit tumble. "You look like shit."

Ray ran a hand over his face and moved back to let him enter. "Yeah, I haven't showered today. Cade and I had a fight last night."

Jonas had a feeling Ray hadn't showered in a *few* days, but he kept that little thought to himself and stepped over the threshold. The first thing he noticed was the mess. Clothes and dirty dishes were scattered all over the entry hall and living room. A far cry from the neatly kept house Jonas had visited on more than one Sunday when he'd come over to watch their favorite team.

"An argument or a fight?" Jonas asked, needing clarification. "I take it you told him he needed to go to rehab."

Ray grimaced. "A fight." He shoved his hands into the front pockets of his black slacks. "Went over about as well as I expected too."

Jonas slapped him on the back. "He's pushing you right now, but he'll come around." Jonas squinted as his gaze connected with a bowl of something on the coffee table. "Damn, is that mold?" He shuddered. "Dude, you need a maid."

Ray had the good grace to flinch. Jonas saw it as a good sign because at least the poor guy knew things were a wreck. Jonas supposed that was step one.

"I know. The place is a pigsty. Sorry."

Jonas shrugged. "Get a maid, problem solved. As to Cade, I have an idea."

Ray's eyebrows shot up. "That's what you said on the phone. What is it?"

Jonas held up a hand, unwilling to let Ray get his hopes up so soon. "Listen, it won't be easy or fun, not for either of you. Can you handle it?"

"If it turns Cade around, I'm all for it."

Jonas was glad to hear it. A dad willing to go the distance for his son was better than one turning a blind eye. Jonas pointed to the stairs. "He at school now?"

"Yeah, why?"

"I need access to your computer."

Ray strode to the desk in the corner of the room and hit a few keys. "There, it's all yours. What are you planning?"

Jonas closed the distance and sat down, then went to work. "Addicted241 is going to send Cade a new instant message telling him the time of the meeting's been changed."

"How will you do that? And, wait, what? I don't want him going to that meeting at all, Jonas."

"I know. One thing at a time. First, go shower." Jonas grimaced. "No offense, but you stink. Second, let your fingers do the walking, dude. Look in the phone book and call a fucking cleaning service. I'll take care of this, then explain everything. Deal?"

Ray stood there and stared at him, as if trying to decide whether he should be offended or not. Finally, he said, "Deal."

Ray turned to go, then stopped and said, "Thanks, man," over his shoulder before heading for the stairs.

"Okay, I'm already lost. What's a sniffer?"

"A network sniffer is a piece of hardware that will monitor your network data." Jonas held up the small black box. "By attaching this to your router, I'll be able to capture all of the traffic coming in and out of any computer on your network." When Ray still looked lost, he explained, "In other words, when Cade gets an instant message from his go-to guy, this baby will record it, and I'll get notified."

"What good will that do? I'm basically already doing that with the chat-snooping program I installed."

"Yes, but this will allow me to take the instant message, alter it, then send it back to Cade. When he logs onto his instant messenger, it'll look like he's received a new message from Addicted241."

"And what will the modified message say exactly?"

"That the meeting is scheduled for tomorrow night instead."

"Wait, if Cade replies back, won't he know that the message was false? I mean, won't Cade's friend tell him the meeting is on as scheduled?"

"We'll have to word the message so Cade knows not to send a reply."

"Okay, but if it's a setup, then what will Cade really be walking into?"

Ah, here came the tricky part, Jonas thought. "A meeting with a narc officer."

Ray jumped out of his chair. "What the hell, Jonas?"

Jonas held up a hand and stood. "Calm down. Cade won't be in any real trouble. This guy is a friend of mine. He's just going to shake Cade up."

He scowled. "Scare him straight, you mean?"

"Yeah. It's the only way I can see to keep Cade from being Valdez's drug mule. If you have a better idea, I'm all ears."

Ray ran a hand through his hair. "Shit. How did it come to this, Jonas? How'd I let my kid down so badly?"

"You're human, Ray. It happens. The key now is to get him back." Just then the doorbell chimed. "And the cleaning service is here. My advice?"

"What's that?" he asked as he moved to let them in.

"Tip them real fucking good. They're going to deserve it."

Ray snorted. "Thanks, asshole."

"Anytime, buddy." Jonas followed Ray out. "I'll be back in the morning to download those traces and modify the message."

Ray nodded as he let the cleaning service enter. Jonas wished them luck, then headed toward his car. Tomorrow night Cade was going to be in for a big surprise when he met with the narcotics officer. If Granger didn't scare the kid straight, nothing would.

Deanna loved Jonas, and she'd all but blurted it out over a video chat, no less. "Crap," she grumbled as she sped up in the hopes of being on time for her meeting with Valerie Rhodes.

The estimate was finished, and Deanna had even wrangled Dean's construction company to do the remodel. But she was having a terrible time concentrating on the road because all she kept hearing was Jonas telling her that she wasn't the only one falling.

Had he been serious? Or had it been lust talking? Pillow talk—men engaged in it all the time, didn't they? She mentally scanned her past lovers. Yes, she thought miserably, men could and would say whatever necessary to get a piece of the action. But Jonas wasn't just any man. He was more honorable than that. Right? Or was she just fooling herself?

Her big mouth was to blame. If she'd kept it shut, maybe Jonas would have been the first to cave. She could've waited a little longer, watched for signs that it was love and not desire he was feeling. "Well, that train has already left the station," she mumbled to herself as she turned down the street where her client lived.

Deanna knew now that the number-one reason she hadn't had a decent, long-term relationship with a man was because her heart already belonged to another. It'd happened the day of their family picnic. Jonas had grinned that ornery grin of his, and Deanna had sunk like a fishing lure. She'd put her heart in a vault that day, saving it for when Jonas would come collecting. Would tonight be that night? Her heart fluttered at the thought.

As she approached the older, two-story brick house, Deanna switched from daydreaming romantic to confident businesswoman. Valerie was a sweet woman. Her husband was an executive at a bank, and Valerie had recently retired. With her kids grown, Valerie had decided to pamper herself a little. The first thing on her agenda was a bigger bathroom with a Jacuzzi-style tub. She wanted Deanna to create a mini-oasis for her. The woman had a vision of something peaceful and relaxing, with tropical colors and a comfortable sitting area. It would be a big project, but an enjoyable one for Deanna.

As Deanna pulled into the woman's driveway and cut the engine, she wrapped her black calf-length wool coat around herself a little tighter. Winter was in full swing and kicking her butt today. She started to get out when her cell phone rang. Deanna looked at the caller ID. UNAVAILABLE. The only person who came up like that was Valdez. She took a deep breath and let it out. "It's now or never."

Deanna hit the SEND button. "Hello?"

"Miss Harrison, it's Terrance. I saw that you called?"

"Yes," she said, striving for confidence. "I wanted to let you know that I won't be able to do the project after all."

"Oh?"

"Yes, something's come up." *Like the fact that you're a drug-dealing loser.* "I'm sorry if I've wasted your time."

"That's unfortunate, but I understand. Business is business, after all. Will you be picking up those fabric samples, then?"

The fabric samples! Damn, she'd completely forgotten about them. "Oh, uh, yes," she replied. "I can swing by tomorrow. Around noon work for you?"

"That'll do fine. Till then, Miss Harrison."

Deanna ended the call. "Done. Whew." Instant relief flooded her system.

As Deanna got out of her car, a gust of wind caught her hair and she shivered. She quickly grabbed her briefcase and jogged up to the front door. Valerie met her with a cheerful hello.

"Come in, dear, before you freeze to death."

Deanna didn't have to be asked twice. "Boy, do you have terrific timing," she said. The warm fresh scent of pastries and the sound of a crackling fire hit her. Deanna's stomach growled even as her body began to warm.

Valerie laughed and took her coat from her shoulders, then hung it on a rack next to the door. "I just took a pie out of the oven. I hope you're hungry."

"Ooh, that sounds wonderful, thank you. I haven't eaten anything today. Been busy."

Valerie shook her head. "You're just like my youngest,

Danielle. She gets tied up at work and skips right past lunch. I get on her all the time about it. Do you like cherry pie, Deanna? The crust is homemade."

Her mouth began to water. "Homemade crust? No way am I turning that down."

"I knew I was going to like you," Valerie said, beaming from ear to ear.

That quickly, Deanna forgot all about her worries and poured herself into the job as she gave her client her full attention.

23

"This restaurant is wonderful, Jonas." Deanna looked around, impressed all over again. "The open kitchen, crisp white linens, and that beautiful Italian mural"—she pointed to the far wall—"make me feel as if I've stepped right into a restaurant in Italy."

"I'm glad you like it. As you've no doubt figured out by now, I can't cook for shit. Unless you count spaghetti and sauce from a jar. But these folks know how to cook good Italian food."

"My dish is delicious." She'd ordered penne pasta with smoked salmon and mascarpone cheese sauce on top. "And the atmosphere is so cozy, and the service is friendly, without being intrusive."

"Cozy, yeah, that was the plan," he murmured as he took a bite of his chicken marsala.

"How'd you know about it?" Deanna wondered if he'd brought other women to the restaurant. Unreasonable as it was, she sincerely hoped not. She wanted Vino's to be their special place.

"You mean because it's located in an ugly-ass strip mall?"

She laughed around a bite of salmon. "Yeah."

"One of those hidden treasures that I'd stumbled on purely by accident. I've only had the opportunity to come here a couple of times, with Wade."

"Of course Wade's been here." She recalled the Mexican restaurant in Miami. "You know, it occurs to me that he doesn't share well with others."

Jonas chuckled. "He likes to keep his cards close to the vest."

She moaned as she took a sip of her Chianti. "I've been so deprived. This wine is excellent, and that's coming from someone who isn't a big drinker."

He winked. "You weren't going out with the right guy, kitten."

Deanna's heart melted at his quiet statement. "Are you the right guy, Jonas?"

"That depends on you." He cocked his head to the side and asked, "Do you think I'm the right guy, Deanna?"

This was it. Her answer could alter everything and she knew it. Should she be honest and tell him that he was the one? Or should she keep it light and say something flirtatious? Taking a leap of faith, and a deep breath, Deanna said, "Yes, I do."

Jonas reached across the table and growled, "Good, because you're definitely the right woman for me."

And because she was too nosy for her own good, Deanna asked, "Have you brought other women here?"

"No. I didn't want to share it with just anyone. I wanted to experience it with someone special."

Deanna squeezed his hand. "I'm glad it was me you brought here, Jonas."

"There's more to this night, kitten. This is just the beginning."

Deanna dropped her fork. It hit the plate with a loud clang, but she didn't bother to pick it up. "More?"

He brought her hand to his lips and placed a kiss on her knuckles. "When we're through, I want to take you back to my apartment," he said, his voice low and intimate. "There's a surprise waiting for you."

Deanna's heartbeat went from a gentle saunter to a wild gallop. "Oh?"

He nodded. "Will you come home with me?"

Yeah, like she was fool enough to say no. "I'd like that, Jonas."

The waiter came over then and inquired about dessert. They both declined. Jonas asked for the bill and to-go boxes. After the waiter left, Jonas leaned forward and said, "You look gorgeous tonight, by the way. I think the waiter is half in love with you."

"Thank you," she said as she felt her cheeks heat with embarrassment.

Since it was going to be their first real date, Deanna had taken extra time getting ready. As silly as it seemed, considering they'd already spent a weekend together, Deanna felt as if she were going out with Jonas for the first time.

He'd told her red was his favorite color, so she'd worn her ruby-red cashmere sweater. With the deep V neckline and above-the-waist hemline, Deanna always felt sexy and confident in it. She'd paired it with her black skinny jeans and black leather high-heel shoes. She'd left her hair down around her shoulders. Judging by the way Jonas kept finding reasons to touch her, she figured the effort had been well worth it.

The waiter came back with their bill, and Jonas quickly paid, then stood and held out his hand. Enchanted by the romance of it all, Deanna placed her hand in his and let him lead her out of the restaurant. Once they were in the privacy of his shiny black Charger, Deanna took a moment to look at him. So rarely afforded the opportunity, Deanna knew that with the darkness surrounding them, it was as good a time as any.

The hard angles of his face appeared even rougher in the low, white light coming from the instrument panel. His dark hair was always a wild, untamed mane, but tonight it seemed as if he'd stepped right out of the jungle. Short tendrils kept dropping onto his forehead, and Deanna had the insane urge to reach out and play with them. Too easily she remembered what he had looked like in the morning when they'd been in Florida. That moment when he'd first woken up, before he'd had the chance to shower and comb his hair. He'd looked positively sinful in that rumpled state.

"You're looking at me," Jonas whispered.

"That's because I think you're hot," she answered with complete honesty. No sense in beating around the bush, she thought. Heck, he had to know how she felt about his body by now.

He chuckled. "Do you know that's one of the things I adore about you?"

Genuinely confused, Deanna asked, "What's that?"

"Your honesty," he stated as he reached over the middle console and entwined his fingers with hers. "You could've tried to save face just now, but you didn't. I like that."

Jonas's forearm flexed with each move of his fingers. He was six feet two inches of gorgeousness, Deanna thought as she sighed. "You work out, don't you?"

He took his eyes off the road for a second and said, "Six days a week, why?"

"Just thinking maybe we could work out together."

"What gym do you use?"

Deanna named the place she usually went to. "It's close to my house and small enough that I don't feel exposed to a bunch of guys looking to hook up."

He nodded. "I know that place."

Her gaze narrowed. "I've never seen you there."

"I haven't worked out there, but I know the owner."

"You know Troy?"

Jonas nodded as he turned down a side street. "He's a good guy." He glanced over at her for a second, then back at the road. "You're on a first-name basis with him?"

"Not really. He helped with an overzealous patron once. The guy kept chatting me up. When I exercise, I want to exercise, not look for a date." She shrugged. "Troy took care of it."

"He's a good guy." Jonas shook his head. "Guys can be such horny idiots." He sent her a quick wink and said, "How about I come with you next time? I could be your bodyguard."

Deanna rolled her eyes. "It was one incident, Jonas. I don't need a bodyguard. But I wouldn't mind a workout partner."

He chuckled. "You just want to watch me bench-press."

Yeah, okay, he had her there. "And maybe that's part of it too," she conceded as she opened her purse and took out her lip balm. Deanna applied it while her gaze surreptitiously zeroed in on the fly of his jeans. Even in the low lighting, she could tell he was hard. Her body burned in anticipation.

Jonas glanced at Deanna and noticed her gaze on his crotch. Even in the dark, where the only real light came from the dashboard and the few streetlights they passed, Jonas could tell she was hungry for him. The knowledge had him turning his gaze back onto the road and pressing harder on the gas pedal.

As his mind went over their video date the night before, and the late-night confession that had followed, Jonas decided now was as good a time as any to lay his heart on the line. "Last night when we were on Skype, I told you that you weren't the only one falling."

"I remember," she replied.

Her response was vague. Too vague. He wanted her open and trusting, the way she'd been when she'd come for him. The way she'd been when she'd told him she was falling for him. "Would it surprise you to learn that I think I started falling for you that day at your family picnic?"

Out of his peripheral vision, Jonas saw her gaze dart his way. "You did?"

"Yeah, kitten," he murmured. "And I have this overwhelming need to make up for all the time we've lost over the years."

"How?"

"You'll see when we get to my apartment."

"The surprise," she whispered.

"Yeah, the surprise." Jonas turned his car into his apartment complex, found his parking spot, and shut off the engine. "We're here," he growled as he turned in the seat to look at her.

"Yes, we are."

He leaned toward her and brushed his lips with hers. "Are you ready for your surprise?"

"Y-yes," she moaned.

"I love when you do that, kitten."

"What?"

"That little stutter you get when you're turned on. It's hot as hell."

"I don't stutter," Deanna insisted.

He smiled at her embarrassment. "Do, too, but don't worry, I've only seen you do it with me."

"You're delusional," she said as she laughed and unbuckled her seat belt.

No, I'm in love, Jonas thought. He wanted to share those words aloud, but he wasn't sure she was ready to hear them. Yet. When he unbuckled his own seat belt and opened the car door, he instructed her to wait for him. By the time he'd jogged around to her side, she'd already gotten out and closed the door.

Jonas frowned. "Is this a control thing for you?"

"Is what a control thing?"

The big doe-eyed look she sent him wasn't fooling him one bit. "Or is it that you think it's sexist?"

"Your need to pay for dinner, carry my suitcase, and open doors for me, you mean?"

"Yeah," he growled.

"No, I think it's lovely," she admitted, her gaze softening.

More confused than ever, he asked, "Then why the hell didn't you wait for me?"

Her lips twitched. "Because I like to drive you crazy."

Jonas cupped the back of her neck and leaned close to her ear. "That ass of yours is going to get a good spanking if you keep this up, kitten."

"Promises, promises," she murmured as she slipped away from him and started walking toward his apartment building. Jonas took a second to admire the view. Son of a bitch, her ass was a thing of beauty.

By the time they'd reached his apartment, Jonas was as hard as a spike and ready to be buried balls-deep inside of Deanna's tight cunt. *Slow down, big guy. There's still the little matter of her surprise.*

Jonas unlocked the door and let her enter ahead of him. He flipped on the light and waited for her to spot the big bouquet of white roses and miniature gerbera daisies. He heard her gasp. Yep, found them.

"Oh, Jonas, they're gorgeous!" She crossed the room, then leaned down and inhaled. When she turned around, Deanna's eyes immediately filled with tears. Every muscle in Jonas's body tensed.

"No crying," he ordered. "Even if it's a happy cry."

She bit her lower lip and looked down at the floor. Jonas took the room in three strides; then he reached behind the vase and handed her the small red box he'd hidden there. "Promise me you won't cry and you can have your other present."

Instead of answering, Deanna plucked the box out of his

hand and gently lifted the lid. After a few seconds, her gaze came back to his and stayed there. She didn't say anything, merely stared at him. Jonas started to worry he'd screwed up. "Uh, if you don't like it, I can take it back."

"Why did you get me this?"

Ah, so that's what had her so quiet. "You can't guess, kitten?"

"I could," she murmured, "but I'd much rather you tell me."

"The daisies are because they're your favorite flower," Jonas explained as he took the necklace out of the box, unfastened the hook, and put it on her. "The ruby teardrop necklace is because red is your favorite color," he went on as he cupped her face in his palms. "And this," he murmured as he pressed his mouth to hers, savoring the delicate sounds she made, "is because I love you with all my heart and soul."

A single tear spilled over and her lower lip quivered. "What I feel for you is so much more than I ever thought possible, Jonas," she said. "You're demanding, romantic, sexy, arrogant, and you've completely ruined me for other men."

"And?" he urged.

"And I love you."

Jonas shook his head. "You sure do know how to put a man on his knees, kitten," he grumbled as he leaned down and lifted her into his arms. "There's another present in the bedroom. Want to see?" he asked as he cradled her against his chest.

She wrapped her arms around his neck and laid her head against his shoulder. "Show me, Jonas."

"My pleasure, kitten," he whispered as he carried her off.

24

When Jonas reached his bedroom, he put Deanna back on her feet and pointed to another box sitting on his bedside table. Deanna frowned. "Bedroom Games," she said, repeating the words on the lid.

"Open it," he quietly ordered.

Deanna lifted the top and peeked inside. Jonas laughed. "They won't bite, Deanna. Take one out and read it aloud."

She plucked a card from the box and opened it. " 'Be your lover's sex slave. Perform any act of foreplay they command.' " She laughed and waved the card in the air. "Did you go through the box and arrange these to your satisfaction?"

Jonas grinned. "No, but that's not a bad idea." He let his eyes roam over her body. "Undress for me, kitten," he whispered.

Deanna's smile disappeared, replaced by white-hot desire. She placed the card on the table and began to do as he bid. Her fingers went to the hem of her sweater, and she tugged it upward. While he watched her bare herself, Jonas started to strip out of his clothes. By the time she had her sweater lying neatly on the end of the bed, Jonas was down to his boxer-briefs. His gaze caught and held on her white lace bra. He leaned forward and cupped one beautiful tit and licked her nipple, wetting fabric and all. Deanna moaned and unhooked the back clasp. When he stood back up, she let it fall to the floor. Next went the jeans. She had to wiggle her hips to get them down, and Jonas cursed at the unintentional erotic display. Her panties caught on the denim and slid down with them. The dark curls covering her pussy looked sweet as hell. She bent and pulled off her shoes, then the clothes. When she stood back up, she was completely nude.

"You do me in, kitten. You're so goddamn pretty."

She clasped her hands together in front of her and said, "Thank you."

Jonas got rid of his underwear, then picked up the naughty card and held it up. "Are you prepared to be my sex slave, Deanna?"

She tipped her head to the side, and her lips kicked up in a sideways grin. "Depends on what you expect from me."

He slid the tip of the card over her mouth. "Your hot, little mouth wrapped around my cock."

Deanna smiled. Somehow appearing both shy and wicked at the same time. Jonas's dick hardened. She bent at the knees and placed both hands on his thighs, then opened her mouth and looked up at him.

"Jesus, you look good like that," he growled as he wrapped a fist around his cock and guided it onto Deanna's waiting tongue. "Lick it, kitty," he ordered.

Her tongue darted out and swiped over the head, back and forth, tasting him as if he were a juicy Popsicle. "I want more," she pleaded.

"You want my dick filling your mouth?"

"Yes, please," she whimpered.

Jonas couldn't speak. In fact, he was pretty sure his brain

had taken a holiday. He wrapped his fist in her hair and tugged her head forward, watching as several inches of his cock disappeared inside Deanna's mouth. She hummed and sucked the bulbous head, swirling her tongue around it a couple of times before teasing the slit. Jonas pushed her head onto him a little more, needing to watch her take it deep. She opened wider, as if hungry for his taste, and Jonas instinctively flexed his hips. She gagged and he quickly pulled out, then watched as a mix of pre-cum and saliva clung to her lips and the tip of his cock, tying them together. She leaned forward and licked it off him, causing Jonas to grit his teeth against the need to fuck her mouth.

He cupped her chin in his palm and forced her head up until their gazes locked. "Another minute of that and you'll be swallowing a mouthful of cum."

She licked her lips and smiled. "You do taste delicious, but I'd rather you came elsewhere this time."

Jonas swiped his thumb over her bottom lip and murmured, "Does your pussy need to be fucked, Deanna?"

She stood and wrapped her arms around his waist, then placed little kisses over his chest. "No more teasing, Jonas," she begged. "I don't think I can take it."

He lifted her and placed her on the bed. "No, no more teasing."

With her hair all around her shoulders and curling around one nipple, eyes half closed with passion, Deanna looked like an offering to a god.

Jonas moved on top of her, then reached down with one hand to cup the silky softness of her mound. She was hot and wet with her juices, and Jonas wanted to drive into her, hard.

He dipped his head and nuzzled the pillowy softness of her round tits, squeezing one soft orb with his hand as he licked the other. Jonas inhaled her sweet, floral scent, deliberately driving all his senses mad.

"You're like a drug, sweetness. I swear to God, I can never get enough of you."

"That feeling is mutual, Jonas," she said as she wrapped her arms around his shoulders and held him close.

Jonas caressed her clit and Deanna moaned. He lifted his head so he could watch as her pleasure mounted. She arched her neck and closed her eyes while his fingers continued their torture. He delved his middle finger into her wet opening, letting his thumb slide over her swollen nub, and heard her cry out his name. Every moan and shudder drove Jonas higher and higher. Deanna's pussy tightened around his finger, and Jonas's dick leaked precum, as if anticipating the tight grip.

"Damn," he growled. "I need my cock feeling that squeeze, Deanna."

"Yes, Jonas, yes," she cried out.

All thought fled as Deanna began bucking wildly beneath him. She was close; Jonas could feel her body climbing higher and higher. He instantly pulled his finger free of her pussy and slid down her body, putting his mouth to her instead.

"Come in my mouth, girl," Jonas commanded as Deanna opened her eyes and stared down at him.

He licked and teased her pussy lips, then plunged his tongue in and out several times. He nibbled her clit and felt her body go stiff as a board. When she plunged her fingers into his hair and shouted his name, surprising him with her climax, Jonas nearly came right along with her.

He kept his mouth against her until the last of her spasms subsided. When he lifted up, Jonas touched his index finger to her lips and growled, "Taste it."

Deanna wrapped her hands around his, then slowly sucked his finger into her mouth and licked it clean. "Mmm, so damn sweet," he murmured.

As Jonas positioned his cock against her pussy, he kissed her lips. He could taste his precum and her pussy juice both; the mixture drove him higher. He slid his tongue down her chin to her throat, then teased her erratic pulse. He felt it speed up and he nipped at it, leaving his mark behind.

Deanna pushed her hips upward, and his dick slipped inside her narrow passage. "God, you feel so good," he groaned. "So damn hot and tight."

She shuddered and he pushed a little farther inside her sweet heat. As her body stretched to accommodate his size, Deanna began to move her hips a little faster.

"Jonas, I feel like I'm on fire," she moaned.

Her breathless voice spurred him on. He pushed a little farther inside, and her inner walls clenched around him. They both whimpered. "Wrap your legs around me, kitten."

She did as he bid, and Jonas slammed into her. She shouted and threw her head back. Jonas couldn't take his eyes off her. The pink flush of her cheeks and the sheen of perspiration on her neck and chest were so damn beautiful.

He started moving, sliding in and out, taking his time at first. Soon it wasn't enough. He rose up and hooked his arms beneath her knees and spread her wider, then thrust in hard and fast.

He never took his gaze from hers as he said, "Once I'm done loving you, there'll be no doubt, Deanna."

Deanna's eyes opened, her gaze locking with his as she asked, "D-doubt?"

"That you're mine. That we belong together."

Deanna felt his declaration clear to her soul. She watched the strain on his face and marveled at his control. But it wasn't what she wanted. Deanna lifted her bottom off the bed, and the motion pushed Jonas's cock inside her so far she felt impaled by him. The feel of him buried so deep was nearly overwhelming.

"Goddamn, I'm going to lose it if you don't lie still," Jonas growled.

"Good. Fuck me, Jonas."

The muscles in his neck were straining, and his sinewy arms anchored her to him, effectively keeping her in place and forcing her to submit. As Jonas reached between their bodies and caressed her clit with one calloused fingertip, stroking her wet heat, Deanna began to come undone, again. Her gaze shot wide as her orgasm rushed over her.

"Now," he gritted out as he drove into her, pumping in and out like a man gone mad. Then suddenly he was joining her, pouring every ounce of his seed inside of her pussy, filling her.

Jonas collapsed on top of her, and they lay sweating and exhausted with his cock still buried inside her sex. Time seemed to stop as Jonas turned his head and kissed her cheek. "I love you, Deanna Harrison."

Deanna's heart soared at the words she never thought she'd hear from him. "I love you, Jonas Phoenix."

Several minutes passed before Jonas lifted off her and carried her to the bathroom, where he spent a great deal of time pampering every inch of her body.

Deanna had definitely died and gone to heaven.

25

The next morning, Deanna found herself perched on top of Jonas's kitchen table with Jonas seated in the chair between her thighs. He was currently in the process of feeding her a chocolate-cream-filled doughnut. In between each bite, he kept her on the very edge of desire by licking and nibbling on her thighs.

"I'm having a terrible time concentrating on my treat with your mouth on me," she chastised. Not that she really cared. With Jonas around, food would always take a backseat.

"Hmm, that's a real shame because I'm not having a bit of trouble concentrating on my treat," he whispered against her inner thigh.

"You're insatiable," she said, a little amazed by his stamina. Even before she'd been fully awake, Jonas had had his hands filled with her flesh. They'd made slow, sweet love and it'd brought tears to her eyes. Afterward, he'd instructed her to take a long, hot shower while he went out to get them some breakfast. When he'd returned, Deanna had been dressed in one of his old black T-shirts, and nothing else. Jonas had dropped the doughnuts on the counter, then carried her back to bed, where he'd brought her to heaven once more.

Now Jonas was dressed in nothing but a pair of gray boxers and treating her as if she were the most desirable woman on the planet. It was enough to make a woman swoon.

When he tried to feed her yet another bite of the pastry, Deanna held up her hand. "I'm going to bust. Please, no more."

He leaned forward and licked her lower lip. "You had a little chocolate on you," he explained.

"Oh," she murmured. To take her mind off the potent, half-naked man seated in front of her, Deanna asked, "So, what are your plans for the day?"

He looked at the clock and cursed. "I need to go to a client's house first, then later head over to Valdez's."

"Valdez? *He's* the one under surveillance?"

"Yep. A case we're working for a friend. Wade took last night's shift. It's my turn."

Deanna frowned. "You don't have to watch him day and night, though, do you?"

"I planted a long-range camera inside his house, one with audio," he started to explain as he stood and took their used napkins to the trash, "and in order for it to record the feed, we have to be within range."

"Oh, wow. That sounds . . . boring."

He chuckled. "It can be." He came toward her and planted his fists on either side of her hips on the table. "So, call me when you get a chance and talk dirty to me; otherwise I might fall asleep and miss something important."

She wrapped her arms around his neck and grinned. "I could do that. I just have a few errands to run; then I'm going home to work on Valerie's design."

He kissed his way over her face to her neck, where he lingered. "Valerie?" he asked, his breath whispering against her skin. "Is that your new client's name?"

"Yeah," she murmured, becoming pleasantly distracted.

He stilled. "Shit, that picture. I completely forgot." He

moved out of her arms and jogged from the room. When he came back in, he was holding an eight-by-ten sheet of paper. "Valdez," Jonas said as he handed it over.

Deanna took it and looked at the small driver's license photo, then nodded. "Same guy," she confirmed as she handed it back to him. "By the way, I already turned down the job."

He cupped her cheek and frowned. "I'm sorry. I know you were counting on that money, kitten."

She shrugged. "I don't want my business to stay afloat if it means taking on clients like him." Deanna considered telling him about her errand to pick up the fabric samples at Valdez's but nixed the idea. It would be a quick trip. She wouldn't even need to go inside the man's house. Just get the samples and leave.

Jonas's cell phone began to ring, and Deanna waited as he answered it.

"Hello?" he said. There was a beat of silence; then his gaze widened. "Oh, hell, man, I'm sorry." Deanna could see the concern on Jonas's face, and she began to worry. "No, your son needs you right now, Ray. You need to be with him in case he wakes up." He paused, obviously listening to whatever the caller was saying, then said, "Yeah, I'll leave here in a few minutes and meet you there."

When he ended the call, Deanna asked, "What happened?"

Jonas passed a hand over his face and let out a heavy breath. "That was the friend. His son Cade is hooked on Valdez's drugs. An ambulance just rushed him to the emergency room. A possible overdose."

"Oh, no! Is he okay?"

"Ray doesn't know. He's headed to the hospital now." He looked at the clock on the microwave. "Look, I need to go up there. Ray's a mess with all this. I'm sorry to rush off, kitten."

She waved away his apology. "Don't be sorry for helping a friend. Do you want me to come with you? The beauty of being your own boss is that you can take a day off if you have to and you won't get fired."

He shook his head. "I think Ray wants to talk to me alone, but thanks for offering." He kissed her forehead. "Go, take care of your errands. I'll call you when I know anything, okay?"

She nodded, but as he started to leave the room, Deanna called him back. He stopped and quirked a brow. "I love you," she said, needing to say it once more before they went about their day.

He crossed the room in two strides and took her mouth in a hard, possessive kiss. "I love you too. Take care of yourself today, kitten."

Deanna shivered, knowing darn good and well that if she lived to be a hundred, she'd probably still get that little thrill down her spine whenever Jonas kissed her.

"You too," she murmured.

As Deanna watched Jonas walk out of the kitchen, she knew the truth—Jonas showing up at their family picnic had been the luckiest day of her life.

Noon on the dot, Deanna noticed as she saw the time on her phone when she turned it to vibrate and tossed it into her purse. She walked up to Terrance's door and rang the bell. Too late, she forgot how much she hated his doorbell. It played an annoying little jingle that grated on her nerves a little more each time she heard it. She just wanted to get the fabric and leave. A gust of bitter cold wind blasted her face, and she pulled her coat closed a little tighter, willing Terrance to hurry. The door opened, nearly paralyzing Deanna with a bout of nerves as realization dawned. A drug dealer, Deanna thought, not a harmless businessman.

"Miss Harrison," he said as he opened the storm door. "Please, come in."

He stepped back to allow her entry into his foyer, and fear

snaked down Deanna's spine. No way was she going anywhere near that particular lion's den. She smiled and hitched her purse up higher on her shoulder. "Oh, no, that's okay. I'm sure you're busy. I can just wait here while you grab the swatches; then I'll be out of your hair."

His smile instantly disappeared. Too late, Deanna realized her blunder—the man was nearly bald. Oops.

"Of course," he bit out. "I'll go get them for you."

He shut the storm door in her face, and Deanna wanted to kick herself. "Great, you've managed to piss off a drug dealer," she mumbled to herself after he disappeared into another room.

Just then, a truck pulled into the drive. Curious, Deanna turned her head in time to see a man jump out of the driver's side. He left the door hanging open as he came toward her, his strides eating up the distance. Two things struck Deanna at once. The first was the crazed look in his hazel eyes. He didn't just look upset; the man was in a full-on rage. The second was the gun he held tight in his right hand.

Too late, Deanna registered Terrance out of the corner of her eye. Unaware of the drama unfolding, he opened the storm door and handed her the fabric. At the same time, the stranger wielding the gun lifted his arm and fired. Deanna screamed and watched in helpless disbelief as Valdez fell to the ground, his body landing half in and half out of the house, blocking the doorway. He clutched at his chest and groaned.

As blood started to form a macabre circle on his chest, Deanna tried to kneel down, her only thought on helping a dying man. The gunman grabbed her by her forearm and shoved her into the house. Next, as if Valdez weighed no more than a bag of flour, the man picked Valdez up by the shirtfront and tossed him into the foyer behind her. When he kicked the door shut, Deanna knew things had just gone from bad to worse.

26

Emotionally wiped from talking to Ray, Jonas drove out of the hospital parking lot and hit the freeway. Cade was going to make it, but it'd been touch and go for the first few hours. Ray had been understandably distraught. Almost out of control. When Cade had opened his eyes and called out for his dad, Ray had calmed and taken charge. He'd been the picture of strength for his son. Jonas had left to give the two of them some privacy.

As he got into his car, Jonas was more than ready to hear Deanna's sweet voice. He missed her. He still couldn't believe she loved him. He, more than anyone, knew Deanna deserved better, but hell if he was going to give her up. She'd handed her heart over on a silver platter and he wasn't about to return it for a refund.

He took his phone out of the middle console, where he'd stored it during the hospital visit, and hit speed-dial 2. After several rings, it went to voice mail. Jonas frowned. "Home," he mumbled as he remembered his conversation with Deanna earlier. She was supposed to be working on that new bathroom design. Jonas hit speed-dial 3 next. It rang four times before the answering machine picked up. Okay, now Jonas was beginning to get a little worried. It wasn't like Deanna to be completely unavailable at both numbers. He wondered if maybe Wade had talked to her. Jonas dialed his friend's cell.

Wade picked up on the second ring. "Hey," he said. "What's up?"

"Have you talked to your sister today?"

"No, why?"

His hand clutched the steering wheel a little tighter. "She's not answering at her house or her cell."

Wade was silent a minute. "Have you called anyone else? Mom? Dean?"

"No," he answered between clenched teeth. "I tried you first."

He heard some clanging in the background. Dishes? Jonas wondered if he'd interrupted Wade at lunch. "How long have you been out of touch with her?"

"It's only been a few hours. I've been at the hospital all morning. Ray's son OD'd."

"Damn, you're kidding."

Jonas rolled to a stop at an intersection. "I wish I were. He's okay now, but he came damn close to meeting his maker."

"Hate to say it, but maybe being so near death will force the kid into rehab."

"Yeah, maybe." Jonas tapped the steering wheel and tried to think where Deanna might be. The only place that made sense was her house. He thought about their night together. They'd only managed a few hours of sleep. Maybe she'd been tired and decided to take a nap. He flipped on his turn signal and said, "I'm going to head over to her place. Maybe she just fell asleep."

He heard Wade groan. "Did she have a long night, you shit?"

This was the tricky part about dating your buddy's baby sister, Jonas thought as the conversation turned awkward for both of them. "Uh, yeah."

Wade cursed. "Christ, I never should've asked."

"If it helps, I plan to marry her." *If I can find her,* he added silently.

"Damn right you'll marry her."

Jonas rolled his eyes. "I should probably ask her first, don't you think?"

"This is Deanna we're talking about." He snorted. "You'll probably have to figure out a way to get her to ask *you.*"

Jonas chuckled, though it felt hollow. He was simply too worried about Deanna. "I'm going to call your mom, see if she's heard from her."

"Deanna did agree to turn down the Valdez job, right?"

"Yeah. She'd already called the bastard and told him to find a new designer by the time I'd gotten around to showing her the picture."

"Good. Oh, about Valdez."

"Yeah?"

"The only thing I got on that video feed was the guy getting a blow job from some girl young enough to be his daughter. He's a real piece of work. Jesus."

Jonas frowned. Something about Valdez was bothering him. "Where are you now?"

"Lunch with Gracie," he answered. "So, with Ray's son out of commission and Deanna far away from Valdez, do you still want to continue with the surveillance?"

He couldn't think about that prick, not until he knew Deanna was safe. "I'll worry about that after."

"She's probably just asleep or something. I'm sure she's fine, dude."

Jonas sighed, wishing the hairs on the back of his neck would get the message. "Yeah, probably."

"Let me know when you hear from her."

"Will do."

They hung up and Jonas hit the gas pedal harder. He had a bad feeling, and his bad feelings were always spot-on. Twenty minutes later, Jonas turned down Deanna's street. The first thing he noticed was the empty driveway. "Shit."

When he pulled alongside the curb in front of her house, Jonas killed the engine. He leaned across the middle console to open the glove box and dug around until he found his lock-picking kit. Jonas tucked it into his leather jacket, then tore out of the car. He jogged up to the front door and rang the bell, then waited. When she didn't answer, he unzipped his coat and went to work. A few minutes later, her lock turned and Jonas was inside.

"Deanna!" he called out, but there was no answer. He took the stairs two at a time, then stuck his head inside the first room he came to. Her bedroom. He recognized the blanket from their video chat. Unfortunately, her bed was empty. He looked into another room and realized he'd found her office. Still no sign of her. Jonas searched every room in the house with no luck. He tried her cell phone again, but nothing.

Jonas returned to his car and for the first time in years, he prayed. Visions of Deanna lying in some gutter cold, hurt, and alone bombarded him. It made him sick to his stomach to think of her like that. The worst part about being an ex-soldier was moments like these. He knew bad things happened to good people every day. It wasn't just an overworked imagination. It was reality.

Jonas grabbed his cell phone off his belt and called Deanna's mother. A few rings later, her delicate voice came over the line.

"Hello?"

"Mrs. Harrison, this is Jonas."

"Oh, hi, Jonas," she said in a cheerful voice.

"Is Deanna with you by chance?"

"No, I haven't talked to her since this morning." For a moment, there was silence on the line. "Is something wrong, Jonas?"

His hopes took a nosedive. Even as he talked, his eyes scanned the sidewalks on both sides of the street. As if she would really go for a walk or a jog in twenty-degree weather. *Great idea, dickhead.*

"Jonas?"

"When you talked to her, did she say anything about where she was going today?"

"Just that she had a few errands. She didn't say what they were."

He checked his watch. Nearly two o'clock in the afternoon. "She's not home and I can't reach her on her cell."

"Did you two argue?" she asked. "Sometimes Deanna goes to work out when she's stressed or upset about something."

"No, everything was fine. Better than fine," he answered as he recalled Deanna sitting on his table professing her love right before he'd had to leave for the hospital. *Please, God, don't let that be the last time I see her.*

"This isn't like Deanna. I'm worried, Jonas."

"I'll find her," he promised.

"Hold on, that's Dean on the other line. Maybe he's talked to her."

"I'll hold," Jonas growled. Twins. Dean and Deanna were twins. A sense of unease skated up and down his spine as he recalled the story Deanna had shared with him about Dean falling and breaking his leg. She'd known before anyone else.

A few minutes later, Deanna's mom came back on the line. "She's in trouble," she said, her voice quivering. "Dean said he can feel it."

Jonas started the engine and put the car in gear. "Has he talked to her?"

"No. He just knows something's wrong." She moaned and Jonas knew the woman was crying. "Oh, Jonas, not my baby girl. Not my sweet Deanna."

"Shhh," he soothed as he took off down the street. "It's going to be okay. I'm going to find her and she's going to be fine."

"I'll call the police." She paused, then in a sturdier voice, she ordered, "Find her, Jonas."

"Yes, ma'am."

After they ended the call, Jonas called Wade again. "I'm heading over to Valdez's."

"I was about to call you. I just got off the phone with Dean. We're both headed there now."

Jonas cursed and hit the steering wheel. "That bastard hurts her and I'll kill him with my bare hands, Wade. One hair out of place and Valdez dies."

"Chill out and think, Jonas," he demanded. "Valdez is a drug-dealing piece of shit, but he's small-time and he's no killer."

Would she have gone to see the man willingly? "I can't figure it. She wanted nothing to do with him, Wade."

"Deanna's smart and she's damned resourceful."

"She's also too damn trusting for her own good. I can see Valdez luring her there for some reason or another. Maybe he was pissed when she turned down the project."

"Don't start speculating. And she's tougher than you think. Have a little faith in your girl, Jonas."

He clenched a fist around the phone just thinking of what Valdez might do to Deanna. Wade was right; for Deanna's sake, Jonas needed to keep a clear head. "Your mom is calling in a missing person's report."

"How far away are you?"

Jonas made a left-hand turn, then looked at the clock on the instrument panel. "I'm ten minutes out." He sped up. "Possibly closer to five."

"I'm at least fifteen and Dean is farther than that. You'll get there before either of us." He paused, then asked, "You have the monitor?"

He looked at the passenger seat. "Yeah, if she's in there, I'll know."

"Only if she's in the living room."

"Yeah," he gritted out. Neither of them wanted to consider the idea that maybe Valdez had her in one of the other rooms in the house—like the bedroom.

"Are we calling the police to the location?" Wade asked.

They both knew the minute Valdez heard sirens he could panic and kill Deanna. "We don't know for sure she's even there. If she is, I don't want to spook him. I'll go in quiet."

"The second the monitor is within range, call me."

"I will," he vowed.

They ended the call and Jonas said one more prayer. She had to be okay; anything else simply wasn't an option. He couldn't lose her. She was his heart, his soul. He'd rather die than be without her.

In his entire life, Jonas had never found so much happiness as he had when he was with Deanna. She made him laugh and curse both. Her sarcasm sent his heart racing. Deanna loved with every part of her being, and he felt like the luckiest man alive because she belonged to him.

He wanted to marry her. To have babies with her. She made him feel capable of leaping tall buildings. Hell, she made him want to be a better man.

As he turned down the road that would take him to Valdez's house, Jonas switched off his emotions and went into soldier mode. When he approached Valdez's driveway, he slowed and turned. He drove up halfway, until the house came into view, then stopped and cut the engine. The first thing he saw was Ray's dirty-ass pickup.

"What the hell?" Jonas muttered; then realization dawned. Vengeance, Jonas thought, and Ray wanted it.

When Jonas saw Deanna's car parked next to Ray's truck, bile rose in his throat. Somewhere in that house, Deanna was trapped between a drug dealer and a vengeful father. He frowned when he spotted something on the front porch, near the door. He was too far away to make out what it was. Jonas reached into the backseat and rooted around on the floor until he found his binoculars tucked beneath the passenger seat. He held them to his face and his heart sank. A pool of blood.

Jonas dropped the binoculars and grabbed the monitor off the seat next to him. He flipped it on and saw a nightmare unfolding before his eyes.

27

Jonas shoved a hand through his hair as he watched the monitor and tried to calm Wade. "Short of telepathy, there was no way either of us could've predicted what I'm watching right now."

"Fuck!" Wade roared.

He heard Deanna's soft voice through the speaker. "She's trying to reason with Ray, but judging by his agitation, it isn't working for shit." He shook his head. "What are the odds of your sister showing up at Valdez's at the same damn time that Ray chose to exact his vengeance?"

"One in a million," Wade ground out. "Is she scared?"

"She looks shaken, but I don't see any marks on her. She appears unharmed. Valdez is on the floor moaning and pleading. Sniveling bastard. Ray is pacing. Every once in a while, he stops and kicks the hell out of Valdez."

"She's alive," Wade stated. "That's what matters. I'm still five minutes out. I say you go in. You?"

"Ditto. Ray knows me," Jonas said. "He trusts me."

"Will he panic?"

Jonas had been wondering the same thing. "Not if I go in alone. He wants Valdez to suffer the way he's had to suffer."

"He's got a gun and he's way off the fucking reservation, Jonas. I don't think reasoning with him is going to work."

Jonas had already given that one some thought. "His son is the key," he said. "If something happens to Ray, Cade's alone. I'm going to use that."

"A distraught father can be damned unpredictable. Be careful. I'll be there as soon as I can."

Jonas couldn't take his eyes off the monitor. The small device was his only connection to Deanna. The only way for him to see with his own eyes that she was alive. "I'm going in the back entrance."

"Got it."

Jonas opened the car door, then thought of something else. "What about Dean?"

"He may not be trained, but that's Deanna in there. No force on earth will be able to stop him from attempting to protect her."

"Just keep him from getting her shot, goddamn it."

"Focus on getting Deanna out of there," Wade ordered. "Let me worry about the rest."

"I won't let anything happen to her. You have my word."

"I know," Wade said.

They severed the connection, and Jonas took off across the yard. With Ray in the front of the house concentrating on Valdez, Jonas knew his best chance of getting in without incident was through the back door. He covered the last two hundred feet, then stepped onto the porch. He looked in a window to the right of the door. The kitchen was dark with no one in sight. Satisfied, Jonas turned the knob. Locked, but the alarm wasn't activated. He took out his kit and went to work picking it. Friggin' thing seemed to take light-years to open.

Once inside, Jonas silently made his way to the living room.

He spotted Deanna on the couch, her hands folded in her lap. When she saw him, she nearly jumped up. Jonas held a finger to his lips and she stayed seated.

"You've destroyed my son," Ray shouted as he pistol-whipped Valdez. "Why the hell should you live?"

"Please," Valdez moaned as he clutched his chest. "I need a doctor."

Ray laughed, and Jonas couldn't believe the sound came from the same man he'd embraced just hours earlier. By all appearances, Ray had completely lost his grasp on reality. Jonas knew this was his only chance.

"Ray," Jonas said in a low, calm voice as he stepped out into the open.

Ray swung the gun around, his eyes wide with fear and rage. When he saw Jonas, he frowned. "Jonas?"

"Yeah, buddy, it's me," Jonas said as he held his hands out to his sides. "I need you to put the gun down now."

"Are you serious? This piece of shit nearly killed Cade!"

"I'm not saying Valdez deserves to live, but you're scaring my girl there." Without taking his gaze off Ray and the gun, Jonas pointed to Deanna.

Ray's gaze darted her way, then back to him. "You know her?"

"That's Wade's little sister, Ray, and the woman I plan to marry." He stretched out a hand. "I need you to take a deep breath and give me the gun."

Ray paled and started visibly shaking as he looked back at Deanna. "I didn't know. I'm sorry."

"She knows that," Jonas said, directing Ray's attention back at him. "But if you don't give me the gun, then we can't fix this. And Cade needs you—now more than ever."

Ray swiped his forearm over his eyes. "He told me he was sorry. That he loved me and didn't want to die." His eyes, so full of anguish, locked onto Jonas's. "Do you know what that does to a man?"

Jonas shook his head. "No, because I'm not a father, but I don't think Cade would want you to do this, do you? He already lost his mother. Don't let him lose you too."

Ray looked down at Valdez and shook his head. "He'll get away with it." He bit the words out, contempt filling his tone. "He always does. He doesn't deserve mercy."

"Maybe not," Jonas conceded. "But your boy deserves at least one parent to see him through high school. Don't let him down, not after everything you've been through together."

Valdez moaned again. Christ Almighty! Jonas wished he'd shut the hell up before he got them all killed. "Karen never would have let this happen," Ray said. "She held all of us together. I miss her so much, Jonas."

"I know you do. It hurts that she's gone, but Cade is still here. He's still very much alive and he needs his dad."

"Oh, God, what have I done?" Ray mumbled as he dropped the gun and fell to his knees, all the fight simply evaporating at once.

Wade and Dean rushed into the room as Jonas closed the distance to pick up the gun. Wade took hold of Ray and brought him outside as Dean went to Deanna. Jonas watched the pair embrace and knew they needed a moment. After tucking the gun into his waistband, Jonas went to check on Valdez. He was still moaning, but Jonas could tell by the position of the bullet wound that he was going to live.

"If you don't stop your blubbering, I swear to God I'll shoot you myself and give you something to really cry about."

It didn't shut him up, but Jonas noticed Valdez's wailing wasn't quite as loud. When Jonas got to his feet and looked over at Deanna, her head lifted. Their gazes held. Jonas opened his arms, and Deanna stepped away from Dean and ran to him. Jonas wrapped her in his embrace, holding her tight. Dean sent him a nod, then went out the front where Wade and Ray were waiting.

"Jonas," she cried as she buried her face in his shirt.

"Shhh, it's okay now." He pulled her tighter, needing to know she was safe. Needing to know she was alive. When he felt Deanna's body shake so violently he thought she'd break something, Jonas looked over at Valdez and got pissed all over again. As far as Jonas was concerned, everything that had transpired could be placed at Valdez's feet.

"I need you away from here," Jonas said as he kissed her forehead. "I need to love you, kitten, to know you're okay."

"I was so scared, Jonas, but I knew you'd come. I . . . I knew you'd figure it out."

"Why were you here?" he asked, still bewildered by her presence inside Valdez's home. "I thought you told Valdez to stuff it?"

She nodded. "I did. I'd only stopped by to get some fabric swatches I'd left here. That's when Ray showed up waving a gun around." She started to cry. "H-he shot him right in front of me. I don't even think he realized I was standing there. He just shot him right in the chest. Oh, God, I'm sorry. I never should've come here at all."

Jonas wanted to kill Ray, but he forced himself to stay calm. Deanna didn't need another crazed maniac on her hands. "Shhh, kitten," he murmured. "You couldn't have known. It's okay now. It's over."

"No," she said, shaking her head. "You don't understand. I could've gotten you killed."

"Huh?"

"When he pointed that gun at you, I thought . . ." Her voice trailed off, and she began to sob harder.

Jonas took hold of her face in both hands and forced her to look at him. "Listen to me, sweetness. You didn't do anything wrong. Do you hear me?"

After a moment, she nodded. "I love you, Jonas."

"I love you, Deanna."

Suddenly the scene filled with cops and paramedics. An officer snapped cuffs on Ray and took him to a waiting cruiser as a couple of paramedics wheeled Valdez off on a gurney. Jonas could only stand by and watch as an ambulance drove off with Deanna, the woman of his heart. He'd never felt so utterly helpless.

"Shock, Jonas," Wade said. "That's all. They just want to make sure she's okay."

"I know," he growled. Her life was so precious to him. It sickened him that she'd been so afraid. "I should've seen the signs."

"Signs?"

"Ray. I should've known he wasn't okay. He was too calm at the hospital."

"Ah, hell," Dean said. "No one could've seen this coming, Jonas."

Jonas shook his head. "She could've died. If I'd only looked a little harder at Ray. Paid closer attention."

"But she didn't die," Wade said as he slapped him on the shoulder. "She's alive and she needs you."

Jonas nodded. "You're right. I'm heading to the hospital."

"See you there." Wade said as he and Dean started for their cars.

"Wait," Jonas yelled. When they looked back at him, he asked, "Did either of you call your mom?"

"Yeah, she's heading to the hospital now."

Jonas thought of the last time they'd had to call Mrs. Harrison to the emergency room. It had been a few months ago, when Wade had been shot trying to rescue Gracie from a stalker. "Dude, your mom deserves a vacation."

Dean nodded. "This is the second time in less than six months that one of her kids has landed in the emergency room."

Wade cursed and shook his head. "We should send her on a cruise or something."

"Good idea. Maybe she'll meet some nice, handsome older man," Jonas said, tweaking the brothers a little. "You know, a companion."

"Go to hell, Jonas," Wade growled as Dean flipped Jonas the bird.

Jonas laughed. "Love you, too, sweetie."

As Deanna sat patiently waiting for the nurse to finish taking her blood pressure, she looked over at her mom and smiled. Her mother looked ready to cry, and Deanna quickly reassured her once the nurse finished and left to get the doctor.

"See? My blood pressure is normal. I'm perfectly fine."

"The doctor needs to examine you still," she chastised. "Just sit tight."

Wade, Jonas, and Dean all stood around, staring at her. "I feel like an idiot with you all here. Ray never touched me, I promise." She didn't think they needed to know about him practically throwing her into the house.

Her mom's lip quivered. "You could've been shot, Deanna." She covered her eyes with one of her hands, her shoulders shaking as she let the tears fall. "Oh, God, I couldn't stand it if I'd lost you too."

Deanna stepped off the table and went to her mom, pulling her into her arms. "I love you, Mom."

Her mother hugged her tight. "I love you, too, so much."

Wade and Dean were there in an instant, and the four of them embraced. When her mom quieted, they released each other. Wade sent Jonas a quick smile. "Heck, Mom, Jonas wasn't about to let our girl get hurt. Believe me, she's in good hands."

"He's right, Mom," Dean said, surprising them all by offering his own complimentary two cents. "Jonas had the situation under control."

Guilt assailed Deanna as the horrible truth hit. Jonas so easily could've been killed, and she'd just sat there, like some ninny, not lifting a finger to stop Ray. As if tuned in to her thoughts, Jonas crossed the few feet separating them and took her hand in his and squeezed. "You okay, kitten?"

She nodded, unable to speak past the lump in her throat. How could she ever explain in words how much she cared about him? How empty her life would be without him in it? She could've lost him—all because she'd needed a few swatches of material.

"Kitten?" she heard Wade ask. Jonas chuckled, which managed to drag a curse from Dean.

"Hush, the three of you," her mother admonished. "I swear sometimes it's like trying to round up chickens with you three boys."

Jonas bit his lip and looked down at the floor. Wade and Dean both snickered. Deanna attempted to smile, but it felt hollow. In her mind, the scene inside Valdez's living room played on a constant loop. Jonas walking in. Ray raising the gun and pointing it at his chest. The crazed look in his eyes as Jonas tried to reason with him. And her, doing absolutely nothing. Bile rose in her throat. The image would stay with her forever.

After a doctor examined and released Deanna, they all had to go to the police station to fill out statements and answer questions. Now, at a little past midnight, Jonas had Deanna in the passenger seat of his car. He'd promised her that he'd take her back to her place, but the silence, and her refusal to look at him, slowly tore at Jonas.

"Wade and Dean took care of your car," he said, hoping to draw her out. "It should be at your house by now."

"Thank you."

Her quiet voice seemed entirely too far away. Jonas began to grow more and more concerned. "Won't you look at me, kitten?"

She shrugged but didn't take her gaze off the passenger side window.

It bothered Jonas that she wouldn't look directly into his eyes. "It's over now, Deanna. You're safe."

She turned finally and their gazes clashed. Her eyes were puffy from crying, and he wanted nothing more than to hold her in his arms.

"It's not that," Deanna said as she clenched her eyes tight and covered her face with her palms.

Jonas reached over and brought one of her hands away from her face, then gave it a little squeeze. "What is it? Talk to me."

She sighed and slumped against the seat. "I keep seeing Ray pointing that gun at you. You could've died and there would've been nothing I could do to stop him, Jonas."

Jonas couldn't be more surprised. "That's what's upsetting you? Fear for me?"

"I panicked and just sat there," she cried out. "I couldn't breathe, Jonas. I thought he was going to kill you and I just sat there."

When she started to cry big, silent tears, Jonas felt like someone was ripping him apart from the inside. "Stop, damn it," Jonas gently ordered as he brought her hand to his lips for a kiss. "Stop beating yourself up or I swear I'll spank your ass."

Deanna laughed and Jonas thought she sounded close to hysterics. "As far as threats, that's a lousy one."

"Why, because you think I won't do it?"

"No, because a spanking from you isn't frightening—it's hot."

Direct. Always so direct. Jesus, he loved her. More than he ever thought possible to love another human being, if he were honest with himself. Now he understood what Wade had found in Gracie. He turned onto her road, then pulled up in front of her house. As he suspected, her car was already in the driveway. Jonas shut off the engine and turned in the seat to face Deanna. She still had tears in her eyes, but they weren't falling, which meant he could breathe.

"You did exactly what I needed you to do back there," he murmured. "You kept your head, which allowed me to focus."

She rolled her eyes. "I wimped out, you mean."

"No," he insisted. "Listen to me. I wouldn't have been able to center my attention on getting the gun away from Ray if I'd been worried about what you might do."

"I love you, Jonas."

"I love you, sweetness," he whispered as he leaned over and kissed her. He didn't want to start something he couldn't finish, so he kept it light. When he lifted his head and unbuckled his seat belt, he ordered, "Come on, I need to get you in my arms."

Deanna nodded. By the time she'd grabbed her purse and had the car door open, Jonas was there. He wrapped his arm around her, and together they walked up to the front. As he looked at the scratches on her lock, he admitted, "By the way, I broke into your house."

Her eyebrows shot up in surprise. "You did?"

He shrugged. "When you didn't answer your phone, I went searching."

She cupped his face in her palm. "And I'm so glad you did, Jonas."

Once inside, Jonas shoved the door closed with his knee and pulled her into his arms. They both let out a huge breath. "Never again, Deanna," he groaned. "I never want to see you in danger again. I swear to Christ I can't take it."

She didn't speak, merely kept her face snuggled against his leather jacket, her arms wrapped tight around his waist. Jonas started to lift her off the floor so he could cradle her against his chest, his one goal to make love to her, when she stopped him.

"I have something I want to show you," she whispered.

"Yeah?"

She reached into her purse and took out her phone, then

turned the volume level all the way up. "It's nearly dead, but it should still work."

Okay, maybe she was still in shock. "You want to show me your phone?" he asked, more than a little confused.

"Call me on it," she demanded, holding it up between them.

"Uh, okay." Jonas took his phone off his belt and hit speed-dial 2. After a few seconds, Deanna's phone started to ring to the AC/DC song "You Shook Me All Night Long." She'd given him his own ring tone. Jonas's cock hardened as he watched Deanna blush and hit END.

Jonas growled low in his throat, then lifted her into his arms. "You ain't seen nothing yet, kitten," he promised.

She laughed and slipped her arms around his neck.

Jonas swung her into his arms and carried her up the stairs to her bedroom. He took his time stripping her out of her clothes, then placed her gently on top of the blanket. When he was naked, he came down beside her.

She frowned. "I want you on top of me, Jonas."

He shook his head and turned her to her side, facing away, then entered her in one smooth stroke from behind. "So sweet," he whispered against her nape. Her flesh molded to his shape. Her body was so hot Jonas thought he'd go up in flames. It'd be one hell of a way to go.

"Faster, please," Deanna whimpered, her need a living, breathing entity in that moment. Jonas ached to pound into her. To drive his cock deep. But not this time. "I want to feel you. Slowly. Every spasm, every drop of your cream as you come undone around my dick. I need to know you're alive, kitten."

"O-okay, but can we get crazy afterward?"

He chuckled and kissed her shoulder. "Yes. For now, just let me love you, sweetness."

Jonas reached around and cupped her breast as he slid gently in and out of her sweet cunt. "We belong together, Deanna. I feel it in my bones."

"Yes, Jonas."

Jonas plucked her nipple, then skated his hand down her body and teased her clit. "When I'm loving you like this, nothing else exists. There are no drug dealers, no bad guys with guns. There's only you and me, Deanna."

"Oh, Jonas. You say things that make me want to cry. It scares me."

"No fear, not with me," he replied emphatically. "I won't let anything happen to you."

She lifted her head and looked into his eyes. "Make love to me."

He leaned near her ear and whispered, "That's what I've been doing since the first moment we kissed."

Then neither of them could speak. The only sounds in the room were of Jonas and Deanna touching and playing. Souls entwined. Every atom of his body seemed to seek nourishment from hers. It was the single most beautiful experience of his life.

When she fell asleep in his arms, her soft, warm body pressed against the length of his, Jonas had a sense that he'd finally come home—and he would do whatever it took to protect that.

The next day, as Jonas watched Deanna whipping eggs for omelets, he received a call from Granger. "What's up?" he asked as he flipped open his cell.

"Thought you'd like to know what we found at Valdez's house."

"Yeah?" Jonas asked, only mildly interested. With Deanna sashaying around the kitchen in her nighty, which consisted of a small white T-shirt and matching cotton panties, Jonas had sweeter things on his mind than drug dealers.

"A search yielded approximately one million dollars' worth of cocaine and another one point three million in meth. Bastard's going straight to jail once he's recovered from the bullet wound."

Deanna bent to pick up an onion peel she'd dropped, and Jonas about swallowed his tongue as her ass came up in the air. "Good riddance," Jonas said as he sat back in the chair and spread his legs wide to accommodate his growing erection.

"My sentiments exactly."

Jonas frowned as he thought of Ray, who even now sat in the county jail. "What do you think will happen to Ray?"

"Man, there isn't a single judge in the entire county who won't go easy on the guy."

Granger sounded almost admiring.

"You think?"

"Some almost consider him a hero, Jonas, seeing as how his little rampage inadvertently gave us a reason to search Valdez's house."

When Jonas thought of how close Deanna had come to death, it pissed him off all over again. "It's going to be a long damn time before I think of him in that light."

Granger was quiet a moment. "If my woman was in a situation like that, I'd feel the same. Take care of her."

"That's the plan." Jonas stood and moved up behind her, then wrapped an arm around her middle and pressed a kiss to the top of her head.

"That kid of Ray's," Granger said. "Cade, I think you said his name was."

Deanna turned in his arms and cupped him through his boxers. He grinned and pinned her against the counter. "Cade, yeah. What about him?"

"He's going to have a rough time of it."

Jonas had to think for a minute; with Deanna's hands on him, his brain often took a holiday. "I think Ray has some family, though. A sister maybe. He won't be going through it alone. He'll be okay."

"Now that Valdez is off the streets, there are a lot of kids like Cade who'll be okay. You feel me?"

"Damn straight," Jonas replied.

They hung up after a few more minutes. Jonas set his phone down, then lifted Deanna and sat her on the countertop. "Now, where were we?"

"I believe we were about to have breakfast," she said as she tunneled her fingers into his hair.

Jonas wagged his eyebrows and slipped his fingers beneath the waistband of her panties and tugged. When she lifted and let him pull them off, Jonas got a good eyeful of her succulent pussy, already damp with arousal. "Yeah, breakfast, and I'm famished." Then he dipped his head and tasted paradise.

Epilogue

One month later . . .

When Jonas woke, the first thing that registered was Deanna's curvy body draped on top of him. He smiled and took his hands on a slow, leisurely path over her shoulders and back, before they reached the plush cushion of her ass. Her bottom was a thing of beauty. He could spend hours kissing and fondling her there. Had, in fact.

He cupped her, filling his palms with smooth feminine flesh, then moved her a few inches to the left so that he could wriggle his cock between her thighs. He rubbed against her clit with his engorged tip, nudging and evoking a throaty little moan from her. Slowly, she started to move her hips, beginning a rhythmic rotating motion even in her sleep. Her cheek pressed against his chest, and one hand splayed wide directly over his heart. His sweet Deanna, so beautiful and giving, and yet she'd decided to fall in love with him. The thought made him want to shout out a vicious war cry.

Intent on loving her the only way he knew how, fiercely and with his whole heart, Jonas moved the wild mane of Deanna's shiny, dark hair to one side and kissed her exposed cheek, savoring the taste of her satiny skin. Her eyes fluttered open and her tongue darted out, licking at her dry, swollen lips. He watched the emotions skitter across her face as she realized where she was and who she was with. When her smile came, easy and unforced, he breathed in relief. Some part of him was still afraid she'd wake up and regret loving him. He was just too fucking glad she didn't.

"Good morning, Jonas," Deanna mumbled, her voice hoarse from screaming out her climaxes from the night before. His sweet little kitty had been an eager participant in the games they'd played, which consisted of whipped cream, body oil, and a pair of fuzzy handcuffs.

"Good morning, kitten," he said as he gently flipped her over so that he covered her with his body.

Her breath came out in a whoosh, and his smile turned devilish as he descended on her already-erect nipple. This morning he was beyond niceties; all he wanted was to be deep inside of her. He sucked her hard nipple into the wet cavern of his mouth, flicking back and forth with his tongue. She arched into him, giving him more, giving him whatever he craved. Jonas licked and bit, then used his hands to plump both breasts together so he could nuzzle his face against her cleavage. He leisurely made his way down her body, lapping and nibbling at her rib cage until he reached her belly, where he let his tongue dip into her little button. She pleaded with him, saying his name over and over.

"Mmm, pussy," he growled as he reached her dark curls. "My favorite morning meal."

He pushed her legs wide, then dipped his tongue into her hot opening. Deanna's hands went to his hair, grasping handfuls and pushing his face against her farther. He sucked her clit, teasing it with his tongue. She vaulted up, coming and shouting his name in wild abandon.

Jonas lifted and sat back on his haunches. "Roll to your stomach, kitten," he ordered. "Up on your hands and knees. I want you from behind this time."

Deanna moaned and turned over, then pushed up on all fours. His cock thickened at the pretty sight. He moved behind her and, using his knee to spread her legs wider for his invasion, Jonas clutched her hips in one hand.

"Does this ass need a spanking?"

She whimpered and wiggled. "God, yes!"

Jonas quickly swatted her. He kept the strikes gentle at first, alternating between each buttock, then harder. She cried out as he spanked her with more force. Over and over, until her ass was good and pink from his hand. "Now that's a pretty sight," he murmured as he massaged the sting away. He dipped his hand between her ass cheeks and encountered her wet, swollen folds. "Damn, you're soaked."

Her pink vulva and pearly clit were completely visible in the early morning light. Jonas wanted to take the time to look at her, to fill himself with the beauty of her, but his dick had other ideas.

"Jonas, I need you," she pleaded.

He took his cock in a tight fist and guided it to her entrance. One silky glide imbedded Jonas deep. When she moaned and reached between her legs, grasping his balls and beginning to squeeze and play, Jonas lost it.

He pulled all the way out, then thrust into her, impaling her in a mad rush for that one elusive thing that only Deanna gave him. His body knew hers and his greedy cock craved her. Only her. Only Deanna. When her supple hips pushed backward, Jonas cursed.

"Harder, Jonas," she cried. "Fuck me."

"Hell yeah."

He plunged into her, over and over, until his passion rocketed out of control. As he lowered his body over hers, caging her in, he kissed her neck, then sucked at the delicate skin, causing blood to rush to the surface.

"Another love bite?" she asked in a breathless voice.

"Yes," he gritted out as he watched a slight bruise appear.

"That's very naughty of you, Jonas."

"You can spank me for it later," he promised.

Reaching a rough, calloused hand beneath her, Jonas rubbed over her distended clit. "Is this my hot little pussy?"

"Y-yes, always," she vowed.

She arched and clenched around him then, her sex cupping his dick like a hot little glove, and they both flew apart.

A few minutes passed; then Jonas pulled his cock free. Deanna collapsed onto the bed, her breathing labored and sweat causing tendrils of her hair to stick to her cheek.

"You take my breath away," he whispered as he stared down at her.

She chuckled and turned over. "It's you with all the wicked ideas, Jonas."

Jonas merely shook his head and dropped to the bed beside her. "Come here, woman," he growled as he reached over and tugged her on top of him.

"Ew," she said, "I'm all sweaty."

He pushed her hair off her face and kissed her forehead. "I like you all sweaty, so be still."

She settled against him. "I meant to ask you last night but we got . . . distracted."

He let his hands massage the length of her back. "By *distracted* do you mean when I squirted whipped cream on your pussy and licked it off?"

She laughed. "Yeah, that."

"A very tasty distraction, kitten."

"Anyway, I wanted to ask about Ray's phone call. What'd he say?"

Jonas frowned as he recalled the conversation. "Cade is doing well. He's staying with his aunt, Ray's sister, while Ray's in prison. It seems like the kid has his life back on track—even though his dad will probably do time for attempted murder. Jesus, what a mess."

Deanna lifted her head and looked at him. "Cade is getting his life straightened out and Ray got the minimum sentence of three years. Those are good things, Jonas. So why did you seem angry?"

"Are you kidding me, Deanna?" he growled. "Ray nearly shot you!"

She laid her back down on his chest. "He was out of his mind with pain. We need to try to forgive him, Jonas."

Jonas coasted his hands down to her ass and squeezed. "I understand the reason behind Ray's rampage, but I'll never forget seeing that pool of blood on the porch. I'll never forget how close you came to dying."

"Neither will I," she said as she kissed his chest. "I'm very glad you saved me."

Jonas knew now was the time. He loved her, would always love her. And the time had come for him to do something about that. Suddenly, his palms grew damp and he felt as if he were going to be sick. Christ, he was nervous! He'd laugh later at the absurdity of that. Much later.

"I love you, kitten."

She lifted her head and smiled up at him. "And I love you."

He took a deep breath, then let it out. "I want to spend my life making you happy, Deanna."

She kissed him. "I like the sound of that," she breathed against his lips.

"I think I've loved you from the moment I saw you at your family's picnic. I just didn't know it then." He leaned down and softly kissed her warm cheek.

"Jonas?"

"Yeah?"

"Will you marry me?"

Jonas jerked. "Damn it, girl, that's supposed to be my line."

She laughed and reached down to cup his dick in her palm. "I was afraid you'd take all day. And I have other plans for you."

At once, Jonas was vibrating with sexual awareness. "Plans?"

"Mmm," she murmured as she rubbed her thumb over the tip of his cock.

"Remember in Miami, when you said I could tie you up and tickle-torture you?"

"Uh, Deanna—"

She shook her head. "Uh-uh, no chickening out."

Jonas smiled and spread his arms out to the sides. "I'm all yours, kitten."

Deanna sat up, then reached across the bed to the nightstand and grabbed the handcuffs. She snapped one around his wrist, then the other. Now he was bound and at her mercy.

"Oh, yeah," she murmured. "This is going to be so much fun."

Jonas groaned. "I've created a monster."

Turn the page for a sizzling preview
of Tawny Taylor's

DANGEROUS MASTER

An Aphrodisia trade paperback
coming November 2011

1

It was heaven. Glorious, nude male bodies as far as the eye could see. Limbs entwined; muscles stretching and flexing; hard, thick cocks gliding in and out of pussies, mouths, asses.

Mandy Thompson's job had taken her to all sorts of places, from the presidential suites of Michigan's finest five-star hotels to rat-infested hellholes in the most dangerous pockets of Detroit. But never a place like this.

Until tonight.

A tray of full champagne glasses balanced on one hand, Mandy stood in the doorway, her gaze meandering around the space, sliding from one beautiful male body to the next. A sigh slipped from between her lips. "Damn, I love my job. I am *so glad* I took this case."

"I told you, you wouldn't regret it." Sarah Gray, her best friend, adjusted her corset before leading her down a narrow walkway that skirted the perimeter of the room. "Just remember, you can't get so carried away that you forget everything I taught you."

Easier said than done. Although Mandy was professional

enough to realize the danger of forgetting where she was, why she was here, and what could happen if anyone made her.

To everyone but Sarah, Mandy was a waitress, paid to tote around trays of champagne.

To Sarah, and to her client, Allison Clark, wife of Mr. Andrew Clark—two-timing trust-fund baby—she was one of the best private detectives in Metro Detroit. Discreet. Thorough. And as tenacious as a bulldog.

Sarah and Mandy made a full circle of the room. Only twice was she stopped by thirsty guests. Then they headed outside, down the main corridor, and into a second spacious room, this one set up as a bondage dungeon.

Sarah stopped in front of a scene featuring a gorgeous man, nude with the exception of an itty-bitty G-string that strained at the seams. He was strapped spread-eagle to a wooden cross. But it wasn't the rippling muscles, pulled taut beneath oil-slicked skin, or the hard penis testing the construction of his G-string that made Mandy feel warm between the legs. It was the look of rapture on his tanned face. It was sexy beyond imagining. It was enough to make her cream her panties.

"Now *that's* how you tell if you're doing things right," Sarah said, her voice a little on the breathy side.

Her own voice husky, Mandy said, "It's no wonder you spend practically every free minute at places like this." Shifting the tray to hold it in front of her body, she leaned back, letting the wall support her. The drywall felt cool against her burning skin. It was a very welcome sensation.

Sarah gave Mandy a little nudge. "I have a feeling you will, too, even after you're done with your case."

"Maybe. Speaking of the case . . ." Mandy pushed off the wall, forcing her gaze from the man on the cross. She closed her eyes for a moment, trying to visualize the man she had been hired to watch. It wasn't easy shoving aside the memory of the man on the cross, but she did it.

Late thirties. Blond hair, wavy and cut about collar length.

Andrew Clark, one of Metro Detroit's richest men, was said to be submissive and prefer male doms and sex partners. He had talked his wife, Allison, a former topless dancer, into signing a prenup. She wouldn't get more than ten thousand dollars in the event of a divorce, unless she could prove infidelity.

Why a gay man who'd married a woman to pacify his father would think a document would be enough to protect him was beyond Mandy. But it was good for his soon-to-be ex.

And good for Mandy's bank account, too. Despite having steady work that paid well, it was getting lean. Lately, she was shelling out hefty money for her grandmother's care. Her maternal grandmother, a woman who wore the "feisty Irish" tag with pride, Grandma Dougherty was the only family she had left, and Grandma Dougherty was the most important person in the world to her. Mandy would live in a cardboard box to keep that woman in the home she loved.

"Do you see Mr. Jones?" Sarah asked, using the code name they'd agreed upon before leaving her apartment.

"Not yet."

"If he isn't in one of these two rooms, he's probably in one of the private suites upstairs." Sarah gave Mandy's arm a tap. "Let's go around to the other side to make sure."

"There are private suites?" Hefting the tray, Mandy sighed. "This isn't going to be easy."

"Like I told you, Mr. Jones isn't much of an exhibitionist. You're probably not going to catch him bent over a horse, a sweet boy fucking him in the ass."

Mandy had seen a picture of Andrew Clark, aka Mr. Jones. Seeing a hot guy fuck him in the ass would be a sight to behold. "Now, that was fodder for one hell of a dream." Fanning her face with her free hand, Mandy motioned with a tip of the head, indicating a nearby scene. The dom was drop-dead, traffic-stopping, panty-dropping gorgeous, and the sub, a man who was younger than him, maybe in his midtwenties, wasn't far behind him in the looks department. "What is it with this party? Every single male is beautiful. I've never seen so many good-looking men in one place in my life."

Sarah shrugged. "Couldn't tell you. But it's one of the things I find most appealing about Zane's parties." She nudged Mandy in the side. "Finally."

"Is it Mr. Jones?" Mandy followed the direction of Sarah's gaze.

"No, it's my subs."

"Did you say 'subs'? As in, plural?" Mandy located a pair of men in their late-twenties, both wearing jeans that fit them like second skins and tank tops that did a lot of good things for their pecs, shoulders, and arms. "Those two?"

"Uh-huh." Sarah gave Mandy a grin, then turned on the charm as the pair sauntered up to them. "You're late." She was still smiling, but there was an evil glimmer in her eyes. Mandy had a feeling those two were going to regret being late. Then again, maybe not. "I have a suite. Let's head back."

"Ladies first," one of the two men said as he gave Mandy the once-over.

Mandy raised her tray. "I'm not playing today. I'm working."

"Too bad."

She was almost sharing that sentiment. Almost.

Keenly aware of the man's lust-filled eyes on her, Mandy gave Sarah a little wave. Sarah and her wonder twins headed in one direction while Mandy headed in another. In the congested main hallway, someone tapped her on the back. She carefully turned to face the back-tapper.

Ohmygod.

The man was too freaking beautiful to be real. His face was the stuff of dreams. His body, of wet dreams.

"Hi." Mandy swung the tray around, assuming he wanted a glass of champagne.

"No thanks." His voice was a deep baritone. It made her nerves prickle, in a good way.

"Okay." Confused now, she gave him one of her brightest smiles. "Can I help you?"

"I guess that depends." His gaze meandered up and down her body. If she wasn't so incredibly attracted to this man, she might've been irritated by his obvious staring, or embarrassed. As it was, she was getting warmer, particularly between her legs.

Aware of how damp her panties were becoming, she tightened her thighs, pressing them together. She reminded herself she wasn't at this party to make new friends. She was there to collect proof of her client's husband's infidelity. "Depends on what?" she asked, infusing her voice with a more professional tone.

His perfectly arched brows lifted slightly. He extended a hand. "I'm Zane Griffin."

She knew that name.

He was, essentially, her boss. She'd been hired by an agency to work at this party, at his party. And if she wanted to make sure she was hired to work future parties, she had better make a good impression.

She placed her hand in his. "Amanda Thompson." His grip was firm. He didn't let her hand go. Now more nervous than turned on, she slightly shifted the tray balanced on her other hand. "You said I could help you?"

Something she couldn't quite read flashed in his eyes. "Yes." He finally released her hand. She placed it under the tray, which was getting a little heavy. He took the champagne from her and set it on a nearby table. "I saw you. In the dungeon."

Immediately, Mandy recalled what the agency representative had told them when she'd first arrived. There was to be no alcohol served in the dungeon. And there she was, toting champagne into the dungeon. Her face burned. "Ohmygosh, I'm sorry. I totally forgot. My friend, who is a guest, was showing me—"

"It's okay," he interrupted. "I'm not making myself clear." He straightened ever so slightly, which made him look that much more intimidating. "It's true—there should be no alcohol served in the dungeon. But that's not why I wished to talk to you."

"Oh, okay." Mandy tucked her now-empty hands behind her back.

"I need someone to work in my private suite. To serve some very special guests there. I wanted to ask if you'd like to be that someone."

This was exactly the opportunity she needed. With any luck, Andrew Clark would be one of those "special guests," and she'd have her evidence by the end of the night. All she needed was one photograph of him either being penetrated or penetrating another person, male or female, to collect her paycheck.

"I would be honored."

"Excellent. This way." Zane Griffin, aka Master Zane, as Sarah called him, placed a hand at the small of Mandy's back and steered her toward the sweeping staircase in the front foyer. Up she went, propelled by his touch, aware every second of the heat of his hand, even through the material of her white cotton blouse. At the top of the stairs, he turned her into the first room. They entered through a pair of French doors into one of the most opulent master suites she'd ever seen.

Immediately inside the French doors was a lounge area, with several cozy couches. A porn film played on a huge flat-screen television hung on one wall, the sound replaced with some sultry jazz playing over unseen speakers. Here and there, flickering candles created soft ambient lighting. On the floor lay a thick rug. It looked like some kind of animal fur. Mandy could imagine lying on that rug, nude.

Zane stopped in the center of the room.

Mandy hung back, closer to the door. "This room is gorgeous."

"Thank you." His gaze locked on Mandy's face, Zane slowly circled the perimeter. "I designed this space." He stopped in front of a painting of a nude woman, hanging over a deep mahogany dresser. He looked at it, and his features softened slightly. "Every piece has a special meaning to me."

"I can tell." Something pulled her deeper into the room. One moment she was standing just inside the door, and the next she was beside Zane, looking up at the painting. The artist had used oils. Mandy could tell by the layered shading and texture. "This painting is very nice. I tried my hand at painting figures in college. It's definitely not my forte."

Zane turned, facing Mandy. Now she felt small and vulnerable and uncomfortable. He was big. Really big. And his body was powerful, his arms thick, his shoulders heavily muscled. If he wanted, he could easily swoop her off her feet, cart her to the nearest bedroom, and . . . do whatever he wanted.

She almost wondered what that might be like.

He leaned close enough for her to catch the slightest scent of cologne, trapping her between his body and the dresser. "Amanda, you know what will be happening in this suite, don't you?"

"I have some idea." The image of this man nude flashed through Mandy's mind. She shifted back, putting as much space between her body and his as she could. It wasn't enough. Not by a long shot.

"You won't be bothered by what you'll see, will you?" He caged her body between his arms, his hands resting on the dresser's top.

"No." But she sure as heck was bothered now. She'd figured this case would be a little awkward, maybe a bit uncomfortable, but she hadn't seen this coming. "I'll be okay." Her voice sounded so small. There could be no way he'd believe her.

Mandy wouldn't have believed it was possible, but Zane leaned closer still. If she inhaled too deeply, her tits would probably touch him. She didn't inhale . . . at all.

"My guests, particularly in my personal suite, must have absolute privacy. You may not tell anyone who you've seen here. Nor are you permitted to take any photographs or recordings. As if he knew she had a hidden camera in her skirt pocket, he slid a hand over her hip. It stopped right on the spot.

Mandy swallowed. She'd been made. Already.

Zane was holding her gaze hostage. That wasn't making her feel any better about being caught red-handed with a camera. "What's this?" His hand slipped into her pocket. But instead of going right for the camera, he let his fingertips graze her leg through the thin fabric of the pocket's lining. The intimate touch made her quake. She wanted to shove him away. She wanted to smack him across the face. She wanted to run out of this place and never come back.

She didn't do any of those things.

But neither did she answer his question. She figured he already knew what it was. And even if he didn't, he would soon enough.

Who the hell was this little chit, bringing a camera to his party? The agency had promised to do a background check on every person they'd sent. This little minx with the tumble of brown waves cascading over her shoulders, the cool gray eyes, and the lush lips had been cleared. But it seemed she shouldn't have been.

What was she up to?

Zane knew he should throw her out on her ass. *Should.* So why couldn't he get himself to do it?

He inhaled deeply, thinking the lungful of air would help him gather the strength to show her the door. Or at least release her and take a step back. It didn't. Instead, that inhalation carried her scent deep into his nostrils, deeper still, until he could practically taste her.

She was scared.

But that wasn't all she was feeling.

Thanks to his heightened senses, he could tell she was ready. To fuck.

Her pussy was wet for him. And damn if he didn't want to shove his cock inside her slick heat and find out how tight and hot she was.

He slid his hand, still deep inside her skirt pocket, around to the back of her thigh and pulled her hips flush to him. He checked her eyes. The pupils were dilated, but her lids were narrowed in defiance.

Damn, she was fun.

"Sir, I'm here to do a job. Not to be a . . . participant."

Her voice lacked conviction. She wanted this, wanted his touch. Wanted his cock. She wouldn't admit it, not with words. But her body couldn't lie.

He curled his fingers around the camera.

Her eyes widened.

"Who are you?" he asked.

She lifted her chin. "I told you my name."

"Yes, I know. But *who* are you?"

Those pretty eyes narrowed again. "I'm the waitress you hired, that's who."

"Sneaking around with a camera." He pressed the object against her thigh. "Are you a reporter?"

She didn't answer.

He pulled the device out of her pocket and, backing away slightly to eliminate the distraction of her intoxicating scent, took a look at it. It was tiny, just under three inches by one inch. If not for the person who'd reported seeing her holding something suspicious, he might never have known she'd carried it in. Somehow she'd made it past his security team. They'd been trained to detect stuff like this.

He'd have to talk to them later about their failure.

He took a closer look at the device. It was a video camera, sold primarily for security use. "Are you a cop?"

She worried her lower lip. "No."

A spark of anger buzzed through his system. He dropped the camera on the floor and crushed it with his heel. Dammit, he didn't need this shit. Didn't need someone poking around, looking to make trouble for him, for his guests.

But . . . she mesmerized him.

More than any woman had. And although she was pretty, he couldn't say exactly what it was about her that made him so hard and tight and hot all over.

He caught her chin in his hand and tipped her head back. "If you ever bring a camera into one of my parties again, I'll make you regret it for a long, long time."

"Is that a threat?" she snapped.

Damn, she had balls.

"No, it's a promise." Not allowing himself to smile, he stepped back, motioning toward the door. "My security team will escort you off my property. Good-bye, Amanda Thompson." He pulled his phone out of his pocket, hitting the button to call Phillips, the man in charge of his security team.

She had the nerve to glare at him. "I don't need an escort. I can see myself out."

"Oh, no, you can't," he said through gritted teeth.

If only she knew how close he was to dragging her back to his bedroom and giving her what she wanted. The guard was for her sake, not his.

The beast inside had wakened.